SCRAPBOOKING THE SUPERNATURAL

MIDLIFE MAGIC IN MARSHMALLOW BOOK TWO

KEIRA BLACKWOOD

D1372725

Dragon Guardian of Water

Bear Warrior of Water

Werewolves of Sawtooth Peaks

Running to the Pack

Defending the Pack

Uniting the Pack

Howling with the Pack

Leaving the Pack

The Protectors of the Pack

Bodyguard

Enemies

Heir

Warrior

Scoundrel

Werebears of Riverwood

Grizzly Bait

Grizzly Mate

Grizzly Fate

The Protectors Unlimited

Can't Prove Shift

Suave as Shift

In Deep Shift

The Protectors Quick Bites

(with Eva Knight)

Midnight Wish

I Dream of Grizzly

The Ocean's Roar

To Catch a Werewolf

Outfoxed

Tactics and Tails

Vampires & Chocolate

Vampire Prince Exiled

Vampire Prince Hunted

Vampire King Dethroned

Spellbound Shifters: Dragons Entwined

(with Liza Street)

Dragon Forgotten

Dragon Shattered

Dragon Unbroken

Dragon Reborn

Dragon Ever After

Spellbound Shifters: Fates & Visions

(with Liza Street)

Oracle Defiant

Oracle Adored

Spellcaster Hidden

Spellbound Shifters: Standalones

(with Liza Street)

Hope Reclaimed

Orphan Entangled

Edited by Liza Street

ew skills were as underrated as sleeping. I would trade my left boob for the ability to drift off as soon as I climbed under the covers at night and plopped my head on the pillow. If the universe was game for bargaining, I'd throw the right boob in, too, to master the art of napping.

I'd been lying still for so long that my memory foam mattress felt like a slab of concrete. My brain wouldn't shut its proverbial trap and relax like it was supposed to, either. It was the perfect storm for another dreamless night.

Sure, everyone hated restless nights. But I was probably alone in my desperation to dream. If I'd had a third boob, that's what I'd trade it for—a quick ticket to Dreamville. Maybe I was going a little wild, throwing boobs around willy-nilly, but some problems call for drastic solutions.

Was a dream witch really a dream witch if she couldn't dream?

Say that three times fast.

I rolled from my side to my back and opened my eyes. My room was pitch black, like a house was meant to be in the middle of the night, but I could make out the shadowy shape

1

of the ceiling fan above my bed. The best thing about the dark was definitely the way my eyes adjusted and made the world look like it was filtered through a layer of old timey TV snow. The worst part was the way stationary objects seemed to come to life, which stirred my imagination all over again. How was I supposed to sleep when the laundry basket was creeping around like it had grown a set of stubby little legs?

Note to self—ask Molly if gremlins were a thing.

No. I was only allowed to focus on sleeping. Dreaming was priority number one. It was hard, though, when I knew there was a whole hidden world of magic out there just waiting for me with open arms.

I closed my eyes and tried to stop listening for sounds of movement. The basket wouldn't move, because there weren't gremlins in my house.

But wouldn't it be cool if there were?

I pulled a second pillow on top of my head to muffle the sounds that were nothing, and block out the sights that were also nothing.

A click that was definitely *not* nothing came from somewhere else in the house. It couldn't be my son Evan, since he was spending the night at a friend's house.

I threw off the covers and grabbed the golden trident that I, with the help of my coven, had pillaged from the vampires' hoard. When I was feeling fancy, I liked to refer to the trident as Sir Pointy McStabberson. The rest of the time, I called it my trusty spork. Weapon at the ready, I tiptoed out into the hall to investigate. After being abducted by a vampire smoke monster, I probably should have been afraid of bumps in the night, but I wasn't.

I was jazzed.

There could be a real live dragon man in my house right now, here to proclaim his undying devotion to me and sweep

2

me off my feet. He could have magicked the front door open with a flex of his chiseled pecs. Yeah, I liked that scenario.

Since I had only met one dragon man, and he was otherwise claimed by my best friend Remi, that scenario was unlikely.

If said bestie had tried to call and couldn't reach me, she had a key. It was probably just Remi downstairs.

Still, there was the possibility the intruder was neither my imaginary boyfriend nor my best friend, thus the need for Sir Pointy.

Quieting my ever-overthinking brain, I took in my surroundings, paying particular attention to the shadowy bits. There was no sign of life in the upstairs hall. I peeked into the bathroom, the closet, and Evan's empty room just in case. No gremlins, baddies, or anyone else to be found anywhere. Then I headed for the steps.

I paused on the landing and looked down over the rail. The front door was closed, and from here everything looked like it was supposed to. Had I imagined the sound? I didn't think so, but I was becoming less and less sure.

Creeping as slowly and as silently as possible, I started down the stairs.

A hiss froze me mid-step.

I hadn't imagined it. There was definitely someone here. A snake monster of some sort, it seemed.

Right about now, it would have been awesome to have Remi's fire power. Snake man would open his mouth to show me his fangs and forked tongue. I'd lob a ball of flame with a wicked one liner. *Fire in the hole, mofo.*

Or if I had Molly's power, I'd grab the snake by its forked tongue and steal its life force until it was a shriveled husk. As its scales turned to dust, I'd wink and make finger guns and deliver an epic, *"Cobra or corpse?"*

But I didn't have either of their abilities. I was the

dreamer who couldn't dream, useful to the coven for my fierce loyalty and the boost I could give them by being nearby. I was a battery for their greatness with no real power of my own.

It sucked being the least awesome one. An ache in my chest was the constant reminder that no one needed me. My teenage son was about to strike out on his own. And then I'd be alone. Which was why I needed to master my power and earn my place in my coven. And until I did, at least I had my spork.

As I reached the bottom of the steps, I caught a flash of light, and then it cut out.

I jumped from the step and faced the direction the light had come from, Sir Pointy in hand.

Standing beside the recently closed fridge and holding a recently opened can of soda was Evan. My teenage son wasn't supposed to be home, so why was he in the kitchen narrowing his gaze at me?

I set the butt off my spork on the floor, totally casualish.

Evan set down his Mountain Dew and flicked his head to sweep his shaggy hair out of his eyes. He asked, "Mom...what are you doing with the trident?"

His voice was even, like this was a totally normal question to ask about my totally normal behavior.

I straightened my spine and frowned at him, because *he* was the one doing something he shouldn't here, not me. "It's Friday," I told him. "You're supposed to be staying the night at Brandon's."

"Brandon's sick. I came home, because this is where I live."

"Okay," I said. "But in the middle of the night? Shouldn't you be sleeping?"

"Mom, it's nine-thirty."

"Oh." I guessed that wasn't so late after all. It had felt like

4

hours had passed while I tossed and turned. Closer to thirty minutes.

"Well," I said, still the adult and the boss here. "No more caffeine after that soda. It'll keep you up all night."

"Last one, I promise." He looked from my pajamas to my messy bedtime bun. "Still having trouble sleeping?"

"Yeah." The weird part was I was freaking exhausted. "It's like the more tired I feel, the worse I sleep."

A little V formed between Evan's brows, barely visible between bits of his thick hair. "Did you try that tea I bought for you?"

"Not yet," I told him. "I'll do it now. Thanks again for picking it up."

"We've got to look out for each other, right?"

No question he was the sweetest, most caring seventeen-year-old in the entire world. I was so freaking lucky. Still, I wished he didn't feel like he had to take care of me. He should have been focused on school, and track, and friends, and girls. Well, not *too* focused on girls. But the point was, he shouldn't have to worry about me.

I set down my trident and hugged him. He patted my back gently, humoring me before pulling away.

"I'll be in my room," he said. "I'm meeting the guys on Discord for a squad battle. You're really okay, right?"

"Peachy," I told him, projecting an air of confidence. Then I went about making myself a cup of tea.

Evan slowly backed away, hardcore scrutinizing me as he headed for the stairs with his caffeine fix and a bag of cheesy chips in hand. I played it cool and checked out the tea box like it was the most interesting thing in the world until he was gone. It wasn't the least interesting thing in the world, with a hooded-eyed sloth wearing a nightcap and button shirt in bed. Maybe my lack of nightcap was the issue. If only.

Tea fixed, I cleaned up and then headed back upstairs. The hot liquid sloshing around in my oversized mug smelled herbaceous, like I was about to drink a whole field of dried wildflowers and grass. It was a pleasant scent, for an essential oil or room spray. Hopefully it tasted nothing like it smelled.

Back in my room, I turned on the light, set my mug on the floor, and sat down on my fluffy rug. If I wasn't going to sleep, I might as well do something to pass the time while I waited for the tea to kick in.

My favorite solo hobby was stashed in a box under my bed. I pulled out the little tote and emptied the contents onto the rug. The first scrapbook I ever created was more or less a baby book for Evan. The fill-in-the-blank jobbies that were available at the drugstore lacked pizzaz. My version wasn't so much a capturing of numbers and dates as a raw and real celebration of his first year in colorful papers and photographs.

The first page was one of my favorites—blue and white striped paper with a photo of the first time I held him in my arms. Like all of the major moments in my life, it wasn't Evan's father, but my mother and my best friend who were there with me. Neither one had been psyched to take this particular photo.

Both Evan and I were bawling our eyes out, faces like wrinkled beets. From the edge of the pic to the border of the page teardrop-shaped blue jewels were arranged and stuck in a spray pattern. At the bottom of the page, I'd used my sparkliest silver pen to write in a curvy script *Kicking and screaming, he stole her heart.*

Perfection.

My current project had the same level of flair, but followed a completely different subject. I was documenting the adventures of my coven. So far, we were still a baby coven of three witches coming into their power. There was a fair amount of kicking and screaming for this baby, too. What the future would hold for us, I had no idea, but I was psyched to find out.

I flipped open the first two-page spread and looked over the wedding photographs from the night where it all began. On the left was the start of the evening, with a selfie of me and Remi getting ready. I had on one of my fancy suits that made me look like I actually had my life together. Remi wore a pretty dress that was sure to show her ex, Dick, that she still had it going on. We were making mock-surprised faces, like someone had caught us on camera when they shouldn't have. There was a cream rose paper behind the photo, and a caption below that said, *Preparing for battle.*

I took a sip of my sloth tea and smacked my lips together at the cringey taste—hits of tea, heaps of grass. The honey I'd added to it helped, as did the cream, but there was no masking the fact that this stuff belonged in barnyard feed instead of my cup.

The next photos were from the wedding, with the background changing to red roses, with a touch of pink between, for an ombre effect. And finally, on the right was a newspaper clipping of Dick's wrecked and flaming car pyre. Behind the clipping, I'd transitioned papers from red roses to fire. The caption beneath the clipping made me grin and chuckle at my cleverness. *Don't be a Dick.*

I flipped through a few more pages to my work-in-progress spot, the smorgasbord of loot. This was where I was going to put pictures of the treasure room we'd found underground, along with some shots of my friends carrying all of the goodies up to the magic shop.

The page was supposed to be blank.

But it wasn't.

Swirls moved across the pages, darkening the white to a cloudy black. I didn't have any paper that could do that. If it existed, I would have definitely bought it and definitely remembered.

Images materialized in the fog—one of me being dragged from my car, suffocated by smoke. My heart stopped. My stomach dropped.

I couldn't blink or tear my eyes away. I just stared at the book.

Another photograph appeared, of the event that happened next, one of me fighting with tears in my eyes as I was chained to a sewer wall.

My eyes burned as tears began to well, and my breath caught in my throat.

No. There weren't pictures of this.

None of this was happening. It couldn't be real.

I reached for the scrapbook to slam it shut. But my trembling hands went through the book as if I were a ghost.

With wild kicks and skittering hands, I crab-ran away until I smacked my back on the bed frame. Pain radiated through my arms and my spine, and I dropped down on my butt.

Pop.

It was a tiny sound, for a tiny creature.

A kitten hovered in front of my face, an adorable animal with fluffy black fur and big round eyes. The fairy wings on its back whizzed, creating almost a pink halo around the kitten. It was the same kitten that had busted out of a scaly egg in a bonfire at Molly's place two weeks ago.

Staring into those pretty blue irises, all the panic I had felt faded. I reached for the kitten—the cutest, snuggliest creature on the planet. A voice in the back of my head screamed for me not to do it.

Run.

CHAPTER 2

*M*y brain was screaming, but my body wasn't listening.

Don't touch it. Run, nincompoop!

The air crackled beneath my fingertips, charged like wooly socks in a static storm. My hand moved on its own accord, like it craved the shock.

Pop.

The kitten disappeared. Poof, gone.

My fingers brushed the air where that floofy monster had been, and I sighed my relief at the lack of contact. Had that adorable little fairy thing forced me to want to touch it? Or was that all me?

Where had it gone?

Wide-eyed and on red alert, I scanned the room for any sign of the kitten. At least it had gone along on its merry way without melting me with its eye lasers or eating my face. I had no idea if it did in fact eat faces or not, or if it had skin-melting powers. That was the problem, or at least the biggest one at the moment—the fact that I knew nothing.

Why was it here? And what was it? And why did I have to have a billion questions but zero answers?

Worse...what if it wasn't gone?

I jumped up from my spot on the rug, knocking my tea over onto my scrapbook.

No! I dove for my book. I had to get the tea off before it soaked in and ruined everything.

My eyes shot open, jolting me away from where I had been and what I had been doing.

I wasn't on the floor. I was supposed to be on the floor. Instead, I found myself in bed, blinking sleep from my eyes and staring up at the ceiling fan through a haze of TV snow. The lights had been on, but now they weren't.

Everything that just happened—had it all been a dream?

I threw off the covers and climbed onto the rug, inspecting the cream fibers by touch. Dry, completely tea-free. If I'd been dreaming before, maybe I was still dreaming now. How was I supposed to tell?

There was a click somewhere else in the house. Based on the quiet sound, I'd guess it came from downstairs. Whatever the cat fairy was doing, it couldn't be good.

I grabbed my weapon of choice, Sir Pointy McStabberson, and crept into the hall.

Nothing out of the ordinary.

At the top of the steps, I heard a hiss.

Wait. This happened before. Was this a dream repeat, or was the first time a *prophetic* dream, and now it was becoming real?

This time I didn't go cautiously down the steps, I bounded down, taking two at a time. Impressively, I did not tumble and land on my face or break any bones on the way.

Evan was standing exactly where he was supposed to be, in the kitchen with his Mountain Dew. Technically he was supposed to be out for the night. But this was exactly how it had happened in the first dream go-round.

"Mom...what are you doing with the trident?"

"It's Friday," I said, ignoring his question. "You're supposed to be staying the night at Brandon's."

"Brandon's sick. I came home, because this is where I live."

"Okay," I said. "But in the middle of the night? Shouldn't you be sleeping?"

"Mom, it's nine-thirty."

"Oh." Right, this was exactly how it had happened before. I didn't seem to know that until the words were already out of my mouth. What could I do that was different?

"Well," I said, "No more caffeine after that soda. It'll keep you up all night."

"Last one, I promise." He looked me over. "Still having trouble sleeping?"

"Yeah. It's like the more tired I feel, the worse I sleep."

This was going down just like it had before, right? The longer we talked, the hazier the dream became, and the less sure I was. Everything was clouded but the fairy cat. When was Molly going to tell us what the fairy cat was, and what to do about it? She'd ended our bonfire party early and been all vague and distant. Two freaking weeks of no communication or explanation had passed.

I liked to think she knew everything, but what if she didn't? She said something about consulting resources for our next move, and I hadn't been able to reach her since. I'd even tried showing up at the magic shop, but the door didn't open for me.

If Molly didn't know what the cat fairy was, we had no leads at all.

Evan furrowed his brows. "Did you try that tea I bought for you?"

"Not yet," I said. "I'll do it now. Thanks again for picking it up."

"We've got to look out for each other, right?"

I set down my trident and hugged him. He patted my back and then pulled away.

"I'll be in my room," he said. "Meeting the guys on Discord for a squad battle. You're really okay, right?"

I offered a reassuring, I'm-completely-sane smile and said, "Peachy."

He backed away, scrutinizing that grin, before heading upstairs and leaving me to make my tea. Only I didn't want tea. I didn't want to sleep. That's where this loop ended before, with me sitting on my rug with a cup of tea and my coven scrapbook, and a winged kitten materializing out of nothingness.

I didn't have to do that...did I?

Nope.

With the steely resolve of a woman in control, I took charge of what was happening, and I made a change. I grabbed my phone from the counter and called the one person who would know what to do.

If nothing else, Remi would roast that little kitty like a marshmallow. As I lifted my phone to my ear, that thought sank in and left a sour taste on my tongue and a pout on my lip.

I liked kitties.

"Hey, Jen," Remi answered on the first ring.

In the background, I could hear the familiar voice of Angela Lansbury. Of course, it was Friday night, so Remi was watching *Murder She Wrote.*

"It finally happened," I said.

"You dreamed." Her voice sharpened as she blurted her guess. "Should I be congratulating or consoling you?"

I fidgeted with my mega-sized spork, twirling the prongs with a twist of the rod. "Both?"

A scuffing sound came through the line, like Remi was on the move. With a click, her TV went silent.

"Tell me everything," she said.

"There was a whole repeated thing, me coming downstairs, talking to Evan—"

"I thought he was spending the night at his friend's house," Remi said.

"Right? Well, apparently not. He's here. And in the dream, I made tea, went upstairs, and opened up my scrapbook. And then something weird happened with the pages. And then the kitty fairy appeared."

"I'm coming over."

"Wait, Remi—"

"Jen needs me," she said away from the phone. "Mm-hmm. Probably not until morning." She paused.

I couldn't hear what Julian said to her in response, just the timbre of his voice.

"Love you, too," Remi said, still muffled, like she had the phone to her chest. Then clear as crystal, "Don't go back upstairs, Jen. I'm on my way."

Before I could protest, the line clicked. I set my phone on the counter and moved to the tea shelf. My fingers brushed over the box with the sloth on it before I made the conscious effort to stop myself.

No repeats. I had to change what I was doing.

I stared at the tea boxes a moment, the sleepy sloth seeming to yawn at me. And I yawned back. Instead of taking the risk, I grabbed a glass and filled it with cool water from the tap.

Before long, there was a knock at the door.

With as quickly as Remi had arrived, she couldn't have walked. When I opened the door, I caught a glimpse of Julian waiting at the curb to see that Remi made it inside okay. He gave a friendly wave and drove off when he spotted me.

If anyone was capable of defending themselves, it was Remedy Todd. Still, it was sweet that Julian had waited. He always seemed to be doing the little things that pushed him well into too-good-to-be-true man territory, like driving his lady to her best friend's house in the middle of the night, just because said best friend had dreamed a scary dream.

Or maybe life had just pushed the bar so low that I was easily and overly impressed with the benign. Either way, Julian was a keeper.

Remi grabbed my arms and inspected me. Had she been anyone else, I probably would have been self-conscious being scrutinized braless and in my pajamas, but this was a safety check made from love. Plus, Remi was wearing sweatpants, and was also sans bra in her favorite REO Speedwagon hoodie. Her mass of crimson curls was knotted up on the top of her head, much like I wore my hair.

With a curt nod, likely signaling that she was satisfied with my unharmed state, she threw her arms around me in the hug that I totally needed, even if I hadn't realized it until that moment.

"I'm so glad you're here," I told her.

"Same," she said as she released me and headed past me into the living room. She lifted her palm, sparking a tiny ball of fire in her palm. "Is it here?"

I shook my head, though she didn't see me as she looked over the space with the same critical inspection she had used on me.

"Not that I know of." I shut the door and followed her into the living room.

She grabbed my spork and offered it to me. I gladly accepted it.

"Show me where you saw it," she said.

I led the way upstairs, to my bedroom. I pointed to where the kitty had been. "I was sitting right here, looking at my scrapbook."

The twitch of her lip was so subtle I almost missed it. Remi wasn't a fan of my project to document our coven's adventures. Most of all, she didn't care for the page where she and Molly were holding hands, both looking like they were one hundred fifty years old. That was only a little older for Molly, but quite a bit more for Remi.

When I'd first shown Remi the page, she'd grumbled about bad memories being left in the past. But whether she liked it or not, it was important to keep a record. One day when the two of us really were a hundred years old, she'd appreciate it. And even if she didn't, I liked looking through and seeing the fun we'd had together. She seemed to like the grade school volumes I put together better, but scrapbooking wasn't Remi's jam in general.

It was quickly clear that there was no supernatural creature lurking under my bed, and Remi poofed her fire away.

"We deserve clear answers about what hatched out of that egg. We deserved them two weeks ago," Remi said, a clear jab at Molly being MIA during our time of need. "She knew."

This was not our first conversation on the topic.

I said, "We can't be sure what Molly knew then, or what she knows now."

"And we're left to guess," Remi said. "Because she's not here. She knew that egg was in my house when I moved in. She told us to run when it hatched. Her ball monster rolled it into the fire and *made it hatch*."

"The evidence is incriminating, sure," I said. "I can agree with that. But we should give her the benefit of the doubt." I tapped the photo of the two of them holding hands and shot Remi my most adorable grin. "Covens need each other. And she did help you save me from the vampire hordes. That has to count for something."

Remi grumbled, sat down on the edge of the bed, and grabbed the TV remote from my nightstand. "Let's watch *Murder She Wrote*. The best episode is on."

"'Who Killed J.B. Fletcher?'"

"You know it."

She flicked the episode on while I straightened up my scrapbooks. Then I joined her on my bed, knowing our conversation was over and I'd come as close to winning as anyone could with Remi.

We watched what was left of the episode we'd both seen a thousand times and then crashed, flame and spork at the ready, ever the vigilant sentries.

CHAPTER 3

When Evan was little, mornings had been chaos. I'd chase him around the house trying to catch him while he crawled under the beds and on top of the dressers, all the while attempting to tie his shoes before he pulled his socks off for the fifth time. Nowadays, all I had to manage was dressing myself and reminding the two of us that we should eat something nutritious before we went out the door and on to our separate routines. Just like with Evan's socks, some days my morning duties worked out better than others. Some days I ate a piece of chocolate and called it breakfast. But I liked to think of that chocolate as more of a benefit of being the boss than a failure of nutrition.

Remi didn't hang out, and instead left just before I hopped into the shower. We said our goodbyes with me agreeing, promising, and swearing, that I'd call should anything out of the ordinary happen.

I got dressed for work and headed downstairs, crossing paths with Evan on the way. Cradled in his arms was a bran muffin, an apple, and a bottle of water, while he tapped furiously on his phone. He glanced up and tilted his shoulders so as not to bash me as he passed.

"You have work this morning, right?" he asked before turning his attention back to his phone. With an abrupt eruption of laughter, he startled me before I could answer. Then he hugged his phone to his chest and looked at me. "Sorry. What'd you say?"

"Nothing," I said.

"Oh." He furrowed his brows and leaned on the stair railing.

"You asked if I was going to work," I said. "And the answer is yes."

"Have fun," he said, and continued on his way upstairs, eyes glued to the phone.

"You, too," I called after him.

Because it was Saturday and he didn't have track this weekend, Evan would probably spend his morning on school work before breaking out the online games with his friends. He was gone before I could ask. I grabbed a cup of coffee on my way out the door, and drove across town.

With a long drag of morning joe, I clicked my car fob and headed up the sidewalk toward my tiny office. *Marshmallow Realty* was written in red above the door. It was a boring moniker, but clarity trumped cleverness, at least in naming a business. Selling real estate was a completely different beast, where cleverness was king.

The lights were on a timer, so there was no way to tell at a glance if my business partner Jerry was in or not. I tried the handle, which didn't give—locked. Coffee in one hand, I flipped my free hand, landing my keys in my palm. As with crafting, I found it best to keep things color coded. Red for realty. It shouldn't have been tricky to pick the right one and get it in the lock, but alas, a tired brain meant fumbling fingers.

Careful as a clam, I slid my coffee cup into my elbow, then grabbed the red key from my palm and put it in its place in the lock. Score one for team Jen.

A cringey crack was my only warning before my cup—supposedly as strong as the less eco-friendly types—flattened against my not-large-enough-to-Hulk-smash-cups boob.

Lukewarm coffee splattered all over said boob, bypassing my jacket and giving my cream-hued shirt the appearance of some kind of wild chocolate lactation mishap. Score one universe. Touché. And this was why I kept extra clothes all the places—Remi's house, the magic shop, my car, and most useful today—my office.

After going inside, I poured what was left of my coffee into the toilet and tossed the cup in the trash. Then I headed for my desk and disrobing.

The door opened with me halfway caught in my shirt, stained bra hanging out. I froze for half a second before I heard a friendly, "Morning, Jen."

Just Jerry.

I finished taking off my shirt and pulling a clean one on.

When I finally looked up, Jerry was leaning on his desk, just across from mine, with a queer look on his face. It was his not-so-subtle judgment expression, where he tipped his sharp chin up, crossed his legs, and clenched his jaw.

"Wanna talk about it?" he asked.

"Coffee accident," I told him. "No big deal."

"Sure, you need to invest in a real cup, but I meant—" He flitted his wrist, gesturing at my head. "Raccoon eyes, frizzy hair. So not you. Tell me there's a man involved and it was so hot you didn't sleep."

"I *haven't* been sleeping." I twisted my lips. Jerry was good people, probably my only friend outside of my coven. As he was a non-magically-inclined type, I was not supposed to spill the beans to him. I wasn't entirely sure I agreed with

Remi and Molly's insistence that the hidden-truth policy was for the best, even though they both had assured me more than once that it was for Jerry's own protection.

"So no man?" Jerry stuck out his bottom lip. "That is a bloody shame."

If I didn't know him, I might have thought his tone meant he was being sarcastic, but this was his sincere voice. It just happened to be the case that all of his tones had a sassy quality.

He went on, "I could always set you up, but you know that."

I waved him off. We'd had this conversation before.

"If it's not debaucherous escapades keeping you up, is it stress?" he asked.

"Can't argue with that."

"Way to be obtuse." His words were flat, and his expression remained cool. "It's the lack of clients, isn't it? There hasn't been anything decent to hit the market in forever. And even for the good ones, like the Bradley place, there aren't any buyers."

I nodded my agreement. We had been having a slower than usual fall season. If I hadn't found boatloads of treasure with Remi and Molly, I would have totally been worried about money. As it was, I was fine.

But was Jerry?

His plastic hair was as perfect as ever, as was his plastic smile. I swear the man was a functional, life-sized Ken doll. But behind the perfect skin and remarkably wrinkleless eyes, there was the truth. His wife had a solid job working for the town, but it wasn't enough.

He said, "I swear, you keep looking at me like that, I'm going to get matching dark circles. And when that happens, there's no concealer that can offer enough coverage."

"Sorry."

"So what's our game plan?" he asked. "Hire a marketing firm for the town, out of our own pockets? Seems like the only way to bring people in. I mean, it's picturesque here if you don't mind having absolutely nothing social or exciting to do. Push for a fancy campaign for...campers?"

Magic was what made Marshmallow awesome.

"We have Tergel's," I suggested. "And *Murder She Wrote.*"

Jerry snorted. "Put it in the brochure, see who flocks here for reruns of *Murder She Wrote.* And for the record, you can stream it anywhere."

"I'd come," I told him.

"If you didn't grow up here, you wouldn't be here, same as me."

Maybe. But I was glad I was here. There was nowhere I'd rather be. What I needed wasn't more listings to split my focus further. What I really needed was more time to focus on my special skill—sleeping. That settled it.

"You should take my clients," I told Jerry.

His jaw dropped. "You only just realized how terrible our little town really is, didn't you? You're not leaving me."

"No, nothing like that." I rifled through my drawers and pulled out the two listings I actually had. Giving them to Jerry was really no big thing.

"Did you lie about the man thing?" He squinted at me. "Rich sugar daddy requiring all your time?"

"Ha. I'm too old for anything like that."

"Girl, you're perfection. Those old bachelors would be lucky to have you."

"Sure," I said, and offered him the files.

He put up a hand instead of taking them. "Tell me what's going on."

"I came into some money," I told him honestly. "What I really need is time."

He searched my eyes, with the sharpness of a hawk,

before offering me a curt nod. "Okay. But when you come back, I'll be waiting for you."

I hugged him.

He squeezed me back. "I mean, any day now, we'll get swamped with new clients."

I shrugged. "You never know. Call me if you need help with anything, but I'm happy for you to take my commissions."

"So long as I can find buyers."

"Right," I told him.

"You need time for your mystery hobby, the one that has you up *all night long.*" He waggled his brows. "Go get it, girl."

I could tell him again that I didn't have a man. Either he wouldn't believe me, or worse, he would. Then he'd have more questions I wasn't supposed to answer.

Nervous but jazzed, I grabbed my things and headed out into the day. I was going to master my magic...if I could only figure out how to make myself nap.

* * *

"ARE YOU SICK?" Evan's voice startled me.

A guilty sensation brought a rush of heat to my cheeks, like I'd been caught doing something wrong. I pulled my eye mask up and peeked at my son who was standing in the doorway with a stooped posture and his lips pursed.

"No, I'm not sick," I told him, my voice crackling in an unconvincing manner. "I'm great."

"In your pajamas, lying in bed in the middle of the day?"

"Yep."

Evan came in and sat on the edge of the mattress. He took a moment, prolonging eye contact, then asked more quietly, "Shouldn't you be at work?

I sat up against the headboard to put the two of us at eye

level. "Listings are lean," I told him. Then I paused before saying more.

Our relationship—and parenting in general—was tricky. Sometimes, when I looked at him, I had to remind myself that he was still a kid behind the facade of manhood. At the same time, I still saw him as my baby, and I imagined I always would.

Generally, I believed in telling the truth to Evan. The same went for everyone else, too. Lies tended to do more damage than good. When Evan was five and told me he thought I was Santa, I told him he was right. When he was eight and wanted to know why he didn't have a dad, I told him Carl had run off as soon as I'd told him I was pregnant. When Evan was thirteen and wanted to track his father down, I helped him. And when Carl unsurprisingly showed his soggy gherkin colors and bailed on their planned meeting, I had held Evan as he'd cried.

But since the supernatural world had thrust itself into my life, *damage* tended to mean a lot more than hurt feelings and awkward conversations. It meant getting chained to a wall in the sewers by a hoard of vampires. Or worse.

The stakes had never been higher, and I didn't know what I should and shouldn't tell my son anymore.

"I'll get a job." Evan turned to fully face me. His jaw was set in determination. "Brandon might be able to get me in at Shop and Go."

"What? No."

"I can contribute," he said. "Better if we're proactive."

"First, no."

He opened his mouth to respond. I lifted a finger, to tell him to wait.

"Second, no," I said. "You need your after-school time for homework, studying, and track."

"Coach would understand if—"

I shook my head. "Nope."

He frowned.

"You have your whole life to work. You're going to be a kid as long as you can. I insist," I told him.

His gaze flicked to my golden crown and spork.

"And before you go getting any crazy ideas about selling my prized possessions," I said, "we're fine."

"We're fine," he repeated in disbelief.

"Yep, peachy," I told him.

"You're sleeping in the middle of the day because there's no listings, no money to be found at work, and you expect me to believe we're not on the brink of destitution?"

"Exactly."

"You've been extra crazy lately, Mom. Ever since Remi's husband bit her. I'm worried about you."

"*Ex*-husband," I said, not disagreeing. "Dick's in Remi's rearview, long forgotten."

"That's not the important point here. You get all up in arms about vampires, go wild with the crosses and garlic, then act like it never happened. You disappear without calling, and then you come home with a trident and a crown. *What is going on with you?*"

Gulp.

"I'm letting Jerry have the listings," I said. "I need some time off."

"Okay..." He squinted at me. "But how can we pay the mortgage, or the power, or anything without a job?"

Maybe it wasn't responsible to tell him about my witchy powers, even if I really *really* wanted to, but I could show him my stash. Clearly this whole money thing was stressing him out, and without some reassurance, it was bound to cause him to do something stupid.

I climbed out of bed and opened my armoire. Under the samurai sword I'd confiscated from a vampire and my neatly-folded sweaters was an unassuming burlap sack. With quite a bit of effort, I pulled it out.

"What are you doing?" Evan asked.

Squeezing my sack—*ha*—I made a grand gesture of tipping it just enough for a bit of the contents to spill onto the floor.

Golden coins, some fancy rings, and a diamond the size of a baseball clattered to the floor. One of the coins hit my little toe, apparently at warp speed, and I hissed and cringed in pain. I guessed I should have been thankful it wasn't the diamond that hit me.

Evan dove to the floor to check out the goods. He lifted the diamond up to the light and looked through it. Then mouth agape, eyes wide, he looked at me. "What did you do?"

I laughed. "Robbed the treasury."

He snapped his jaw shut, and glowered, making it clear he didn't think I was funny. "Where did you get this? Is it the same place you got the crown? I'd thought it was fake. Now..."

He'd assumed I liked playing dress up and bought costume pieces. I happened to bring them home after being kidnapped, only Evan thought the whole event was some kind of boyfriend thing, like I'd actually spent the night over at someone's house. At the time, Evan hadn't pushed when I was evasive and didn't give answers. He always made this squinched up, disgusted face when he looked at the spork. He was probably afraid that I'd tell him the spork and crown were a sex thing.

"If your boyfriend gave you all of this, we're going to have to talk about him. It'd be just like you to finally let yourself date and then you find a Nigerian prince or something. And not even the fake email scam kind of Nigerian prince."

"There's no boyfriend," I said.

Evan stared at me like I was the most exasperating human

on the planet. He ran his hands through his hair, looking like he'd dig trenches in his scalp. He was expecting more of an explanation, and he deserved one.

"It's vampire loot," I told him. "After our triumphant defeat of Weaty and friends, Remi, Molly, and I claimed the treasures in the hidden room underground."

"Oh, I get it. You're into LARPing."

Sometimes it was like we didn't even speak the same language.

I asked, "What is LARPing?"

"Live Action Role Playing." Evan gave me a look which said the strangest part of this conversation was that I didn't know what LARPing was. "Where a group of adults dress up with their friends and play make believe, like a fantasy novel come to life."

"Right," I said, still confused.

"And someone ridiculously wealthy must be involved, if this stuff is half as real as it looks. I can't believe you're getting paid to play games." His grin overtook his face. "I'm proud of you, Mom."

"Thanks?"

Evan proceeded to tell me things about games that sounded like the one he had decided I was playing. Apparently LARPing was nerdy, and also a big deal. It was nice to see Evan thinking something I was doing was cool, even if it wasn't true. The whole lie thing felt less good.

We refilled my bag of loot and I stashed it back where it belonged.

"What are you going to do now?" I asked.

"More schoolwork, I guess. Though I'm getting ahead now. Everything that has to be done is done."

I nodded. Schoolwork was important. "How about a movie?"

"I have just the thing," he said. "Meet you downstairs."

Since finding out supernatural creatures were real, I had a lot more interest in watching monster movies than I used to. If vampires were real, who knew what other truth gems existed in those horror flicks, just waiting to be discovered. And Evan was an expert.

He'd seemed surprised the first time I asked him to show me one, but horror movie night was turning into my favorite part of our weekly routine. Usually we didn't watch on the weekend since I was working during the day and after Evan typically had plans with friends, but today I got lucky.

I hurried downstairs, gathered the requisite supplies, and waited for Evan on the sofa while I snuggled up in a blanket.

There were three requirements for our movie hangouts. One—popcorn. I mean, duh, it's a given. Two—my supernatural movie notes journal. If I let some relevant-to-reality tidbit pass through my brain without jotting it down, I'd kick myself for it later. No one likes getting kicked. Three—the newest of the rules—the villain had to be a legit monster. After the second showing of serial killer villains with no supernatural inclination, I declared those films torture and banned from my viewing pleasure.

Evan joined me in the living room and pulled a VHS tape from behind his back.

"I think you're going to like this one," he said.

"Oh yeah?"

The cardboard case was battered like he'd dragged it behind his car. The last time he'd shown me a VHS, I'd been surprised that he even knew what they were, given everything was going digital or disk. But he'd explained that some of the best old flicks were never made into DVDs. I loved that my kid could see merit in the format that I'd grown up with. The only problem was the lack of subtitles. Evan wasn't a fan of them. But I hated to have to ask what people were saying every other scene.

I lurched forward to get a better look, and immediately regretted the ungraceful jolt when my back pinched.

Evan popped the tape into the player. *"Vacations with Vampires."*

"Awesome," I said in a jovial tone, though really I was a bit less than enthused. We'd watched quite a few flicks about bloodsuckers, and I was hoping to move away from them and the memories associated with them. "I hope there are some other paranormals, too. Branch out and whatnot."

"It's horror comedy on a tropical island."

That was different. "Wouldn't the super sunny beach be inconvenient for vampires?"

"That's where the comedy comes in." Evan hit play and sat down beside me.

I put the popcorn between us, readied my journal, and watched the opening scenes. A young David Cassidy clone in a half-open Hawaiian-print shirt slid a pair of Ray-Bans down his nose, winked, and flashed a very fake fang. He flexed his arm as a group of shirtless men with short shorts ran across the screen.

Oh yes, I was going to enjoy this film very much, just probably not in the way my son had intended.

$\mathcal{R}$idiculous, gory, and macaroni-level cheesy, *Vacations with Vampires* was my new favorite monster movie. It was fake enough that it didn't trigger panicky feelings. It was funny enough to make me spit popcorn across the room, even though the best parts didn't seem to be intentionally hilarious. And the man candy was sweet enough to make my eyes happy while not making the film awkward to watch with my teenage son.

The plot was pretty non-existent, with the lead character being both a fang-toothed murder machine and a detective who was supposed to catch the murderer. He ended up being more bad guy than good, given the whole penchant for biting thing.

As the credits rolled, I caught Evan staring at his phone screen, smiling from ear-to-ear. There was a gentle blush on his cheeks that said whoever he was texting was more to him than just a friend.

"Great movie," I said, tapping my knee into his.

He set his phone down on his thigh. "I knew you'd like it."

His phone dinged.

He squeezed his palm over it but didn't pick it up. He squinched his lips together.

"You have somewhere else you want to be," I guessed.

"I hate to watch and run, but a couple of the guys from track are meeting up for food."

"Just guys?" I raised my brows.

"Might be a few of the girls, too. I don't know all the details yet."

There were definitely going to be girls. Selfishly, I wanted to ask him to stay and spend more time with me. But that wasn't what he needed.

"Go," I told him. "Have fun."

"Brandon wants to try a do-over. I'll spend the night at his place if that's all right."

"Isn't he sick?"

"He says he's feeling better," Evan said. "It was a dairy accident."

Enough said. That boy's intestines exploded when someone waved a slice of cheddar at him.

"No girls stay for the sleepover," I said. Not a question.

Evan raised his hands in defense, his expression sincere. "Of course not."

I nodded, told him I loved him, and watched him go. The funny thing was, I'd never minded being alone. Would it be nice to have a partner to share my life with? Sure. But I was okay without. I'd always had Evan. Soon it wasn't going to be just nights spent at a friend's house. Soon he'd go to college, move out, and I'd *really* be alone.

Left to my own devices, I ate a slice of leftover veggie lasagna for dinner, had a glass of wine, and crashed early with a full and bloated stomach. When my head hit the pillow and my heavy eyelids fell shut, I didn't have to stare at the fan and hope for sleep. It came to me all on its own.

* * *

Dale Corduroy, Vampire Detective trotted across the sand. His feathered hair bounced as he swished his head back and forth in sloth-paced motion. Plains of orange-tan skin flexed and bulged, every inch but his dingle dangle exposed, the seemingly shrunken bits tucked away in shorts so short I expected said bits to fall out one of the leg holes at any moment.

The sun soared high in the sky, burning bright. It seemed that only when I acknowledged the existence of daylight that Dale did, too.

He squinted, looked up, and slid his sunglasses down from the top of his head to the bridge of his nose. His mustache twitched. Translucent tendrils of clouded air lifted from the top of his head.

I pointed. "That doesn't look good."

The air blackened into smoke, and all at once, Dale's entire body burst into flames. With all the masculinity of a school girl in a princess dress, he screamed. The shrill noise stabbed right through my head, and I cringed.

Dale ran for the treeline, and upon reaching the shade of a towering palm tree, stopped, dropped, and rolled in the sand.

With a knot in my stomach, I approached, wishing there was something to do to help.

A bucket of water appeared in my hands. As soon as I dumped the water over the flailing vampire detective, the bucket was full again. Something about the whole scenario felt off, but I couldn't peg the cause. Instead of worrying about it, I emptied the refilled bucket, extinguishing the last of the flames.

Dale popped up from the sand, uninjured and completely dry. This seemed normal and appropriate.

"Fank you, Jennifer Jameson." His Transylvanian accent broke as his false teeth separated from the roof of his mouth. He pulled down his sunglasses and winked at me. "You saved me."

This guy was supposed to be a vampire, right? The wiggly teeth weren't enough to convince me otherwise. So why wasn't I scared of him? And why had I helped him instead of celebrating his demise over his funeral pyre?

"Because you're dreaming." The dark voice seemed to come from everywhere and nowhere at the same time. And it had nothing to do with the orange-skinned vamp. It was deep and palpable, like the bass level thrum of a classic muscle car, vibrating through my limbs and straight into my pants.

I spun around to search for the source before turning my face up to the sky. The sun was gone. The sky was dark, the moon hidden behind thick clouds.

"Are you reading my thoughts? I asked. More importantly, I had to ask, "Who are you?"

The mystery voice didn't answer.

As the sensations of the voice faded, the silence it left behind was cold and numb. My chest tightened. I didn't know who the voice belonged to, or where he'd gone, but I wanted him back.

Dale Corduroy brushed the sand from his oiled chest, then walked toward a dense jungle that had only been a cluster of a few trees a moment before. That was weird. Everything was weird.

Perhaps there was something to Mr. Mystery's theory. If I was in fact dreaming, did that mean Dale Corduroy wasn't real?

Dale poofed away like he'd never been here at all.

None of this was real.

"You're real," the mystery voice said. "And so am I."

* * *

MY EYES SHOT open and I scrambled, heart racing for the dream journal on my nightstand. There was a short window after waking before I forgot most—if not all—of the details from my dreams. It was important to record those details before it was too late and they were gone forever.

I scribbled down notes about the voice and what it had said. Rating my feelings was trickier. What emotion had Mr. Mystery evoked? Well, I hadn't seen him. He was just a voice. My palms were sweaty, and my heart was still racing. So, fear. Also, intrigue. Who was he, and how did he find me? Or was he part of my mind? It was entirely possible that *he* was *me*. That seemed the most likely. Why would he *not* be a figment of my mind just like everything else I'd experienced?

I climbed out of bed, my muscles sore for having been *resting*. That was the norm these days. I'd tried a number of different mattresses, some soft, some firm, and everything in between. I was the living embodiment of the princess and the pea, only there was no pea and no end in sight.

After a quick shower, some aspirin, and a fresh set of clothes, I was more or less ready for the day. I checked my phone for the usual texts from Evan when he went to a friend's house for the night.

All was well, so I plucked the orange juice and champagne from the fridge and headed over to Remi's place for our weekly Sunday brunch date.

Buckthorn House was more Remi than ever. Since I'd been over last, the wood had been repainted in the same punch-in-the-face red that had been used decades ago. There was no longer any sign of fire damage, but the scent of char had forever soaked into the house's wooden bones. Children still walked on the opposite side of the street when they passed, as everyone but Remi had done when we were kids.

It was beautiful in a non-inviting way, just like my best friend.

Booming on full blast, the sound of "Rebel Yell" seeped through the front door. I tried knocking, but Remi unsurprisingly didn't answer. Equipped with my own key, I let myself in.

"Remi!" I called from the entry.

She knew Molly and I were coming for brunch, but it was still polite to give warning in case she forgot and was doing the Talladega tango with her man, Nurse Hotpants. It was a crime for her *not* to take advantage of such a tasty man at every opportunity, and I had told her so, more than once.

Yeasty scents saturated the air, making my stomach rumble for whatever bready goodness she was baking.

"Remi," I hollered again, as I made my way toward the kitchen.

"In here."

The music went from blaring to almost too quiet to hear. I stepped into the kitchen, where Remi was dancing and holding a wooden spatula in front of her mouth like it was a microphone as she mouthed the words to the song. She had batter splattered across her face and streaked over her long-sleeved t-shirt and sweatpants.

Her messy bun bounced back and forth on the top of her head as she perfectly mimicked Billy Idol's mannerisms. Feeling the rhythm in my bones, I shimmied over to the radio and turned the knob back up a couple of notches, just in time for the next round of chorus. Remi pointed her spoon at me, and grinning from ear to ear, I tried to replicate her awesome impression of the ultimate punk rock icon. My version was much less impressive, but I didn't care. This was what life was all about.

I used to think the world revolved around my baby. And it did, while he was a baby. As Evan had needed less and less of my hands-on attention, I lost a little of who I thought I was. If he didn't need me to change his diapers or tie his shoes, who needed me and what for? Who was I on my own?

And that's where Remi came in. She was my constant. We'd been besties for forever. She was always there to remind me that I didn't have to be everything to someone else to be happy. I was enough.

I set our mimosa supplies on the counter. Remi grabbed my hand and lifted, gesturing for me to do a twirl. I did, laughing, and then lifted our arms and offered her a turn. I snapped a pic of the two of us with my phone, immortalizing the jubilant, candid moment.

The song came to a close, and I was left a little dizzy with a grin that spread from ear to ear. Remi turned the music back down, grabbed a pair of wine glasses, and said, "Good morning. How'd you sleep?"

The fun drained from the room with those weighted words. *How'd you sleep?* She may as well have asked me if I liked kicking puppies.

I raspberried the air in an elongated exhale. "Weird."

"No more cat monsters, right?"

I shook my head and took a seat on the stool at the counter, helping myself to a mimosa. I poured one for her, too.

"Good. Stay on high alert. Maybe it was nothing, but this is Marshmallow. Nothing might not really be nothing."

"Yeah," I said automatically.

"Anything else in your dreams that could be a prediction? Anything to watch out for?"

"Nope. Just the regular kind of weird."

"Glad to hear it. You *are* going to master your power," she said, her eyes glowing with contentment.

Remi had been so much happier since she'd banished her vampire ex from town. No surprise there. She also had found herself a sexy dragon man, started the business she'd always wanted, bought the house of her dreams, and gained awesome fire powers. Everything was coming up Remi lately, and I couldn't be happier for her, even though her awesomeness punctuated everything hot mess about my life.

I decided not to respond to her mastering comment, as I appreciated her vote of confidence, and didn't want to whine with impatience. *Power now, please.*

"Where's Nurse Hotpants?" I asked, using my fave nickname for Julian.

"Work." Remi swirled her glass, took a sip, then headed to the oven and pulled out a loaf pan.

"What's that?" I asked, shamelessly lifting my nose in the air and filling my lungs with the scents of freshly baked bread. "Tell me it's not one of those vegetable loafs."

"The carrot and zucchini breads are quite popular," she told me as she flipped the bread onto a rack to cool.

"That's not what I asked, and you know it."

I could hear the smile in her words as she spoke. "I do know."

"So?" I waited for her real answer.

"Honey wheat with cinnamon nut swirl. Nothing green, I swear."

"Or orange," I added. "Carrots are orange."

"No vegetables of any color. Scout's honor."

She knew that I knew that she was never in the scouts. Still, I was sure she was just messing with me. She also very well knew that I ate my fair share of vegetables, and didn't need them to be slipped to me like I was a toddler. If she said it was veggie-free, it was.

"So your weird, non-cat dreams, non-prophetic dreams," Remi said, "were they yours?"

"Yes?" I took a sip of my mimosa, then repeated with more conviction, "Yes."

I'd only dream-walked the once, accidentally finding my way into Remi's head. That left me oh for two—no prophecies, no dream-walking.

"What else have you been up to?" Remi asked. "Watch anything interesting with Evan?"

"Mmm," I held up a finger and threw back the last gulp of my mimosa. "Evan found my stash."

Remi turned around, bread cutting knife held in her fist. "Not the porn stash, right?"

"What? No." Thank the universe for that. "My cash stash. And for the record, you look really scary when you do that with the knife."

She looked at her hand and the weapon she held, then set it down and leaned across the counter from me weapon-free. "Better?"

I nodded. "But *found* isn't exactly the right word. I showed him."

Remi's brows shot up.

"He found me in bed, in the middle of the day, and he was worried. I told him I wasn't going to be working—"

"You're not going to work?" Concern filled her voice.

"It's all good." I waved her off. "We're having a slow stint, and Jerry needs the money more than me. So I'm stepping back and letting him have my listings. I mean, I don't need the money."

"But you like your job."

"I do," I said. "But I'd like it more if I could figure out this whole dream witch thing."

Remi squinted. "I can appreciate that. But Evan—"

"I know. I know. You don't think I should tell him things, even though for the record—"

I stopped myself before I said it was Remi who introduced Evan and me to the supernatural world.

"I regret Evan being involved in any of that," Remi said. She sighed and headed back to the stove to cut the bread.

I screwed up. I hopped up from my stool and moved to her side.

"I'm sorry, I didn't mean to imply," I said. "You shouldn't regret anything that happened."

She snorted as she cut into the bread.

"Seriously," I told her. "We could both be dead if Evan hadn't told us all that great monster stuff."

Remi shrugged, then shot me a pointed look. "That may be true. But we both need to be careful."

I knew exactly what she meant we should be careful about. The more people knew, the more danger they were in, or so she thought. But really, I figured they were in the same amount of danger, more or less, only if they knew it, they could look out for it. Still, I wasn't one-hundred-percent decided on the sentiment. And when Remi was so sure she was right, as a general rule of thumb I listened to her.

"I didn't tell him everything. And anyway, he thinks we're doing some kind of weird game and that it's all make-believe."

I grabbed a plate, a piece of bread, and a large slathering of butter while Remi seemed to consider what I'd said.

"That's good, I guess."

I glanced at the clock.

"Where's Molly? I figured she'd be as ready as I am to discuss the whole fairy cat thing. Did she say that she'd be late?"

"I haven't heard from her," Remi said, not sounding at all disappointed about that.

But we'd all agreed to do brunch. Molly was supposed to tell us everything she'd learned about the cat fairy that had hatched from the egg in our bonfire two weeks ago.

"She's probably miffed that we're meeting here instead of Robertini's like she wanted."

"I don't know," I said.

"Oh, I know that look," she said. "Don't waste your time worrying about Molly Fernsby. She's having a harder time figuring out what's going on in Marshmallow than she expected, or this is a power play. Either way, if anyone can take care of herself, it's Molly."

The last part was true, but I wasn't so sure about the others.

"I've missed brunch being just you and me, anyway," Remi said.

"Yeah, it's nice to spend some time when one of us isn't in crisis-mode."

"Exactly." Remi took a bite of her slice of cinnamon bread. She made a hmmpfh noise, then shook her bread at me. "Could use carrot."

CHAPTER 5

*E*ven if Remi wasn't concerned that Molly flaked on brunch, I was. The two of them had a weird blind spot for each other, where they couldn't see how amazing the other was. There were moments of appreciation here and there. With time, I hoped they'd come around and truly embrace each other.

I wasn't going to wait for Molly to contact us. When I left brunch, after eating way too much, I headed straight to her place.

To the naked, non-magical eye, the forest on the corner of Bukavac & Vanth was just that—a forest. Before my first prophetic dream, all I could see was a lot full of trees. But now, I saw the truth. Roots lifted from the ground and twined together to create a big ball of a building. An itty-bitty baby tree grew from the top, much too small for such an elaborate root system. Between the front door and the street, a wooden sign stuck out of the mossy earth reading *The Magic Shop*.

Just being here made my skin hum, like the air itself was pure magic.

The big circle of a door at the front of the building usually opened by itself, a grand invitation to enter. Today, it did not.

"Hello, door," I said to the wooden circle. "I'd like to come in, please."

Maybe I shouldn't have expected a door to respond, but I kinda did.

However, it did not respond.

"I'm going to knock on you now, cool?"

When the door again did not respond, I rapped my fist against its surface, once with hesitation, then twice more with feeling.

Nothing.

I tried the knob in case it was unlocked, but no such luck. Disappointed, I turned to go, but a flash of movement caught my eye. It looked like a blue ball the size of a watermelon barreling through the tall grass next to the building.

Before he popped up to his feet, I already knew it was Fernando. What exactly Fernando was, I had no idea, but the little dude was definitely distinct. He was a cyclops bouncy ball with the most wicked smile in existence.

I headed toward Molly's companion, meeting him half-way. He stopped rolling and slid his hairy feet under himself. Long, skinny arms popped out of his sides, and his unibrow rose with his cheeks as he grinned.

"Greetings, Fernando." I held out my hand for a shake.

Instead of grabbing my hand with his, he darted forward, taking half my arm into his mouth.

I may have screamed. I definitely recoiled.

Fernando slipped off of my wrist slowly, leaving my arm wet and sticky. My sleeve and jacket were pasted to my skin. It could have been worse, given the very sharp, very nasty-looking nature of his teeth.

"Uhh," I said, trying to gather my thoughts.

Fernando made a gurgling sound, which was how he spoke. It sounded like a hippopotamus choking on a large bird, while underwater.

"I wish I could understand you," I told him.

He did a little jig, going side-to-side.

"Right," I said, mostly to myself. Remi definitely told me Fernando was able to communicate by gesturing. I just had to try to remember which thing she said meant yes and which one meant no.

"I'm still not picking up what you're putting down," I told him. "Let's do an exercise so I can work out your code. Sound okay to you?"

He did a little back and forth jig, bobbing from stubby foot to stubby foot—which either meant yes or no...

"The sky is orange," I said.

He held out a boney arm and waggled his finger at me with such enthusiasm that it seemed he was aggrieved I'd even suggest such a thing.

"It's blue, like you," I said.

He did his little dance again.

"Okay, cool. Dance for yes, angry finger for no."

He blinked at me, and either agreed or retorted in a garbled muffle of strange noises. It was also possible he was telling me something completely unrelated. I chose to believe he was congratulating me on figuring him out.

"So, my friend." I tapped my lip with a finger that had not been in Fernando's mouth, trying to figure out what to ask him first. I had a couple of questions in mind. First was Molly. It would be good to know that all was well, and if it wasn't, I needed to know right away so I could help her. "Is Molly home?"

He shook his finger back and forth.

"She's not here." I nodded. "Do you know when she will be back?"

He did his little yes dance.

"Great," I said, encouraged. "When?"

He replied with a string of sounds that was reminiscent of a very hangry stomach.

"Right, not a yes or no. Well, I'd love for you to ask her to call me when she gets in. Please do that. And while I have you, remember the bonfire?"

He did his yes dance.

"And you told Molly the egg needed heat. And then you rolled it into the fire. But then the kitty thing is somehow bad? Right? So why would you help it hatch exactly? And I know that's not a yes or no question." I sighed. "So I guess my question is, is the cat fairy really bad?"

Fernando covered his eye with his arms. His brow dropped, and his mouth seemed to disappear in a tiny frown.

"I'm sorry," I told him. "I didn't mean to—"

Quicker than he'd appeared, he rolled away into the woods. I stood there a moment, debating if I should go after him, but decided better of it. Maybe next time I came by, I'd bring him a gift to show him how sorry I was. I hadn't meant to cause him distress. I also didn't know how life had been at home for him since the bonfire. Was Molly mad at him? Had *she* known what was going to come out of that egg?

No reason to dwell on questions I couldn't get answers to, at least not right now.

When I got home, I expected to be alone, but Evan's car was parked in the driveway. What a nice surprise.

I parked beside his yellow Prius and strolled toward the front door. A bristly breeze gusted past, pulling my coat and hair in its wake. A clacking sound drew my attention. I glanced over to Mr. Geffin's exuberantly-decorated yard next door. Half of a cardboard person stuck out of the side of a tree. She was only legs and butt and witch's broom, and she whipped about like the tube man at the car dealership.

There was something about Halloween season that made people obsess about witches. And in that obsession, witches became one of three types—the scary ones with hairy warts who ate children, the mostly-naked ones, and the dumb ones who couldn't handle their flying brooms. What was up with that? And what would Mr. Geffin think if he knew there was a *real* witch living one house over?

What would Jerry, my business partner, think if he knew about me? Would he see me the same if I told him what was going on in my life?

Would Evan, if he knew?

My kid was the best. He'd probably tell me to put my powers to use picking lotto numbers. With a little chuckle to myself, I headed inside.

It was quiet on the first floor, with no sign of Evan in the living room or kitchen. But my clothes were neatly folded in a pile on the counter, and the pan I'd left soaking in the sink last night was clean and put away. I really did have the best son ever. He was probably in his room playing games or doing his homework.

I cupped my hands and hollered so as not to startle him like a silent creeper. "Hey, I'm home!"

There was no answer, but I didn't expect one, so that was fine. Evan was probably listening to music. But that meant when I inevitably did startle him, I had a good defense. I did *try* to warn him.

I went to the kitchen and fixed myself some hot chocolate. There was zero room in my belly for lunch after overeating brunch at Remi's, so I didn't need anything to eat. Evan might. I'd have to ask. We still had tofu stir fry leftovers, and I'd bought him some lunchmeat last time I'd gone to the store, so that was an option, too. If he hadn't eaten yet, he would definitely want a sandwich.

Marshmallowy hot chocolate warming my hands through

the mug, I headed up the stairs to check in. After I did or didn't fix Evan some lunch, I could spend some time on my scrapbook. Whenever Molly got back from whatever she was doing, we'd do the brunch thing or a bonfire or some kind of gathering, and I'd show Remi and Molly the proof of how amazing we were together. It was a long shot to expect the two of them to be instantly friendly after such a rough start, but we'd bonded over the Weaty incident, and they just needed a reminder to prod them in the right direction.

I could hear faint, muffled noise coming from Evan's room. It was that banging mess of sound he considered music, probably playing way too loud in his headphones. His door was cracked open, so I did a little knock and then popped it a bit farther with my foot.

Evan's headphones were on the floor beside his computer chair. I wasn't sure why I fixated on that. I stared a moment, before I saw *it*.

Evan was sitting in his chair, the light of the screen making his face pale. His mouth was agape, and in front of his monitor was a little black kitten with fairy wings.

Panic welled in my veins.

Everything happened in slow motion.

I screamed an epic battle cry and dove forward. Forgotten, my cup flew from my hand. Hot chocolate sprayed out, raining brown liquid and marshmallows everywhere.

The cat fairy snapped its head in my direction. It lifted its cheeks, flicking its whiskers and flashing tiny kitten fangs.

My arms chopped through the air as I tried to grab the furry monster.

Before I could reach it, the kitty fairy hissed, then disappeared with a pop.

My hand landed on the keyboard that was covered in searing brown liquid and sticky marshmallow. But I hardly noticed.

I dropped to my knees beside my son. It was difficult to see with tears filling my eyes, so I impatiently blinked them away. Evan's eyes were vacant. His body was languid. His eyes slid shut and his head fell back.

I grabbed his shoulders and shook. No, this couldn't be happening. Not to Evan. The cat fairy did something to him, but what? Tears and snot ran down my face and my limbs shook with panic.

A soft rumbling snore came out of his throat.

He was alive, but unconscious—asleep.

"Wake up!" I shouted.

Nothing.

I couldn't breathe. I couldn't think.

There was no time to consider what to do next. I had to act.

I patted his cheeks, hard enough that he should at least try to smack my hand away. I pinched his arm. I yelled in his face. I pulled his hair.

Nothing worked.

His chest rose and fell. I found his pulse on his neck, steady. But he wasn't making any more noise. He wasn't responding at all to me.

When reason failed, there was still magic. I had no idea how, but I had to go into Evan's dreams and drag him out. Accepting defeat wasn't an option.

I grabbed his hand and squeezed my eyes shut, and prayed like gherkin's backside that I could fix this.

CHAPTER 6

*F*ear was a powerful motivator. Determination was, too.

There was no time to nurture my dreamy magic powers and wait for them to grow. I was a firecracker of resolve, poised to burst through whatever walls were blocking me from reaching my son.

I would find him in the dream world, and pull him out of it. It was the only acceptable solution. I would save him, because I had to.

Somehow, smashing my eyelids together so hard I might have peed my pants a little worked.

No longer sitting on the floor in Evan's room, I found myself in an unfamiliar place. Two suns lingered on the horizon of a lavender sky. Buildings reached up toward the clouds, crumbling gray shapes with broken windows and zero character or distinguishing traits. They were blocks, not architecture, belonging in some depressing dystopian alternate reality.

Where was I?

As I took a step forward, my foot crunched on gravel. I

looked down and found that I was wearing boots—combat boots. I also had on military-esque fatigues with a cream and gray pattern like I was some kind of desert commando. Nothing like a little soldier gear to boost confidence.

My legs flickered, the military garb momentarily replaced by the loose-fitting blouse and pants I'd been wearing before transporting here. Real me was still sitting with Evan in his room. This was definitely a dream. Was it possible that this was Evan's dream? If this was my dream, wherever I was had to be derived from something familiar, right? Shouldn't I know where I was?

Thinking too much about the weirdness of a dream could screw up everything. Maybe. I had no idea what I was doing.

As quickly as my clothes had changed to the clothes I'd been wearing in the real world, they transformed back to the unfamiliar fatigues. But a hefty gun appeared in my hands, too. I really wasn't much for guns. My knee-jerk reaction was to throw that death-machine to the ground and pretend I never saw it. So, that's exactly what I did.

"You shouldn't do that," a deep, disembodied voice said out of nowhere.

There was a dangerous edge to it, one that sparked a reaction on a chemical level throughout my body.

"What's it to you?" I asked, spinning around.

There was something familiar about the voice, like I was supposed to recognize it, like I'd met this guy before. Was *he* the cat fairy? If so, kitty had a sexy voice.

On edge, and totally not turned on, I squinted at the buildings on either side of the street, searching for whoever was here. One broken window after the next offered no evidence of anyone here but me.

Whoever he was, and whatever he wanted, I wasn't interested. I had a mission.

"Mom?" A feminine voice came from behind me.

I spun around to where there had clearly been no one standing a moment before.

A woman was there, with soldier garb just like mine, but when I looked at how they fit her, it was obvious that they were not at all the same. On her, they were curve-hugging. On me, they offered the level of flattery of a shapeless blob.

I remembered the deep voice from before, telling me to keep the gun. It was still there on the ground, just behind me. Did I need to pick it up? If this woman turned into a monster and ate me, would I wake up in the real world? Would I be able to save my son?

I grabbed the gun, even though it made me feel icky. Evan was worth it.

When I stood back up, the woman was still standing where she had been, just a few feet away. She had a gun in her hands, too. Hers was pink instead of black, though, and for a moment, I wished we could swap.

She took a few steps closer and grabbed my wrist. I looked at her face, really seeing her for the first time. She wasn't a woman at all, but a teenage girl, and an adorable one at that. Her hair was in a pair of golden knots behind her ears, like an updated version of space buns. She had dewy skin, a button nose, and big lashes over sparkling hazel eyes.

"You're Mom," she said with a tilt of her head.

"Why are you calling me that?" I asked, and then it hit me. Maybe this wasn't my dream. What if it was Evan's?

The girl gave me a confused look. "Mom is Mom."

"Right," I said and looked down to where she was still holding onto my wrist. She was some kind of dream person I guessed, and clearly not the most intelligent one. Was she someone Evan knew from school?

She pulled my arm. "This way, Mom."

I followed, again wondering about the semiautomatic rifle. Was the totally-not-sexy, super deep, caress of a voice trying to trick me into hurting this dream girl who was trying to help me find Evan? There was no indication that she was bad.

"Where are we?" I asked as we turned down a narrow alley.

The girl opened a door. Her face flickered, switching through a range of expressions before returning to a steady state. She blinked and gestured to the open door. I glanced inside, but there was no inside to be seen. It was just a black rectangle for a threshold. It looked solid to me. Was it even a doorway at all?

The girl shook her head and gave me a shove, knocking me into the black wall. Only when I hit it, I went through, and appeared not inside a building, but out in a...jungle?

The landscape transformed from industrial wasteland to tropical paradise. The gun in my hands was gone, replaced by a wooden staff with a massive shiny gem at the top, which I completely approved of. My clothes were different, too. Instead of the military getup, I had a flowing purple robe with rainbow swirls all over it. I double approved.

The girl walked through the black rectangle that stood in the middle of the jungle with no other door-ish features about it. As soon as she was safely on the grassy side, the door completely disappeared.

In a clunky, pixel-like glitch, the girl's outfit changed. Instead of fatigues or a wizard robe like mine, she had a micro bikini with a skirt that was so short, it was more of a belt. This was not the kind of dream I wanted to step in on... well, maybe it would be if the dreamer was anyone but *my son*.

Her gun was gone, too, replaced by a giant, rose-colored sword. At least that part was cool.

"I really should have asked your name by now," I told her, keeping my eyes locked on her face.

"Evan," she said. "We are all Evan."

Before I could ask what in gherkin's name that was supposed to mean, an exact replica of the girl stepped out from behind her. This one was wearing armor. And a third version of the girl appeared from behind her, decked out in a jester's outfit.

"Well," I said. "This is interesting. I guess whoever you're supposed to be, Evan thinks about you a lot."

The jester danced over to me, bells jingling in her hair and on her curled slippers. She paused, leaned in, and clapped her hands together in my face. I, being a real person, flinched. When she pulled her hands apart, a photograph floated between her palms. It was a group of kids, including a few of Evan's friends who I'd met. They were gathered around a desk at the front of a classroom with a whiteboard covering the wall behind them. Beside Evan was the girl whose iterations surrounded me. In the photo, she wore a pair of big glasses, along with the space-esque buns from the first dream iteration, and she was laughing, face red and her hand on Evan's shoulder. He was beaming at her, clearly enamored.

"Who is this?" I asked the jester girl and pointed to her real-world clone in the photo.

The jester snapped her hands together, disappearing the pic. She dropped her chin and shot her brows up to her hairline in an exaggerated expression of surprise. And before I could respond with more than a frown, she bounded away, jingling as she went.

I'd just have to ask Evan when this was all over.

I was wasting time I didn't have. Ready to give up on talking to any version of the girl, and get back to finding Evan, I turned to go.

The bikini girl raised a hand and smiled at me. "Her name is Erin."

Erin, huh? Clearly she went to school with Evan. Given the very unrealistic feel of my surroundings, game-like even, it seemed likely Erin played games with the guys, too. If so, no wonder he was into her. All of the group probably was, since she seemed to be the only girl. I was definitely going to have to investigate this further. *Later.*

"Thanks," I said. "Where is Evan?"

"We are all Evan, Mom," the jester said.

Ugh. This was getting old fast.

Bikini Erin pointed in a direction. "Past the grogin's nest."

Without further ado, I marched down the path, between gigantic fantasy-esque trees. Whatever a grogin was, I didn't care. I needed to reach my son.

Swaying orange petals emerged from behind a bush. A human-sized flower danced out into the path, tiptoeing on tiny green vine legs like a ballerina. It was lovely, but it was also just another obstacle in my path.

I hurried around the flower to continue on my way.

But Armor Erin yelled a deafening, "Grogin!"

I glanced back.

The group of Erins dove at the flower, tearing and slicing at it. At first I was going to call them out on the crazy, but then the center of the flower turned into a mouth and tried to bite them. So Jester Erin bit it.

Frozen in shock, I stared wide-eyed only a moment before regaining my senses and hurrying past. It couldn't be much farther. My chest tightened and my eyes burned as tears began to form. He was close. I could feel it.

I broke out into a run.

My slipper-covered feet pounded against the dirt path as I barreled ahead and around a curve. When I got through the trees, I found him.

Huddled into a ball, Evan lay alone in the center of a clearing. My breath caught in my throat. This was it. I'd found him, and we'd wake up together, and everything would be okay. It had to.

"Evan, I'm here!" I ran to his side and dropped to the forest floor.

I reached out to grab his shoulders. But my fingers met air.

Evan faded, his shape a ghost, and then he disappeared completely.

The tears I'd successfully held back fell.

So close. I was so freaking close.

Before I could figure out my next move, my surroundings began to fade just as Evan had. I stood, gripping my staff hard. The ground beneath my feet remained the same, but where trees had been around the edges of the clearing, there was sand and then water. Nothing but beach in every direction.

A dark shadow overtook the sky, making the world nearly black. Exciting action music appeared from nowhere. This was like one of Evan's video games, and I was about to face the boss. All I had to do was win, and Evan would reappear...right? Defeat a game-style monster with my stick, and no way of knowing how that worked. Easy peasy. *Ha.*

Two giant, tree-sized legs dropped down on either side of me. I peered up to see the underside of a skyscraper sized-man's underpants. No—short shorts.

The giant bent his head down in front of me, his neck twisting unnaturally. He smiled, revealing a set of fangs nearly as tall as I was—*Dale Corduroy, Vampire Detective.* Evan's version was a lot more horror-esque than the one I had dreamed up.

With a fierce battle cry, and the force of all my emotion behind it, I swung my staff as hard as I could and bashed the monster vampire in the face.

The staff bounced back with a *boing* that really put a dent in my courageous resolve. Dale Corduroy laughed, then he bolted right for me head-first.

Fangs flashed. Everything went black as he scooped me into his mouth.

I swung around wildly and tried to find something to grab onto in the darkness, but everything swirled and whirled like a riptide, and then the world stilled.

I was on my back, dizzy, devoured by the giant.

This can't be how it ends.

I had to save Evan. I had to save myself. But how?

In the darkness, a familiar voice seemed to come from everywhere and nowhere at all. "It's time for this nightmare to end."

"Yeah, that'd be pretty great," I said, to whoever. "But I can't give up and wake up. I can't stop until I free Evan from Dale Corduroy."

"You wish the giant to be defeated?"

Where did I know this dark and luscious voice from? I should know. Was it in this same dream that I'd heard it before? Why couldn't I remember?

"Yes," I answered.

"Granted."

A slice of light cut through the black. I squinted at the sudden brightness. Through the tear, a blanket of fur came into focus. A giant, hot pink wolf stood in the light, floating on thin air. He was as big as a bus, and his fur waved in a breeze that didn't exist. I probably should have been scared of the wolf, but I wasn't.

He winked at me. Then opened his mouth and sucked the blackness in. Like a tornado, the air whirled, pulling in flowers and sticks. Shadows circled and disappeared into the vortex of the wolf's mouth, leaving streamers of light and scenery in their wake. Following the dark was a set of giant hairy legs. Dale Corduroy shrank and clawed for purchase, but completely disappeared into the wolf. The pink of the wolf's fur slowly faded, like he was bathing in black ink.

I stared, mouth hanging open, wordlessly shocked and left sitting in the sand.

And then the world rippled, and the wolf jumped into the distortion.

"Wait," I said, too late.

And then I heard a groan.

Evan was lying on his back beside me.

"Evan!" I dove at him and squeezed his shoulders.

He gasped, and his eyes shot open. "What...where..."

With a squee of delight, and a foggy brain full of confusion, I woke.

CHAPTER 7

"*M*om?"

Evan's voice held an urgent tone.

The light was too bright and hurt my eyes. I squeezed my already closed lids tighter shut and rolled my head to the side, crunching something cold and greasy under my cheek.

I opened one eye to see what I was lying on. Doritos bag. I closed my eye again.

"You need to clean your room," I said, slurring my words with lethargic lips.

My heart was light. I was supposed to be sleeping. This was nice.

But the floor was hard.

Why was I lying on Evan's floor? A small scritch in the back of my head, just an inkling, suggested I was supposed to know the answer.

"I'm taking you to the hospital," Evan said.

Well that was a buzzkill.

"What?" I bolted upright. "No."

The movement made my head spin and throb and ache all at the same time. And then reality all came back in a rush—

59

the cat fairy, Evan falling unconscious, the girl in the micro bikini. And the hot pink wolf. Not just hot pink, but also *hot*. At least his voice was. There was something man-like about him, in addition to his rich, dark chocolate voice. But I couldn't put my finger on it.

I shook my head, then immediately regretted it as a fresh punch of pain smashed between my eyes.

"Hospital or Remi," Evan said.

Easy ultimatum.

"Remi."

Evan headed for the hall.

"No, wait." I grabbed his ankle.

He frowned down at me.

"Don't leave. You're not allowed to leave my sight ever again."

"Yeah, that's reasonable." Evan's brows shot up and he tilted his head like he was just waiting for me to hear my own words, and realize how crazy I sounded.

I fumbled at my pants pocket and pulled out my phone. "Here," I said, offering it to him. "Call Remi. But stay here."

Worry took over his features and he sat down on the floor beside me.

"I was only going to get my phone," he said. "I would have come right back. I wouldn't leave you like this. I'm really worried, Mom."

I started to nod, but then stopped when it made my brain rattle. "I know."

Wiping a bit of drool off my cheek, I took in our surroundings. It seemed Evan had stayed in his chair, while I'd crashed on his floor. My rain of hot chocolate had dried into a splatter of cracked crust over just about everything. An image moved across the computer screen, the photograph from my dream of the group of kids hanging out together. And then I noticed the window. The curtains were open, and outside was completely dark. How much time had I lost in the dream? More than that, had Evan shared my experiences? If it was his dream world, and the Erins all thought they were Evan, could Evan remember, too?

We sat together on the floor while he made the call. Based on overhearing this end of the conversation, Remi was already on her way over. After Evan hung up, I gave him a moment before assailing him with all of my questions.

"What do you remember about today?" I asked.

The lines of concern on his face deepened, and his brows dropped even lower.

I tapped his knee and offered what I hoped was a reassuring smile that proclaimed my stable state of being totally fine. "Just humor me."

"Okay. I came home from Brandon's, and finished my English paper."

"Interesting."

"What's that supposed to mean?"

"What time did you finish your paper?" I asked.

"I don't know. Before you came in and collapsed, I guess."

"Show me your screen," I said.

"What? Why?"

I gave him one of my Mom looks, the one that said do as I say because I say so. The two of us got up off the floor, and Evan sat down at his desk while I hovered over his shoulder.

"Sure, fine." He moved his mouse.

There was a document open on his screen, with half a page of conventional paragraphs, and another half a page of *hjssss*-es, as if he hit the computer on S, and didn't stop for— quick check of the page count— one-hundred twenty-seven pages.

"No," Evan said. "No, no, no, no. This doesn't make sense. I was working on this all day!"

"It's okay," I told him. "It was the cat fairy."

He looked over his shoulder at me. "You *do* need to go to the hospital. I'll call Remi back. She can meet us there."

"No," I said. "It's the truth. I'm not delusional, I swear."

With a flat expression, Evan looked unconvinced. Fair enough. It was decision time, and I needed to make one. Hiding the truth from Evan hadn't protected him from the dangers of my world. I should have followed my instincts this whole time and divulged everything.

"Here goes," I said. "I'm a witch. A dream witch."

"Your character for the LARPing," he said, without judgment.

"I don't even know what that means," I said. "It's real, not a game. I'm a dream witch, and Remi's a fire witch."

Evan's jaw went slack and he stared at me in stunned silence.

So, I continued. "And you remember when Remi got bitten and I was sure it was vampires."

He nodded.

"I was right. Vampires are real, and I got kidnapped by one and almost got eaten. But we defeated the smoke monster vampire witch eater, and we confiscated his loot. And I got the sword and the crown, and my spork, and—"

"Trident, Mom. It's a trident."

"Sure," I said with a wave of my hand. "And so there was also this egg, and this blue guy, Fernando, rolled it into a fire and this super adorable cat thing with butterfly wings popped out and it was the cutest thing I'd ever seen. But it poofed away, and today I saw it right here." I gestured to the air. "And it *did* something to you."

"I don't know what to say," Evan replied.

"Tell me you believe me."

He looked down at his hands on the desk, and flexed his fingers, then said without meeting my gaze, "I believe...that you think all of this is true."

I let out a frustrated caveman growl. And I felt bad about cavemanning it up, because really, it was a lot to expect anyone to believe. I hardly believed the wild tale that had spewed from my lips, and I had lived it. How was I supposed to prove the truth to Evan if he didn't remember anything about what happened?

"So," I said, "I had to go into your dreams to wake you up."

"That's the craziest thing you've told me so far," he said. "And that's saying something."

"I can prove it," I said, maybe a little too excitedly. "Erin."

Something shifted in Evan's eyes. "What about her?"

"You've never mentioned her to me, right?"

He thought about it a second, then said, "I don't remember telling you about her, but maybe in passing, or—"

"You haven't," I said. "She's the girl on your screensaver. She is *all* over your brainspace."

Evan paled and shrank down in his seat an inch.

"Ha." I pointed at him. "You believe me."

He didn't argue. "If even a part of what you say is true—that's a big *if*—you have to promise to stay out of my dreams. We need boundaries."

"Fair enough," I agreed. "I promise to stay away from your dreams so long as there aren't any emergencies, in which case, all bets are off, and I do what I have to for the sake of keeping you safe."

"Mom, trust me, I'm a teenage boy. You don't want to know what I'm dreaming about."

I nodded my agreement. This whole tell-the-whole-truth-and-nothing-but-the-truth approach had gone much better than I'd expected. Now I only had to figure out how to stop a magical creature I knew nothing about, and pray that it hadn't damaged my kid in ways I couldn't yet predict.

Easy peasy?

CHAPTER 8

he dead-eyed delivery guy was young. Generally I compared young people to my own kid for a guestimate. Given the explosion of acne on his face paired with the small smattering of frown lines around his mouth, I pegged this guy as slightly older than Evan, probably in his early twenties.

He chomped a piece of gum and held out the bag of Chinese we'd ordered without saying a word. Remi had prepaid over the phone, so I signed the receipt the delivery guy offered, then headed back to the kitchen where Remi and Evan chatted.

Upon her arrival, my bestie had given me a once over. I told her I willingly ended up on the floor, for important dream magic purposes. She'd looked from me to Evan and back to me. Since I'd clearly told him at least some of the truth, Remi didn't press for details and instead ordered Chinese posthaste. Clearly, food was required for the level of conversation we all needed to have.

As I returned to the kitchen, I caught the end of Evan telling Remi his version of events.

"So then she tells me that the fairy knocked me unconscious." Evan snatched the takeout bag from the table as soon as I set it down and rifled through for his personal package of egg rolls.

Remi steepled her fingers on the tabletop and looked up at me. "You must have been terrified."

I let out a sigh of relief. She wasn't going to judge me for telling Evan all about the supernatural. She was simply here to support us. Everyone deserved to have a best friend like Remi.

"I was scared." I pulled out the hot and sour soup, passed it down to Remi, and found my pepper tofu at the bottom of the bag. I took a seat and grabbed a set of chopsticks from the center of the table. "That fear is why I could actually use my dream powers, or at least that's my working theory."

"That makes sense. When my powers started, it was being upset that ignited me."

"Because you catch on fire," Evan said, in a half-question half-statement.

Remi held her hand out, palm up, and summoned a tiny ball of flame.

The orange light flickered across Evan's wide eyes. His smooth jaw went slack.

"That's amazing," he said. Then he turned to me. "So what does your dream magic do?"

Clearly he was looking for some spectacular display, equal in awesomeness to Remi's flame ball.

"Well." I shifted in my seat a bit. "That's still up for debate. Molly—"

Remi leaned in and said softly to Evan, "Molly's the nasty witch I was telling you about, the one with the life magic."

Evan nodded, and kept his eyes on me.

I continued, "Molly says I have The Sight, which is a way of explaining my prophetic dreams."

"Like seeing the cat fairy in your room before it appeared in mine," Evan said, taking all of this in stride.

"Yeah, but that one was weird," I said. "Because it changed. And then there's the dream jumping. I dove into your dream world, but that was the first time I did it on purpose. The second time ever."

"What's the story with the first time?" Evan asked.

Remi cringed. I couldn't blame her. That dream had been of a sexy interlude between her and her dragon man, Nurse Julian Hotpants.

I cleared my throat. "It was one of Remi's dreams, and um...personal. Also, it might have been her dream, or maybe reality. We didn't discuss the details that closely to determine which."

"Well, those are impressive powers, too, Mom," Evan said in a not all patronizing tone. But I didn't have to be told that sometimes dreaming things that might happen, and having no control over it, was not as cool as Remi's fire.

"We can't wait for Molly to show her face," Remi said. "We need answers. What is this cat thing? What does it do?"

I nodded. "I went to her place after brunch today, but she wasn't there."

Remi shrugged. "Well, then we'll look through her stuff and find out what she's hiding."

"I'm not convinced that she's hiding anything," I said.

"Sure." Remi lifted her spoon to her lips and blew on the steaming contents. "We won't know for sure until we pin her down and make her talk."

"Your plan is to assault an old woman?" Evan looked from Remi to me and back again.

"She heals remarkably quickly," Remi said between sips of soup.

"We're not assaulting anyone," I said. Well, probably not.

The night was young. But I knew Remi wouldn't actually hurt Molly on purpose, and that was what mattered.

"Well, have fun, and don't get into trouble," Evan said. "I'll be upstairs finishing my paper."

He popped the last bit of egg roll into his mouth and put his plate into the dishwasher.

"Nope," I said. "You're coming with us."

"If I don't finish my paper—"

"I'm not leaving you alone. That *thing* could come back. Or maybe it did some kind of mind control, and as soon as you're alone, it flips a switch, and you run into town throwing molotov cocktails at the local businesses."

"Wow," Evan said.

"What? We don't know," I told him. "That's the truth."

Evan looked to Remi with a pleading expression. "Tell her that's crazy."

"Actually," Remi said, "I agree with your mother."

Evan sighed.

"But we're not taking him to Molly's," Remi said to me. "Who knows what's going to happen when we get there."

"I have to go," I said to Remi. "And you should go, so—"

"He can stay at my place," Remi said.

I considered this. "Julian *is* the perfect babysitter."

"Not a baby," Evan said.

"Oh yes, he has all that medical training, plus the whole —" I did a claw gesture with my hand.

Remi nodded. "It's decided."

"Don't you need to ask Julian first?" I asked Remi.

"I'll call now, but I don't think he'll mind. Evan is a good kid."

"Hello?" Evan waved his hands in the air to draw our attention. "Who is Julian?"

"Remi's dragon lover," I told Evan.

"Don't worry," Remi said. "He won't bite."

"Right." Evan headed for the stairs.

"What are you doing?" I asked.

"I'm packing a bag," he said over his shoulder. "And my laptop. Because no matter what crazy you're up to, I need to write this paper."

Responsibility for the win. I was so proud.

* * *

AFTER WE DROPPED Evan off with Julian, we drove straight to Molly's. Remi stormed toward the front door like she was a battering ram. I was a little concerned she meant to break it down if Molly didn't answer, but before she reached it, the door opened on its own in that inviting way it usually did.

The interior of the shop smelled like lavender and sage, and somehow also like a used book store, with an overall vibe of being snuggled up in a fluffy down comforter. When I breathed in, it was like inhaling the power of the universe. It was like I could do anything, because I wasn't just me anymore. I was a powerful witch.

Bookshelves lined the walls, each filled with one-of-a-kind volumes that most people would never have a chance to see, let alone read. Fernando tore across the floor, a lumpy blue ball looking like he would crash into all of the tables and crates, but near-missing them all. And at the stone table in the back, with her nose in a book, sat Molly in a green dress, with her silver hair sparkling as if in sunlight.

"You missed brunch," Remi said, making her way to the round table.

Remi still had that storm-the-castle way about her, so I hurried after to try and minimize the incoming damage. Remi took a seat across from Molly, who didn't acknowledge her.

"No apology?" Remi snatched the book Molly was reading. "No excuse?"

"I've been busy. We needed answers, remember?" Molly lifted a silver brow at Remi, then turned to me. "How's the dreaming going, Jennifer?"

I sat down on the stone bench between the tense pair. "There's no easy answer to that one."

"We need to know about the flying cat," Remi said.

I bumped my bestie's shoulder with mine, a reminder I was here for her. She patted my knee.

"Wherever you've been, tell me you learned something useful," Remi said, a touch of desperation taking the sharp edge off her words.

"It's as bad as I feared," Molly said. "The egg belonged to a Kukudhli demon."

Demon.

"Wait, back up," Remi held up her palm like a stop sign and closed her eyes. When she opened them again, she stared hard at Molly. "Those are the guys you said founded this town, right? Baddest of the bad? I believe Julian said something along the lines of the kukudhli making vampires look like kittens."

Molly reached across the table and patted Remi's hand. "He wasn't speaking literally, dear."

My chest tightened, and my pulse pounded in my ears as memories of the cat fairy replayed in my head. It was a demon kitten, and it had done something to my son.

"I know that," Remi said, between gritted teeth. "But I thought they were all supposed to be gone, wiped out, no longer a threat."

"Clearly that is not the case," Molly said.

"But wait," I broke in. My voice came out a little high and a little fast. "Babies can't be all that bad, right? Kittens are snuggly, adorable babies, even if they're demon kittens, *right?"*

Molly and Remi turned to me with concern etched onto their faces. Remi grabbed my hand.

"Tell me," I said. "I have to know everything. Right. Now."

"It was in her son's room," Remi told Molly in a soft voice. "She found Evan unconscious."

Molly paled, which only made me feel worse.

"It didn't touch him, did it?" Molly asked.

"Not that I saw," I said.

Remi squeezed my palm tighter.

"Did your son wake?" Molly asked. "Can he speak?"

"Yes," I said.

"That's a good sign," Molly told me with a sympathetic smile. "Little is known about the kukudhli, or the extent of their abilities."

With the wary way Molly worried her lips, I knew there was more. *"But—"*

I waited for her to answer.

"All the literature is conjecture," Molly said.

Remi looked at the cover of the book Molly had been reading when we'd arrived. *"Compendium of Demonology,"* she read. *"Extinct Species Edition."*

"Claims of extinction are clearly exaggerated," I whispered under my breath.

"Clearly," Molly said. "Which is why I mentioned the uncertainty of my findings."

"If you had this book, and you knew there could be answers in it, why didn't you tell us? It's been *two weeks,"* Remi said.

I happened to agree with Remi on this one.

"It's not my book," Molly said.

"What did you find?" I asked.

Molly frowned and looked up at the ceiling.

"Please."

"Nothing is certain," Molly said. "Accounts imply the kukudhli may hold psychic influence."

"What else?" Remi asked. "Specifics."

"There are no specifics, only legends and stories," Molly said. "You can read for yourself if you wish. But you'll need passing literacy in Algonquian."

Remi's frown deepened. "There's something you're not saying."

Molly's blue eyes flashed with an emotion I couldn't read. "Like other demon spawn, the young are unlikely to possess the magical potency or quantity of powers of a mature demon."

"What else?" Remi asked.

Molly pinched the bridge of her nose. "It's possible they consume, among other things, human flesh."

"Flesh?" I jolted to my feet and slammed my hands down on the stone table, a move I immediately regretted as pain shot up both arms. "You're telling me this thing is a psychic face eater, and it did something to Evan?"

"I wish I could offer you some reassurance," Molly said. "If the demon had eaten a piece of your son, it would be obvious. But I am willing to look at him for you. Heal any damage the demon may have caused."

The tofu and peppers churned in my stomach, threatening to make their way back up my throat.

As far as I could tell, there wasn't a sign of anything wrong with Evan, aside from the fact that he couldn't remember what had happened. "Yeah, okay, thanks."

"What kind of possible damage are we talking about?" Remi asked. "Jen dreamed the demon hatchling would be in her house before it happened. What are the chances it'll return? Psychic mind reading or—"

Molly shrugged and looked down over the side of the

table. Fernando was standing there with a tray of tea. She took it, thanked him, and fixed herself a cup.

"Help yourselves," she said, gesturing to the tray.

I didn't think I could drink anything right now. I couldn't make myself sit back down either.

"Chances are the hatchling was only exploring," Molly said. "It may have popped up a number of places around town by now. While it's possible it has caused trouble, it is also equally likely it hasn't."

"Because kittens are never destructive," Remi said. "And baby sharks never bite anyone. I'm sure baby demons are harmless, which was exactly why you yelled at us to run away when it hatched, right?"

Remi's sarcastic tone seemed to agitate Molly, who narrowed her eyes at her.

"Why did you do that if you didn't know what it was?" Remi asked.

"Don't be silly," Molly said, dismissing her question with a wave of her hand.

"I'm actually curious about that, too," I said. "I asked Fernando why Remi was supposed to watch the egg, and why he rolled it into the fire. He didn't answer me."

I spotted Fernando's big eye peeking out from behind one of the shelves across the room. When he noticed me noticing him, he popped back behind the shelf.

"And then you disappear instead of giving us answers," Remi said. "We deserve answers. We're a coven with no secrets, aren't we? Sisterhood of the magic words and whatnot."

Molly took a sip of her tea and rolled her eyes.

"Stronger together, right? I believe you said that well before we all proved it to be true," Remi said.

"Obviously," Molly agreed. "But I don't have an answer for you."

"Why not?" Remi and I asked at the same time.

"Because Fernando has no memory of the egg," Molly said.

Just like Evan and the hatchling.

"Fernando?" I waved in the direction the blue ball had been. "I'm not mad at you. I don't blame you. I only want to know what happened."

He didn't come out.

"It's no use," Molly said. "He's been particularly hard on himself since the incident. He won't eat. He hardly sleeps. He needs time."

"We could bribe him with those glow worms in the freezer out back," Remi said.

Eww.

"What?" Remi asked, looking from me to Molly and back again. "He eats them. It's not like I said we should threaten him or something."

"I said he needs time," Molly said. "Not brute force."

"It was meant to be a nice thing," Remi said in a raised voice as she shot up from her seat.

Now we were both standing. If it bothered Molly, she didn't show it.

"Of course it was meant to be helpful," I said. "We know."

Molly didn't say anything.

"What if the demon made Fernando do things, and that's the same thing that it did to Evan?" I asked. "What if he's under the influence, too?"

"Did his skin change colors?" Molly asked.

"What?"

"Fernando used to be purple," she said.

"And you didn't think his skin changing colors was odd?" Remi asked.

Molly ignored Remi and continued. "Based on my tracing of the egg, Fernando's skin and fur have been blue since his first contact with it. Does your son have any outward sign of discoloration?"

"We would have mentioned it if Evan was blue," Remi snapped.

"Then it's unlikely the same thing was done to him," Molly said. "As I mentioned, I should examine the boy."

That was something, at least, and maybe the best I would get. I prayed Molly wouldn't find anything wrong with Evan. But the knot in my stomach would not relent.

I nodded my agreement. "Okay, let's go."

CHAPTER 9

*a*fter a quick poke and prod of Evan's cheeks, his feet, and his armpits, Molly seemed satisfied that Evan was fine. Evan, on the other hand, did not think Molly was fine. He was sure to tell me he'd prefer never to see her again. He also preferred to return home for the night, but that wasn't in the cards, either.

The two of us crashed at Remi and Julian's place, and Evan didn't argue under the condition that I let him go to school the next day. He also made me promise that I wouldn't go with him. Reluctantly, I agreed.

So we slept in the living room of Buckthorn House, each of us on our own comfy sofa, and me mostly not sleeping while watching over him in case of demon attack.

My eyes burned from not blinking. My stomach howled as my intestines tried to tear their way out of my torso. Panic mode eventually left every one of my muscles sore and fatigued.

Eventually I crashed, half because of utter exhaustion, and half because part of me knew I'd find more answers in dreams than in the waking world. Or at least that was the hope.

* * *

THE WORLD WAS MIDNIGHT BLACK. I drifted through nothingness with the sense that all was not as it was meant to be. It was a nagging feeling, interrupting an otherwise pleasant float through starless space.

I tried to shrug off the sensation. But instead of disappearing, it grew, sending thorned roots through my head and my chest. My lungs couldn't expand as the tendrils squeezed. I couldn't breathe.

Of course, no one could breathe in space. As if realizing the truth made it come true, my lungs froze and my throat closed. I clawed at my neck, frantic to do something to save myself.

Stars appeared in the darkness, pins of blurry light.

Breathe. I had to breathe.

Unless I *didn't* have to breathe. Again, the thought seemed to alter reality, and it was fine that I couldn't breathe.

But I wasn't floating in nothingness. I was in a giant ball pit as deep as an ocean, full of black balls. Swimming upward wasn't easy, but I worked my way through it, pushing the cool plastic with cupped hands. I kicked off as best as I could, but there was nothing solid to kick off of.

Those dots of light became less blurry, focusing into blinking eyeballs. And the plastic became warm and furry. And it *purred.*

All the eyes turned to me, a thousand tiny kittens covering every inch of me and every inch beyond. They purred as they licked me with tiny wet sandpaper tongues. And they purred as they scratched my skin apart with their blade-like claws.

* * *

MY EYES SHOT OPEN, and for a moment I had no idea where I was. The ceiling was too pretty to be in my bedroom, and this was definitely not my bed. A sheen of sweat coated my skin, making me feel sticky and gross as I lifted my head from the pillow.

Right. We were crashing at Remi's place, in the living room.

I looked over at Evan, who was lying still. *Too still.* My already racing heart pounded harder against my ribs. Images flashed through my brain—of Evan's pale, lifeless face with vertical irises in his eyes. It was crazy. He wasn't half-cat, and he was fine. I told myself this, but I wouldn't be able to rest until I was sure.

For the first time since he was little, I crept across the room and checked to see that he was breathing. No matter how much time passed, or how grown up he became, he would always be my baby. Not that I would creep into his room under normal circumstances now that he was a teen, but after almost losing him to a demon—I gave myself a pass this time.

His chest rose and fell exactly as it was supposed to.

Content that all was well, I climbed back onto my sofa, this time sans blanket, and let myself drift back to sleep.

* * *

SOMETIMES DREAMS WERE stories where I made choices that felt all too real. Sometimes dreams felt like movies that played on their own while I remained a passive observer. As a girl stepped out into a field of wildflowers, I decided this dream was the latter.

Sunshine warmed the girl's skin and kissed her wild

golden hair. She looked to be no older than five or six, with a crooked toothed grin and bare feet. Grasses bent and made way for the girl as she ran, twirling through the field in a scratchy dress. Color didn't seem to have meaning here, but I knew that the fabric was purple, just as I knew that this was the day she'd ruin it in the mud.

Her mother would be cross. The family was supposed to get pictures taken.

Something else was in the field, too—something friendly but afraid.

The girl danced ahead, enjoying the feel of the dirt between her toes and the flowers on her hands. She didn't realize that someone else was there. A rustle ahead was the girl's only warning before she happened upon a plump chicken.

The girl lifted the bird from the ground and held it as it shook, not knowing that the bird wasn't only a bird, but a human girl, too. The chicken's name was Brianna.

I was fairly certain I was supposed to know who Brianna was. There was a feeling of familiarity to both the name and to the hen. That familiarity had nothing to do with the brown and white feathers of the bird or the wild look on her face.

Brianna leaned into the girl, comforted that she was no longer alone, though she was still lost and far from everything that she knew. But covens are family. You're never so lost that your coven can't help, even if you are a chicken.

Storm clouds rolled across the sunny sky, and then I became the girl, only I was an adult version of me. Brianna scratched my chest with her claws.

"Shh," I told her with a gentle pet on her soft feathers. "We're okay."

And we were. Probably.

With the dark clouds came a dark feeling. Something bad was coming.

I turned on my bare heel and walked at a brisk pace the way the girl had come.

"Jenny," my mother called.

But the house I was supposed to be returning to wasn't there. There were only miles of wildflowers, and an ominous sky.

Unsure what else to do, I ran.

The dirt didn't feel nice against my feet anymore. It was too hard, and it hurt. The sun didn't warm my skin. The air was cold and damp and penetrated through to the bone.

From the corner of my eye, I spotted a person. When I turned my head to see who it was, he was gone.

I turned my attention ahead of me once more, just in time to notice the man *right* in front of me. Skidding on my bare feet, I slid into his chest and dropped to the ground. Rain poured down from the sky in sheets, soaking both me and the ground, and covering my purple dress in mud. *My mother was going to be so mad.*

Brianna disappeared, no longer in my arms, or anywhere on the ground around me.

Blinking through the water dripping down my face, I looked up at the man standing before me. His shorts were short, with orange Hawaiian flowers printed on baby blue fabric. There was nothing covering his bare chest except for a carpet of black curly hair. And then he flashed his fangs.

Vampire.

I crawled back as best as I could before the vampire lunged. On instinct, I lifted my arms in defense and closed my eyes. It was a terrible defense. Impact was inevitable, as was my death. But the vampire never landed on me.

Peeking slowly through one eye first, like that was

somehow going to spare me from getting eaten, I found everything was frozen.

The tropical vampire was suspended midair. So was the rain.

I moved to the side, right out of the vampire's murder path, and rose to my feet. Water droplets moved for me, getting me wet when I touched them, but otherwise existed as still, floating orbs in the air.

Weirded out by the experience, I reached a finger in front of me and poked a droplet. It turned to water on my finger and dripped down my hand.

"Brianna?" I called out for my feathered friend.

"She's gone." A deep voice came from nowhere. Like so much else in the dream, it felt familiar.

"Who's there?" I asked, spinning.

"It's me. It's always me."

A bear stepped out from its hiding place in the grass. No, that wasn't right. He didn't hide. Without any idea how I knew, I did, with certainty that he had been there waiting for me to see him the entire time.

"You don't remember, do you?" The bear's white fur flooded with color, vibrant stripes of blue and purple and red and orange.

When a bear appears out of thin air, logic says you run. But the hum in my limbs wasn't exactly fear. It was excitement. I mean, I was talking to a rainbow bear.

"What am I supposed to remember?" I asked.

His bear eyes sparkled with amusement.

He thought I knew him. Searching my memory, I tried to analyze what exactly about him was familiar, because there was something. I just didn't know what it was.

"I've waited for decades. I can wait a little longer," he said in that dark voice that penetrated right through me.

Did he say *for* decades or *four* decades?

82

"Wait for what?"

"You, Jenny. It's always been you."

No one but my parents had called me Jenny since I was little. Had the bear caught that detail from earlier in the dream, when my mother called me back to the house? I stared at the rainbow bear, and I didn't feel like he was deceiving me. I felt like I was supposed to hop on his back and go for a ride, flying through the clouds.

"Nightmares can only touch you if you let them," he said. He scooped a bundle of grass in his bear claw, and tossed it into his mouth.

And then he winked.

Aha! I knew exactly where I'd seen him before. This was a dream, and I'd met him in another dream, only he hadn't been a bear then; he'd been a wolf.

"I know you," I said, but the words were silent. I had no voice.

Wind howled, whirling the grass and wildflowers in a spiral around us. The raindrops disappeared from the sky. I tried yelling a string of nonsense just to hear my voice, but it was eaten by the wind.

The bear opened his mouth. Wider and wider it stretched, until his jaw was taller than me. The air poured in, taking the wildflowers with it. Dale Corduroy got sucked in, along with the grass and the earth, and the sky and the clouds. Everything disappeared into the bear. Everything except for me.

* * *

I JOLTED upright on the couch where I'd slept. Remi's living room smelled delicious, like I could fill my belly on air and be completely satisfied. There was a light on in the kitchen, but none shining through the edges of the curtains from outside. It must have been early, but it was always difficult to tell this time of year with sunrise not happening until around seven.

I glanced over to the other couch. Evan was already up, his blanket folded neatly on top of his pillow. But his backpack was still here, so he hadn't rushed off to school just yet.

Memories of my dreams were fading fast, and I didn't have my dream notebook here with me. So as not to lose everything, I ran over to Evan's backpack, opened the little zipper and snagged a pen without snooping.

Rainbow bear = pink wolf. I stared at the words I'd written on my arm. There. That should do the trick. I'd caught the most important bit, hopefully, and committed it to memory. There was something else. A field? I wasn't sure.

I put the pen back in its place, and followed my nose to the kitchen. Evan was sitting on one of the stools at the counter eating, while Nurse Hotpants pulled a tray out of the oven. Both had their backs turned to me. I didn't even check out Nurse Hotpants's butt as he bent over because I was a good, respectful friend, and those buns belonged to my bestie.

"Good morning, Jen," Julian said before turning and flashing me a friendly smile.

Evan looked up from his plate, his golden-brown hair sweeping just over his eyes. "Oh, hey, Mom."

"Good morning," I said to both.

"I need to brush my teeth and head out," Evan said.

"Need me to drive you?" I asked. "I can take you back to the house to get your car or take you right to school."

"Nah. Julian took me by the house to grab my car last night. I'm all set." Evan held up a pair of keys, then popped the last bite of what looked like an overstuffed omelet into his mouth. He took his plate to the dishwasher and said over his shoulder, "But thanks anyway, Mom."

"Yeah, sure." I stood there, completely not needed by my very grown-up son.

He kissed my cheek as he hurried past. "Meet back here after track?"

I hadn't thought about track. It wasn't exactly fair to expect Evan to give up his life. Part of me wanted to grab him and tell him to stay here indefinitely until I knew the world was safe. But that was never going to happen entirely. There would always be some danger in life, which was part of what made it magical.

"Let's plan on going home," I said. "I'll call if something changes."

"Sounds great." Evan left the kitchen, bustled about, and hollered a goodbye as he left.

And that's when it hit me—I'd forgotten to ask about his paper. I grumbled at myself before remembering I wasn't alone.

Julian was weirdly quiet. It must have been a dragon thing. Definitely not a man thing since they were typically all burps and stomps and farts.

"Would you like something to drink?" he asked. "We have tea, coffee, milk, and juice."

"Water would be great," I said. "And I don't mind serving myself."

I grabbed a glass from the cabinet and filled it from the faucet.

"Omelet?" Julian asked.

"Yes, please," I said. "But only if you really don't mind."

"I don't mind."

"Okay, then yes."

"What would you like in it?"

I glanced at the stove where there were two other omelets going.

"Whatever you and Remi are having," I said. "Where is she, anyway? Still in the shower?"

Julian nodded. "She just turned the water off. She'll be down soon."

I was amazed by his hearing, but also kinda glad no one in my house could do that. There were plenty of things I did that I was glad there weren't witnesses for.

"And you probably don't want what I'm having."

"Oh yeah?" I asked. "Meat, right?"

"Yes, there's that. But I was referring to the ghost peppers."

I wrinkled my nose.

"How does spinach, mushroom, onion, and tomato sound?" he asked with a smirk.

"Perfection."

"Wait till you taste it," Remi said, sauntering into the room in a Led Zeppelin t-shirt and a pair of sweatpants. She tossed her sopping wet red hair to the side and patted it dry before slipping the towel over her shoulders and pulling me to the stools. "How'd you sleep?"

"Weird," I said, showing her the note scrawled on my arm.

Her mouth stretched into an O shape.

Julian slipped two plates in front of us.

"Thank you," I said. "And thank you so freaking much for watching Evan. I don't think I said last night how much I appreciate it."

"You did," Julian said. "And you're welcome. It was nothing."

"We're family." Remi tapped my hand before digging into her breakfast.

Family, right. Something about my dream had me thinking about my mother. I needed to call her and check in. Details were already mostly faded away, as they tended to do whenever I didn't scribble everything down in my journal. It didn't feel like it had been a prophetic dream or anything, but better to be safe.

I took a bite of omelet and it was pillowy heaven in my mouth, and also an explosion of flavors. An involuntary reaction, I moaned my appreciation.

Remi swallowed and grinned at me. "Right?"

"Can I eat breakfast here every day?" I asked.

"Of course you can," Remi said. Then her gaze fell to my arm. "What is this about exactly?"

"I didn't have my dream journal this morning," I said. "Making do."

"And this—" She squinted to read the words upside down. "Rainbow bear. That's a large, hairy gay man, correct?"

"What? No," I said. "He's a literal bear, with fur colored like a rainbow."

Remi shrugged. "Rainbow bear and pink wolf duo—hmm, okay. Are they the next big bad we have to look out for?"

I couldn't say for sure yet, but the feeling that lingered, even if I'd forgotten everything else, was that he was on my side. "No," I said. "I don't think so."

"Have you heard of rainbow bears before, Julian?" Remi asked.

"No," he said.

I wasn't sure if I should be relieved or disappointed, but the swirl in my gut suggested the latter.

A loud bang came from the front of the house, like an elephant had slammed into the door. Remi and I jumped. We all turned.

There was a second bang, and a third.

Julian whooshed down the hall at an inhuman speed. Remi and I scrambled off of our stools to follow.

Before Julian could reach the end of the hall, the door burst off its hinges and skidded across the floor.

Standing in the doorway, shadowed in the bright light of

the just-rising sun was a man not-at-all appropriately dressed for the crisp autumn weather. The only thing he had on was a pair of floral short shorts.

It couldn't be, yet it most definitely was Dale Corduroy, Vampire Detective.

CHAPTER 10

The monster movie character standing in the doorway flipped his feathered brown hair to the side, revealing his set of pale green eyes and a mouth full of fangs. In person, even with his ripped abs, those vampire teeth ruined any appeal Dale Corduroy may have otherwise had.

Remi summoned a ball of fire as Julian barreled toward Dale.

I stood still, holding my breath, waiting for the realization that I did not in fact need to breathe because this whole thing was a dream. But my lungs slowly felt like they were filled with lead.

Julian shoved Dale Corduroy out into the lawn and tackled him to the ground. Steam rose from the vampire as the first shreds of morning light hit him. He hissed and thrashed wildly while Julian kept himself away from the vampire's teeth.

"Who are you?" Remi asked, stepping up beside the two. She lowered the fireball next to the vampire's face. "You won't like what happens if you don't answer."

I stood in the doorway still holding my breath, until I couldn't, and I gasped for air.

"The sun, Dale Corduroy's only veakness," the vampire crooned in his very fake Transylvanian accent. Then equally unbelievably, he added, "Nooooo."

"This isn't a dream," I said to myself.

A gust of frigid air blew through the yard and right through me. My teeth clattered and the little hairs all over my body stood at attention. I rubbed my hands over my bare arms and covered my nips with my elbows.

Holy purple nurples, *this was all real.*

In a flash, I scrambled for my phone from my jacket hanging just inside the door. If ever there was an occasion to snap pics, this was it.

"Corduroy? Seriously?" Remi scoffed, then she glanced back at me when she heard my camera click. She turned her attention back to Dale. "Sounds like a seventies porn star. Is that what you were before you were turned? I guess the hotpants fit the theme, the Burt Reynolds mustache, too. All you need is a pair of roller skates."

"I sense no lie in his words," Julian said. "But there is something off about his scent. This man is not a vampire."

"The night is my mistress, mwahahaha." Dale Corduroy opened his mouth wider, showing a set of fangs that certainly looked real.

I hurried over to Remi's side to get a better look at the vampire's face—and to snap a close-up of those fangs.

Dale's skin boiled with the touch of the rising sun, so he was hardly recognizable. But that voice and those short shorts—there was no denying it was him.

"He looks like a vampire to me," Remi said. "If he's not, then what is he?"

Dale Corduroy's eyes went wide. With a pop, he burst.

Dust flew outward in every direction, covering the three

of us. And as the cloud of gray faded with the wind, sparkly confetti rained slowly to the ground.

"I might know the answer to this one," I said, slowly lifting my dust-covered hand.

Julian rose to his feet. He and Remi both looked like they'd been hit with a talcum powder bomb. I imagined I looked exactly the same. They stared at me waiting for answers.

Okay, just one more pic. I turned and caught the three of us in an epic selfie. That was a shoo-in to my scrapbook, no question.

"His name is Dale Corduroy, and he's a vampire detective in a movie I recently watched," I explained.

"Dale Corduroy is the character or the actor?" Julian asked.

"Character," I said.

"So the actor dressed up as his character, got turned, then came to Marshmallow and knocked down our door for...reasons?" Remi's frown made the gray mask on her face crack and exaggerate the lines of her expression.

"He wasn't a vampire," Julian said.

"Right." Remi frowned. "He used really convincing makeup and magicked up some superstrength with what, drugs? Dale Corduroy like-y the bath salts?"

"It's not a new movie," I said. "Totally old school. The actor should have aged since then."

"So he got magicked a few decades ago," Remi said.

A boy on a bike looked over at us as he zoomed past. Remi scowled at him. A few moments later, a woman jogged in the same direction. Her expression was one of concern as she looked at us and slowed to a walk.

"Everything okay, Julian? Remedy?" she asked.

With a quick sweep of the ground, I found no evidence that the powder and confetti had ever been a vampire. Good thing, because I had no idea how we'd explain a *disembodied foot*. A set of hairy toes stuck over the end of a neon orange flip flop. Clearly not *all* of Dale Corduroy had exploded.

"Peachy," Remi said in a flat tone to the woman.

No one seemed to have noticed the foot except for me. I inched closer to it, keeping a smile plastered to my face and looking anywhere but at the foot.

"Baking accident," Julian said in a friendly tone. "Everything is fine."

"Oh." The woman chuckled. "I hope the kitchen's okay. It would be a tragedy if I had to get Jason's birthday cupcakes somewhere else."

She glanced at the doorway, broken from its hinges. I took the opportunity to station myself between her and the foot.

"Everything is fine," Julian said in such a way that *I* almost believed him.

"Okay then," she said with a wave. "See you later."

Julian waved back as she jogged after the boy. Remi was a brick of tension, scowling at the retreating pair.

A *puft* sound made me turn, only to find the foot had exploded into dust and glitter like the rest of Dale Corduroy.

"Jason's a soggy gherkin," she grumbled. "Little brat called me a cow after running me down on that bike of his."

"There will be no sabotage to the cupcakes," Julian said.

Remi rolled her eyes like they'd had this conversation before.

"Sounds like he's gherkin's merkin," I said, helpfully.

"What's a merkin?" Remi asked.

"It's like a furry bikini bottom," I told her. "You should look it up."

Julian smirked, but the amusement quickly faded. "We should go in and get cleaned up. I need to get that door fixed as soon as possible."

"Right," Remi said.

As we headed in, Remi turned to me. "We'll look up the Dale Corduroy guy, see if there's anything on Wikipedia about him."

I nodded. "Okay, but I don't think that was the actor."

"What do you mean? You think it was an impersonator?"

"No," I said. "I think it was really Dale Corduroy."

"But he's not real," Remi said, squeezing my shoulder.

He seemed pretty real to me, both in the flesh, and before in my dreams. It hit me in the hall—Evan could have passed by Dale Corduroy on his way to school. What if he didn't make it there safely?

I pulled my phone from my pocket and panic-dialed the school.

"Jen?" Remi peered around the corner from the kitchen.

I pointed to my phone.

She nodded and offered me a wet dishcloth. I gratefully accepted it and used it to wipe the vampire dust from my face.

Melinda, the front office lady, answered on the third ring. "Marshmallow High, this is Melinda, how can I help you?"

Julian easily lifted and carried the door from the yard. I headed up the stairs to get out of his way.

"Hi. This is Jen Jameson." I pinched my lips together to stop from adding, *no relation to the porn star,* as someone with my name so often does. "Could you confirm for me that my son Evan made it in safely this morning?"

"Of course," she said. "Is everything okay, ma'am?"

"Mm-hmm," I said as convincingly as possible. "Weird morning. Everything is fine."

Clicking sounds told me Melinda was busy pulling up the info on her keyboard.

"Yes," she said a moment later. "Evan arrived on time for homeroom."

"Great," I said. "Thank you."

With a sigh of relief, I hung up and used the little gingham towel to wipe down my hands and forearms. The red and white squares of the fabric turned an ugly shade of brown.

"We need showers," Remi said, appearing next to me on the landing. "Your extra set of clothes is in the closet. I'll take the upstairs bathroom, you take downstairs?"

"Sounds great," I said. "What about Julian?"

He seemed to have disappeared after setting the door up beside the hole where it was meant to fit.

"He'll shower when he's done," Remi said. "He ran out to the store for door supplies. He said something about the frame being split, so he needs to buy wood to fix it. He'll be a while."

"Okay then," I said. "Thanks."

I grabbed my extra clothes from the hall closet, grateful for my preparedness, then headed straight to the shower.

The water was hot and wonderful, until it wasn't. After a few quick minutes, the water turned icy, which was fine, because I was eager for Remi to prove me wrong about Dale Corduroy. Whoever the actor was, he had to have been turned right after filming. Or this guy was an impersonator. But deep down, the more I thought about it, the surer I was that none of that was true.

Logic was overrated.

Dry and dressed in a billowy lavender blouse, and even more billowy white pants, I headed back to the kitchen.

Remi was already on her stool, phone in one hand, fork in the other. She turned the screen toward me and said, "Look."

I took the seat beside her, no longer hungry. Sad, given how good Julian's eggs were. On Remi's phone was a photograph of a middle-aged man sporting a white tank top and a beer gut.

"Dad bod," I said.

"Right?" Remi chuckled. "The first thing I thought when I pulled up the actor's info was wow, he looks so old. Then I realized he's about the same age as us."

"I hate it when that happens."

"Same. It looks like TMZ has him in California getting caught with hookers...last night, looking like this. Pretty different from the guy who torched himself in the sun in the front lawn."

"Yeah," I said.

"So we're leaning toward impersonator, right? The only thing that doesn't make sense is how sure Julian was that he wasn't a vampire."

This had to be the work of the cat fairy, finally flexing its psychic control over Evan. I knew Molly said his skin would have changed color if the cat had messed with him. But he'd dreamed of the towering giant Dale Corduroy when the demon had knocked him out. It was the only reasonable explanation.

"He's not—was not—an impersonator. He was the movie character, and I think *Evan* might have brought him to life."

Remi blinked at me and set her phone back on the counter. "Well don't hold me in suspense. Tell me."

"When I went into Evan's head, there was a giant towering over him, holding him captive. We'd just watched the movie with Dale Corduroy."

Remi was quiet, too quiet. She thought I was being crazy, believe-everything Jen. She was the skeptic. It was the normal dynamic, and I couldn't expect her to believe me without solid evidence.

Finally, she responded, "You're the dream witch. How do we harness and nurture your gifts to make sure this doesn't happen again?"

I was the dream witch. "What if it wasn't Evan? *What if it was me?*"

"You are amazing," Remi said. "Maybe this is the next evolution of your magic. Either way, we need you in full control of your powers. Tell me how I can help."

I grinned from ear to ear and squeezed my bestie in a big hug, and then together we hatched our plan.

CHAPTER 11

The more I thought about it, the surer I became that it was me who had conjured Dale Corduroy, and not Evan. Evan had shown no signs of weirdness and his skin was its usual peachy hue. Me, on the other hand, I was exploding with weirdness.

There was lots to do before my evening dream hangout plans with Remi. Phone calls took up a big chunk of my day.

I checked in with Jerry, because somehow not working and not knowing what was happening at our business was almost as stressful as actually being there putting in the work hours. *Almost.* It was also amazing, because even if my brain decided I should worry about it, I didn't have to put the time in at the office or show houses.

After chatting with Jerry, I scrolled my phone, picked my favorite photos, and printed physical copies.

My mom was my next call. She told me about the additions she and her gardening club were making to the park at the center of town, the changes in my dad's sleep patterns that had him preferring the recliner in the living room to their bed, and the water yoga class she was teaching at the senior center. When it came time to regale her with the stories of how great I was doing, I changed the subject to how Evan had been missing the weekly overnight he'd had at her house when he was little.

She called my bluff, of course, as mothers always do. Still, she happily agreed to have him sleep over. He might not be thrilled about being forced out of the house for another night, but this was day one of the dream experiment, and it was safer if he was not at home. Plus, it gave me one more night to watch out for kitty demons before Evan inevitably returned to his room.

Molly was my last call. Evan would be home from practice at any moment, and I knew he was not going to be happy when I told him my plan. Good thing I was prepared—with his favorite pizza.

After a few rings, I figured Molly wasn't around. Just before I hung up, she answered.

But she didn't say anything. She did make some strange mouth-breathing sounds though, a lot like Melvin Murderface would from the closet in the movie *Camp Murder* I'd watched with Evan on one of our movies nights.

"Hello? Molly?" I was a little concerned by the lack of talking, plus she must have done a lot of running to get so out of breath.

"Hmmmgrrff." The response was garbled and deep, and definitely not Molly's voice. Fernando must have answered for her.

"Hi, Fernando," I said, leaning my elbows on the kitchen counter. "It's Jen."

There were scuffling sounds on the other end of the line.

"Can you please give Molly a message for me? I made a monster come to life from my brain, and I'd appreciate her help in figuring out what to do next. Remi and I are going to work on my powers tonight and I'd like it to be a whole-coven event. Say nine?"

"Blurggffff."

"Thank you, Fernando," I said, having no idea if he was going to tell her or not. "Bye."

I hung up and decided right there and then that I needed a better method of communication with Fernando. Maybe there weren't any ways to understand him on the phone, but maybe there was something I could do to help in person.

With a few clicks on my phone, I searched my fave online store for chalkboards. It turned out there were lots to choose from. And then I found *the one.* It wasn't a chalkboard at all, but instead a small whiteboard with a decorative chain meant to hang the piece up on a wall. It would be just perfect to go around Fernando's head, hopefully. It was possible it'd sit right over his eye.

I didn't even know for sure if he could write, or if so, if his writing would be as unintelligible as his speech. But if the board didn't work out, I'd hang it by my fridge for grocery lists or notes or something.

One click.

There was only one thing left to do while I waited for Evan to get home—put my freshly-printed pictures into my scrapbook, of course.

Flipping through my stack of celebration papers, I stopped on the perfect page. Rainbow hued sprinkles decorated a matte pink that was probably supposed to be a confection of some sort. But the colorful sprinkles matched perfectly with the confetti that had burst from the walking, talking Dale Corduroy piñata.

I arranged the paper and photos on the blank page, debating which would look best where. The clattering of keys at the door alerted me to Evan's arrival. I cleaned up my crafting supplies and prepared for the inevitable incoming tension.

"Hey, Mom," he said as he stepped inside. Then he sniffed the air. "Do I smell pizza?"

"You sure do," I said, showcasing the box like Vanna White with her letters.

Evan put his coat on the hook and set his backpack at the bottom of the stairs before joining me in the kitchen. His expression was guarded. He crossed his arms and didn't brush his hair back as it fell over his gray eyes.

"Tell me," he said.

"Tell you what?" I asked.

"You're trying to butter me up before bad news," he said.

"I can buy pizza without it meaning anything." I opened the box and waved a hand in a flourish for emphasis. "Mushroom, pepperoni, sausage."

"It's not half veggie," he said, not showing any sign of softening his resolve.

"So?"

"So you don't eat this. I do."

"Right," I said. "A mother can't do something nice for her wonderful son who she loves wholeheartedly?"

His stomach rumbled. "I won't eat a bite until you tell me."

"Fine, fine," I said. "But it's not bad news. You *get to* spend the night at Gram and Pop's house tonight. Yay."

Evan sighed and dropped his arms. "Why?"

I could be vague in my response, but I was done with lying to my son, even if it was by omission. It was exhausting and it did neither of us any favors.

"I'm exploring my powers," I said. "I accidentally made a dream come to life—and not the happy kind. If I don't get my magic under control, who knows what could happen."

"You shouldn't do it alone. What if you bring to life something terrible and you're too asleep to defend yourself?"

"I thought of that," I said. "Remi's coming."

"Okay then." Evan leaned on the island across from me and grabbed a slice from the box.

Okay then. I guessed we were good. That went better than expected.

"But at some point, Mom, you're going to have to let me sleep in my own bed. You're a witch. We live in a town with dragons and vampires. Whether you like it or not, magic is a part of my life, too."

That was fair.

"The vampires are gone," I said.

He sharpened his gaze and twisted his lips in a look that said I clearly knew that was not his point. That was fair, too.

"I guess at some point I'll have to let you stay in your room," I said. "But not tonight."

"Not tonight," he agreed, then returned to his pizza.

Evan spent a little time in his own space, while I prepped for the night's adventure. Candles and wine seemed appropriate for our witchy gathering, but then I decided it was more date-like. Slumber party was more apt, with the sleeping bags and bedding gathered in the living room.

I put the candles away, pulled out some snacks, and put on pajamas.

Evan came back downstairs when he was all set to go. "I'm heading out," he told me.

"Love you."

"Love you, too, Mom."

He opened the door and went to step out.

"And Evan," I said, making him pause. "Just in case I'm wrong, and it's you who created Dale Corduroy from your cursed kitty psychic powers, be careful."

He blinked, stared at me a beat, then said, "Okay. Bye."

It wasn't long after Evan left before Remi arrived. I recognized her knock and let her in.

She hung her jacket on the hook, kicked off her shoes, and stretched. "I'm ready," she said. "Where's Molly?"

"I'm not sure if she's coming," I said.

"That woman." Remi frowned. "I can't believe she's ditching us again."

"Wait," I said. "I left a message with Fernando. She might be coming. If she's not, it's probably my fault for relaying her invitation through a blue creature who doesn't actually speak human."

She didn't acknowledge what I'd said about taking responsibility. Instead, she added, "If it's just the two of us, we either don't have someone to spot for danger or we can't dream together."

"I know," I said. "Give her time. What about Julian?"

"He's working. If Molly doesn't show, I say we go to her place and grab her."

"That sounds like kidnapping," I said. "That's generally frowned upon."

"Molly is no kid," Remi said. "The woman is as old as whatever came before dirt."

"I heard that." Molly's muffled voice came from behind the front door.

"She has young ears," I said with a grin.

I hurried to the door to let her in.

Remi had once described Molly as a grumpy Yoda, hobbling around giving cryptic advice. I didn't see her that way. Molly looked ethereal as always in her flowing dress. I didn't know how she did it, but she had a glowing way about her, like she was a Greek goddess. Her cheeks were rosy apples when she smiled up at me.

"I received your message," she said. "I wouldn't miss it."

"I'm so glad." We did a quick, friendly hug, before I showed her to my living room.

"You have a lovely home," she said.

I guessed this was the first time she'd been here. Crazy, since it felt like I'd known her forever. That was just one of those things about her, I decided.

"Thank you," I said. "It's not magical like yours, but I like it."

Molly took a seat as far from Remi as the furniture allowed. The two looked at each other.

Remi did a bro nod, like Evan and his friends did with each other. She said, "Hey."

"Hello," Molly replied.

Good. This was all going well so far. With the two of them, the threshold for civility was relatively low. I sat down between them and pointed out the snacks on the island, in case anyone wanted anything. Remi grabbed the tray with the veggies and the hummus, set it beside her, and chomped carrots like an angry bunny.

Molly ignored her and said to me, "Tell me about the dream you brought to life."

"He was a vampire, who Julian said wasn't really a vampire," I told her. "He's from a movie."

"Interesting," Molly said. "Where is this dream vampire now?"

"On Remi's lawn, washed away with the laundry, and probably blowing with the wind to who knows where," I said.

"Did the vampire explode on its own or did the two of you dispose of it yourselves?"

"I think it was the sunlight," I told her. "His skin broiled and bubbled a bit before the pop."

Molly nodded as if all of this made perfect sense to her,

for which I was glad. It sounded fairly crazy to me, and I'd witnessed the event firsthand.

"Did you collect any of the dust for further examination?" Molly asked.

"When we were covered in vampire, you expect that the first thing we'd do is get our test tubes and science kits?" Remi's tone was a bit defensive.

"A sandwich bag would do just as well," Molly said.

"No," I said. "We got showers. We didn't collect his bits."

"Did you intend to bring your dream to life?" Molly asked.

I responded with an emphatic shake of my head. "No way."

"All right then." Molly rubbed her hands together. "Shall we begin?"

Remi set the snack tray back on the counter, took a seat in the recliner, leaned back, and popped up the foot rest. "Ready."

That left me. I lay on the sofa, nervous but a little excited, too. I looked up at Molly, who stood over me. "I haven't even explained the plan to you yet," I said.

"You and Remedy share the longest and deepest bond," Molly said. "You'll find her. I'll be here."

"Yeah," I said. "That's the gist of it."

She gave me a small smile and patted my hand. "You can do this."

I appreciated her confidence. If I remembered my task, and if I was able to focus hard enough on finding my bestie, maybe I could do it. But I had to fall asleep first.

Eyes closed, I tried not to think. There was something about focusing on not thinking that always made me think harder. Now that dream Dale Corduroy had died in the real world, was he gone from my dreams forever? Or because I was thinking about him, would I see him even more often than before?

What if I couldn't find Remi? How had I done it before? I'd grabbed Evan's hand when I'd dived into his dreams, so maybe I needed that contact.

The gentle purr of Remi snoring in the recliner a few feet away told me that she was already asleep and waiting for me.

Holding her hand was the trick—maybe. I had no idea what I was doing, so everything was theory at this point. I tried to stand up and walk over to her, but my body wouldn't move. Opening my eyes proved to be impossible, too.

A sleepy mumble escaped my lips.

Get up now, and I'd never get to sleep.

Soft fingers curled over my hand. "Shh," Molly whispered. "The three of us are in this together. Rest now and think of Remedy."

A cold rush of magical energy washed up my arm. I wasn't in my living room anymore. I was floating in endless blackness. There was a serenity to it, like being wrapped in a snuggly blanket with the perfect mug of hot chocolate cupped between my hands.

Content to remain just like this forever, I tried to remember what I was supposed to be doing. There was something, for sure.

Molly's voice echoed through the darkness. "Think of Remedy."

Suddenly I was walking down a sidewalk toward Remi's house. I held a book to my chest. The binding felt familiar against my fingertips.

My backpack pulled on my shoulders, and someone else was there—Remi. She had the most adorable round cheeks, wild short curls that Tommy Butler had said made her look like Ronald McDonald. She also had on a *Fraggle Rock* t-shirt.

I touched my head and found the signature crooked braids I'd sported for most of my childhood. *We were tweens.*

It was the book in my hands that grounded me. Without opening the cover, I knew there were pictures inside of our magical adventures. Somehow holding it reminded me that this was a dream and I was here on a mission.

"And then we can go to the mall. I finally saved enough to get that pair of jellies," Remi said.

She looked at me, waiting for my response. Our feet moved in unison. The sun beat down on us, but there wasn't any warmth, only a cool surging feeling in my arm.

"I'm sorry, what did you say?" I looked at Remi.

She stopped walking and grabbed my shoulders, catching me in that fiery gaze of determination she'd always been a master of. "Matching jellies, remember? What's going on with you?"

"Is this your dream or mine?" I asked, squeezing my scrapbook.

Ten-year-old Remi wrinkled her nose. "What?"

The grass on either side of the sidewalk burst into flames and the sky darkened. I peeked upward and found a giant dragon blocking out the sun. He winked at us.

Remi's dream. This was definitely not mine.

I squished Remi's cheeks with my hands, somehow transforming into adult me when I did so. "You're Remedy Todd, forty-year-old fire witch. And I'm in your head, coming to hang out and dream with you."

Confusion slipped from Remi's face as she, too, transformed into her true, adult self.

"You did it," she said. "You found me."

"Easy peasy," I replied, a smile spread from ear to ear. "Now let's wake up and do it again."

CHAPTER 12

Slumber made time wonky. Sometimes it seemed like hours or days would pass in the dream world, while in the waking world it would be a matter of minutes. Other times while dreaming it felt like only a few minutes had passed, but the whole night had gone by.

Unfortunately, I only managed to find Remi once before day broke. I rubbed the sleep from my eyes and rolled to my side, only to discover my bestie staring at me from the recliner, and Molly beside her on a barstool, also staring at me.

"Is there drool?" I rubbed my face finding none.

"No," Remi said. "You're good."

"Then what?" I looked from one to the other.

"It's morning. Nothing extraordinary happened," Molly said.

"That's good, right?" I asked, confused. "Also, I do consider hanging out with Remi in her dream fairly extraordinary."

"It's good," Remi agreed. "We were just *discussing* what to do next."

The way she said "discussing" paired with the dirty look she shot Molly suggested they'd been arguing before I woke.

"Okay," I said, and waited for further explanation.

"I want to go again," Remi said. "But Molly here is ready to give up already."

Molly rolled her eyes. "Dream work must be done at night. It's already morning, I haven't slept a wink, and *some* of us have other responsibilities."

I knew she meant it as a dig about Remi, but it was me who wasn't working at the moment. And it was me who needed this to be priority number one.

"None more important than Jen," Remi said. "We need to support each other. We need to help Jen nurture her abilities."

"And prevent another dream creature from terrorizing the town," Molly said. "You think I don't know the stakes?"

"It's fine," I said.

Both women looked at me.

"You're both right," I said. "We can't spend all day and night sleeping. It's just not practical. You two should go ahead and do whatever it is you need to do. I'll seek you out tonight while you're asleep."

Molly grabbed her things, and gave my hand a squeeze. "I don't mind watching over you again at night if you need me. After some rest."

I thanked her, and she left.

Remi, still hanging out in the recliner, yawned. Then she cringed. "I need to brush my teeth. Stat."

"There's a spare toothbrush in the bathroom," I told her.

I went to clean up last night's snacks in the kitchen, but found everything already done. I really did have the best of friends. Coming over to help me with my magic *and* cleaning up—what more could a witch ask for?

Remi returned, her face pink from washing it, and a

mischievous grin playing on her lips. She pulled a pair of eye masks out from behind her back. "So we're going back to sleep, right?"

I nodded emphatically. "Yes, please. Lemme just check in with Evan first."

My phone was on the counter beside my scrapbook. Putting aside thoughts of the phone, I reached out and ran my hand across the binding of my scrapbook first, and then the bumpy faux-snake skin cover.

Molly had given me two books upon my first visit to her magic shop. One was a journal to record my dreams. The other was a book written about dreaming. Most of it was impossible to follow, but with my hand on my coven scrapbook, a passage came to me about totems. Dream witches often used real world objects while dreaming to ground themselves. Maybe my scrapbook was my totem.

"Everything good with Evan?" Remi asked.

"Uh, I haven't checked yet."

"That's okay," she said. "I should call Julian to check in. Meet back here after?"

"Perfect."

I set to work preparing two mugs of sleepy tea while I called Evan. When he didn't answer, I checked the time. And of course he didn't answer, because he was in class. I texted him that all was well, and called my mom to make sure Evan was in fact at school and hadn't psychically conjured anything.

He was fine.

After I hung up, I met Remi back in the living room with tea in hand. A few sips and we were both ready to return to our sleeping places and lie down to rest.

It took longer to fall asleep this time, but when I did, I knew exactly what was what, and I went right for Remi, armed with my scrapbook and lucid determination.

Barefoot in her front lawn, fire danced across Remi's skin. Her wild curls lifted from her shoulders as she stared down her ex-husband, *Dick*. He had on a pair of Dale-Corduroy-style short shorts and nothing else. The smug look on his half-melted face stirred within me the urge to punch him square in the nose. That was nothing unusual. I'd hated Dick long before he'd turned a vampire.

Dick's short shorts burst into flames, as did the overly-gelled helmet of hair on the top of his head. Squealing like a newborn piglet, he ran in circles across the lawn as the fire spread over his skin.

"Hey," I said to Remi as I stepped up beside her.

Letting go of the flames that encased her and the hard set of her stance, she said, "I think I like this dream."

"Samesies." I held up my scrapbook for her to see. "This is my anchor."

Remi's brows knitted together.

"To remind me that I'm dreaming."

"Sounds helpful," she said. "Good thinking."

Just like Dale had, Dick exploded in a cloud of dust and confetti. This time, fortunately, we didn't get coated in a layer of gray powder. But Dick's appearance here suggested that soggy gherkin was still taking up some of Remi's brain space.

"You haven't seen Dick since the sewers, right?" I asked.

"Nope," Remi said. "I think the vampire-in-the-lawn thing must have me thinking about him a little. Anyway, we're here. I know we're us, which means you're making progress, right? So what's next?"

Those were great questions. But sadly, I had no answers. "I'm not sure," I said.

"You're a dream goddess." Remi rubbed her hands together. "Let's do everything."

A goddess, huh? It was an exaggeration, sure, but it did make me sound pretty awesome.

I considered what I would do if there were no rules and no constraints. Easy peasy. "I've always wanted to fly."

"Yes." Remi beamed at me. "Let's do that."

Right. Gravity had nothing on me. I grabbed Remi's hand and squeezed tight. I told myself I had rockets for feet, and I jumped.

My legs rumbled with combustive power, and we shot up into the sky. Our surroundings went from suburban yard-scape to endless, open blue.

As the world below faded away, clouds surrounded us. They weren't like the white fog of reality as seen through an airplane window. Up close, they looked like solid, fluffy things that I could stand on.

I had to touch one.

With no free hand, I realized I needed to do something with my scrapbook. If I dropped it, who knew if I'd remember that I was dreaming? And I refused to let go of Remi. So I wedged the book into the waistband of my pants. It wasn't as hard as it should have been. Half in, half out, the book stayed put.

Remi watched, but didn't say a word.

With the deepest voice I could produce and a waggle of my brows I said, "Is that a scrapbook in your pants or are you just happy to see me?"

She smiled. "You are so weird."

"I know," I told her, and gestured to the bookish bulge in my trousers. "But it's this or I let you go."

"Let me go and I'll pinch you when we wake," she shot me a warning glare.

I laughed and reached out, scooping a bit of cloud into my hand. It was pillow-soft, and somehow I knew, right then, that the clouds were made of cotton candy.

I shoved it into my mouth.

"What are you doing?" Remi laughed.

The sugary goodness melted against my tongue. It was more strawberry than strawberries, and I could eat the whole sky full.

"You have to taste it. Do it. Do it." I offered Remi a handful.

She took it, gave it a skeptical once over, then shoved the cloud into her mouth. "Chocolate chip cookies," she said.

"And for *no calories,*" I added. "Mine tasted like strawberry."

"I wonder if they taste like what we want them to or if each cloud is different."

"Only one way to find out," I said, and yanked her arm.

We soared the sky to another cloud. We shared a look, then each grabbed a handful and stuffed our faces.

Sweet cream. Earthy vanilla. Notes of drippy, sticky waffle cones, and childhood happiness.

At the same time we said, "Vanilla ice cream."

Remi's gaze moved past me and over my shoulder. Her eyes glassed over and her jaw dropped.

I whipped my free arm wildly in the air to spin around and see what was behind me. As it turned out, that what wasn't a what, but a who.

And that who was a smokin' hottie.

The first thing that struck me, aside from the sheer confidence about him as he floated in midair and leaned casually on a cloud, was the silver mohawk that topped his head. It seemed to have a powerful presence all of its own, a peacock-like mating call to lure us lady folk.

A gray button-down shirt had the privilege of being wrapped around his clearly athletic torso. Tattered jeans hung from his hips. I didn't know which piece of clothing I should be most jealous of.

"Underpants," I whispered to myself. "I'd enjoy being his briefs."

An uncharacteristic eruption of laughter burst from Remi.

"It's your dream," Mr. Mystery said. "You make the rules."

Listening to his voice was like skydiving at midnight into a crowded concert stadium—as dark and dangerous as it was thrilling, and it touched me all the places.

He winked at me and said, "But for the record, I prefer boxers."

Imaging what that would look like was the inevitable response to his boxers comment—taut tan skin over bulging muscles, shadows marking the valleys between. Yummy.

"I like him," Remi said, and elbowed me. "Set me down somewhere safe before you transform into his boxers."

The idea rolled around in my head. No. I couldn't do that, could I?

"Not this time," I said.

"Next time," Mr. Mystery said. The corner of his mouth pulled slowly up to the side, revealing the panty-meltingest grin I'd ever seen, and then he popped a handful of cloud into his mouth and disappeared.

Remi squeezed my hand. "That man is sex on a stick."

"Yes," I said, staring at the place he had been. "A stick I would love to lick. *Mansicle.*"

I wasn't sure I'd ever been so attracted to a man. And it wasn't just the whole hotter-than-sin vibe he had going on, either. Something about him was so familiar, but I couldn't put my finger on it. Sadly since he disappeared, I couldn't put my fingers on him, either.

"If he comes back, and you want to do your licking thing, I'm happy to jet," Remi said. "This magic practice is important, but I love you enough to wait in the next dream over until you're done doing your thing."

"It hasn't just been a dry spell," I said. "It's a thousand-years-abandoned in the no-touchy-desert bad, Remi."

She gave me a commiserating look of pity.

"But I'm not here for the dream men," I said. "We have a mission. I'm sticking to it."

"Even if he lets you be his underpants?"

I swallowed hard. "Yep."

"Okay then. Can we visit other people's dreams, too?" Remi asked, pulling me back to our floating dream reality.

"Maybe? I've only visited you and Evan so far. I don't know if it has to be people I'm connected to or if it can be anyone."

"Strangers probably wouldn't be thrilled to know someone just flew into their head to spy on them," Remi said.

"True. Imagine what we could learn though. Let's see if I can, but maybe not a stranger. If it works, we don't have to stay if it feels wrong."

"Of course," Remi said. "But who do we know who's sleeping right now?"

"Molly," we said at the same time.

Squeezed tight to my bestie's hand, I jumped from the clouds, straight up toward space. I didn't know why that felt like the way to go, but it did. Everything dream-related here was uncharted territory, and we needed to rely on my intuition.

Beyond the sky was blackness and stars. Up here, everything shined brighter, which may or may not have been the case in the real world.

I closed my eyes and pictured Molly. There was a feeling, a pull. "That way," I said, pointing.

We swam through space, toward a shimmery green star that somehow I knew was where we'd find her. When we reached it, the shape became clearer. It wasn't a star, but a ball of light with thorned vines twisting and pulsing around it.

"Is that her?" Remi asked. "The thorns *are* very Molly."

"Yep," I said.

Who knew what would happen when we touched her light? I adjusted the scrapbook in my pants and reached a tentative hand forward, unsure if I should be doing this at all. How would Molly feel about us coming into her dream uninvited?

Remi gave my shoulder a little shove. "Do it!"

Instantly we were transported somewhere else. Black space was replaced by green and brown woods.

"This is Molly's forest," Remi said. "Behind the magic shop. You did it."

"How can you tell?"

She pointed to a little stone well. "That's where the tentacle monster lives."

"Oh." I took a step back, even though there was plenty of distance already. "So we probably don't want to get too close to that."

"Stay behind the red sand and we'll be fine," she said.

There was a line in the grass around the well that hadn't been there before, or maybe I just hadn't noticed. But it was vibrant as a rose.

Soft footsteps approached.

I turned and found a woman running through the trees. Her hair was long and blond, her dress ridiculously classy and emerald green. She had rosy cheeks and an ageless look about her that I immediately recognized. *Molly?*

Running by her side was a little girl, maybe six or seven, with wild red hair. She, too, wore an old-timey dress much too elegant for playing in the woods. Give the girl a set of jellies and a short haircut, and she would have been a dead ringer for my best friend at the same age.

"Remi," I whispered. "That girl looks just like you."

The woman stopped running and turned to us. The girl disappeared, fading away like a ghost on the wind.

"She's not me," Remi whispered back.

The woman opened her mouth, and a booming shriek shook the forest, ripping the trees from the ground. It was the opposite force of the pink wolf, a gale wind instead of a black hole. I covered my ears, offering some protection against the sound, and fought to keep my footing against the wind. My head rattled so hard I thought it might burst.

Remi flew back, disappearing with the trees.

Before I could react, she was gone. It was only me, and the fury of the woman before me.

"Molly, it's me," I tried to say, but I couldn't hear the words.

Adrenaline flooded my veins. Fight or flight—I didn't want to do either. My pulse boomed in my ears, and I couldn't think.

The wind howled around the woman in a storm of rage. Two words carried across that gale.

Get Out.

CHAPTER 13

I bolted upright, only to find Remi doing the exact same thing. We were both coated in a sheen of sweat. She stared at me with wide eyes, a look of shock I imagined was mirrored on my own face.

Something was wrong with her neck. It was craned to the side like she'd broken it.

"Are you okay?" I asked.

She shook her whole body as she would have shaken her head. "Nope. I can't move my neck."

I raised a hand over my mouth and whispered, "Molly broke it."

"Nope. Couch sleeping."

I cringed knowing exactly what that was like. "I'm sorry."

But, better than serious physical damage from our coven-mate.

Remi asked, "Remember when we were younger and we could crash anywhere and not get injured *by sleeping?*"

"No. That sounds fake."

She chuckled. "Another lifetime. That was Molly though for sure, right? In the dream?"

117

I nodded. "And what was with the girl who looked like you?"

"Someone's going to have to talk to her. You're the obvious choice."

"Why am I the obvious choice?"

Remi gave me a you-better-be-joking look.

"Okay," I said. "I'll talk to her. But I'm not thrilled about it. She was clearly not pleased to see us lurking in her dream."

"Not lurking, visiting," Remi said. "She needs to get over it. We're a coven, and you're a dream witch. You're bound to bust in and see people's secrets. It's just a fact of life."

"We did all agree that we were supposed to tell each other everything. Any secrets you want to air now? You know, before I start busting in and finding everything out?" I asked.

"Nah," Remi said. "You know everything there is to know. Worst thing you'll find visiting me is—"

"Sex stuff," I said with a nod.

She laughed. "I was going to say setting everyone I'm annoyed with on fire. But speaking of sex stuff—who was that Adonis in the clouds?"

At the time, I hadn't been sure. Now that I was awake, I was certain.

"Rainbow Bear," I told her, not knowing if he had a name. "Hot Pink Wolf."

"Hot, for sure. Wait. The probably-not-our-next-villain Rainbow Bear?"

Remi sat down on the sofa beside me, stiffly moving herself like she was in a full-body cast, and turned my arm to look at the faded words I'd written in permanent marker. I'd nearly forgotten about discussing Rainbow Bear with Remi and Julian.

"The same," I said.

"Who is he? Is he a dream witch, too? Or is it warlock because he's a man?"

118

"I don't know."

"Well, he certainly seems to know you," she said. "Remember how you pushed me to give Julian a chance?"

"It was more a gentle nudge than a push," I said.

"Ditching me at the bar so I'd talk to him—that was your idea of a nudge?"

"I didn't shove you into his lap," I told her.

"I guess I should count myself lucky for that."

We shared a quiet moment of fond reminiscence.

"But," Remi continued, "it's my turn to give you the gentle nudge this time."

"I don't even know if Rainbow Bear is real," I said. *And I call him Rainbow Bear.*

"Maybe he thinks it's hot," she said. "He did choose to appear as one of the Feeling Friends, right?"

It had been forever since I'd thought about my favorite kids show. We used to watch the fluffy stuffed animals explore emotions together every Saturday morning. When our parents wouldn't let us hang out, we'd watch from our respective houses while on the phone with each other for the entire thirty-minute block.

"He's not exactly a Feeling Friend," I said, "but I get your point."

"Because you want to feel him." It wasn't a question.

"Who wouldn't?" I said. "So what now, breakfast? I don't think I could sleep another wink, plus my muscles feel like an elephant slept on top of me."

"I have a cupcake order to fill, for that turd of a kid Jason Morrison."

Jason...Jason. I tried to place that name. "The one from the bike incident?"

Remi nodded. "And I will not put laxatives in the batter, because I am not spiteful."

"That's really big of you," I told her.

119

"Yeah," she said in a flat tone, "thanks."

Clearly she wasn't thrilled about having to restrain herself. But she was doing the right thing anyway.

"I think I'm going to go for a run," I said. "I need to wear myself out or I will never be able to sleep again tonight."

"You do that," Remi said. "And I'm going to ice my neck while I bake. See you again tonight?"

"Heat for the first twenty-four hours for injuries," I said. "Then ice."

She nodded. "Thanks."

Over a day had passed without incident, longer since our brief cat encounter. It was time to let Evan sleep in his own bed, and Remi and I needed to do the same or who knew how mangled we'd be by tomorrow morning.

"Let's meet up in our dreams," I said.

"From our own beds?" she asked hopefully with a rub of her crooked neck.

"Yes."

"I love you so hard."

"Samesies."

"But you'll call if you need me," she said, rising back up from the couch.

"Always."

After Remi left, I showered and ate even though I wasn't really hungry. Brushing my teeth was absolutely required, with my breath smelling like hot garbage. No reason to offend Molly worse than I already had.

Halfway out the door, I stumbled upon a package. I pulled it back inside and opened it up. It was Fernando's whiteboard. Score!

Whiteboard in hand, I ventured back out into the cool afternoon. On a typical day, I'd drive the short distance to Molly's place, but today I was set on expending as much energy as possible, so I walked. It was a brisk pace, not quite a jog, and helped warm me up as I went.

Halloween props decorated lawns along the way. Pumpkins sat on steps, cotton spider webs stretched across porches, and fake tombstones stuck up out of the grass.

I'd told Remi I was going to wear myself out by running, but it was better to run later, after I'd taken in all the sights, and when I didn't have something to carry and potentially poke my eye out with if I fell. Yep, running would be great on the way home.

When I reached the corner of Bukavac and Vanth, I spotted Fernando by Molly's front door. His eye darted from me to the yard, like he was considering making his escape. I still had no idea what I'd done to make him scared of me. My best guess was the questions I'd asked last time about the egg incident.

"Hi, Fernando." I gave him a friendly wave, hoping he'd understand my good intentions. "I brought you something."

He lifted his arm hesitantly and waved back.

I stepped up onto the porch. He didn't roll away. So far, so good.

"Since only Molly understands what you're saying, I thought you could use this." I held out the whiteboard to him.

He didn't take it.

I sat down beside him, putting us at eye level. From here he was a lot less cute and a lot more intimidating. His mouth stretched, revealing layers of gigantic needle teeth. For politeness, I tried not to pull away. Even though it was clear his mouth could envelope my head like a spiky helmet of painful misery.

On the ground between us, I set down the board, forcing my gaze from his teeth. I showed him the chain. "This can go over your head if you want."

His giant eyeball followed my movement.

I popped the lid off the marker and showed him how it worked by drawing a pair of happy stick figures holding hands, well one stick me and one ball him.

"You can write words on here. But I probably should have asked if you knew how to read and write first, huh?"

He snatched the marker from my hand, then checked with a look for my reaction. His unibrow dropped lower and lower as he gauged my expression. I smiled, totally non-threateningly.

"There's an eras—"

His forked tongue shot out of his mouth and smeared away the drawing, leaving the board wet but blank.

"—eraser on the lid," I said. "But that works, too."

Fernando gripped the marker in his fist in a way that reminded me of how Evan held his first crayons as a toddler. He ran lines slowly across the board, then turned it to face me.

The word "sorry" took up the whole board. But I could read it. And he could write it. Win!

"You don't have to be sorry," I told him. "We're friends, and I know the cat-egg stuff wasn't your fault."

He smiled, which turned out extra creepy from this angle. I caught a flash of a half-eaten glow worm still wiggling between his needle teeth.

He licked his board, and wrote another word. "Frens."

"Friends?" I asked.

He did his back and forth yes dance. Then he popped the chain over his head to wear it. A perfect fit, the board hung down below his eye but didn't fall off because of his arms. He said something I couldn't understand and rolled away into the grass.

I rose to my feet and brushed what I could of the dirt from my backside. It still felt wet and cold, and sore from sitting. My gray pants were slightly discolored with the addition of dusty brown.

The door didn't preemptively open for me as I approached, so I knocked.

No one answered.

Fernando's familiar gurgle pulled my attention to the side of the building. He waved for me to come with him, with the word "frens" remaining on his board.

I did as he suggested and followed him around to the other side of the building. He stopped at a chest freezer I recognized from coming by when Molly had been in the hospital. Remi and I had collected a bucket of glowing worms from the freezer that Remi rightly thought Molly could use to heal herself.

"Do you want to show me the glow worms?" I asked Fernando. Maybe he was still hungry.

He licked his board and wrote "no" with a backwards N. It was adorable.

"Can you take me to Molly?" I asked. "I owe her an apology."

Fernando reached up and took my hand.

We walked out into the woods to a place I recognized from the dream world. The well looked almost exactly the same as it had in Molly's dream, only the stones were more weathered. It made sense for the well to have aged, too, given how much younger Molly had appeared in the dream. But dreams could be tricky and make no sense at all, so it was best not to put too much stock in particular details.

In a set of sensible work clothes and a thick coat, Molly stood with her back turned by the well pulling a chain out from its depths. A pile of bird cages lay on the ground beside her.

"Don't just stand there," she said without turning. "Help."

I hurried over and grabbed the chain, helping her pull.

The metal was rough and cold, and difficult to budge. I glanced at Molly out of the corner of my eye. Her gaze was downcast, and I couldn't read anything from her expression.

This was my chance, ready or not, I had come here to talk to her. I took a deep breath. "About this morning—"

"Don't," Molly said.

"I need to tell you—"

"You really don't," she said. "Your gift is in dreams. You cannot be expected not to visit the other witches in your coven. Even when the timing isn't convenient."

I wanted to say I was sorry, but she clearly wasn't having it. I considered starting with how I didn't mean to see something private, but it felt like rehashing the same apology she'd stopped me twice from starting already.

"Thanks for understanding," I told her. "I didn't know if I could visit other people, or just Remi and Evan. So I figured you were likely asleep and—"

She shook her head and set down the chain, then turned to face me. There was no anger apparent on her face, only a wistful glaze over her cloudy blue eyes. "Never apologize for your gift," she said. "You caused me no physical harm."

I'd caused her emotional harm. I pinched my lips together to stop myself from telling her how sorry I was.

"I dream of her often," Molly said. "You would have seen sooner or later."

"Who is she?" I asked, hoping I wasn't pushing too much.

"My daughter."

"Oh."

I had no idea that she had a daughter. Really, I knew almost nothing about Molly's personal life. She wasn't an easy nut to crack.

"I know what you're thinking," she said. "My Lily looks like Remedy."

"She does," I agreed.

"The two shared more than just looks," Molly said with a sad smile.

"Shared? Past tense?"

"Lily died," she said.

I couldn't imagine the immense level of sorrow that must have come with losing a child. "I'm so sorry."

"It was a long time ago." She turned her back to me. "Come, help me finish with these cages."

With that, the conversation was over. I hoped with time, Molly would let me in more. I wanted to really know her.

I fell in behind Molly and picked up the chain. Remi had mentioned doing this for Molly before. She'd said the cages were to catch some kind of little face-eating creatures that were attracted to magic. I walked with caution because I preferred to keep my face, thank you very much.

We pulled the chain through the woods, not talking at first, until Molly spoke again. Over her shoulder she said, "Tell me more about the dream you brought to life."

"Dale Corduroy? Well, let's see. For some reason he's a vampire, but also he chose a tropical island as his home. His most distinctive feature is definitely his short shorts."

"Do you think that's what kept him in your subconscious?"

The short shorts? "Like am I super into his package?"

Molly stopped walking, shrugged and gave me a you're-the-one-who-said-it expression.

"Maybe," I admitted. "But when I watch horror movies with Evan, I always dream about the monsters for a while. I'm not particularly fond of being scared."

"Then why watch them?"

"Well, it all started after I learned that magic was real. Evan knew all kinds of helpful tidbits, so I figured why not go straight to his source and watch the movies, too. You never know when zombies or mummies might turn out to be real nowadays."

"And if watching the movies is bringing them to life?" She gave me a total mom voice, somehow both shaming and encouraging me to come to the same conclusion she had.

And I hadn't thought of that, so she did have a point.

"Okay, so maybe no more horror movies," I said.

"Good."

If not watching movies was the cost of keeping nightmare creatures from coming to life, it was worth it. But that wasn't our only problem lately. "What about the kitten fairy?"

"The baby kukudhli," Molly said. "If anyone had seen it, Tergel would have heard. You know how bartenders are, central gatherers of secrets and information."

"So has Tergel heard anything?"

"No. Not yet."

"What about your friend with the fortune cookies?" I wasn't the only one who had prophetic powers. Molly's big friend with the old school suits excreted those little almond cookies that you could get at any Chinese carryout, but his fortunes were special. They actually came true.

"The cookies have not provided relevant demon tips as of late," she said.

With the way she popped "relevant" in there, I was left to assume that there were quite a few demon happenings that she wasn't going to tell me about.

"This is Marshmallow," she said simply, like that explained it.

I guessed it did. The town was supposedly founded by demons.

"What is Tergel?" I asked, remembering Remi's mention of the bartender's tail. At the time I hadn't been able to see it.

"Demon," Molly said. "And harmless."

"Harmless demon—isn't that an oxymoron?"

"No."

Her answer was blunt. At least she didn't say *I* was a moron. It seemed the appropriate response, or maybe that was just me.

We finished planting the cages around the perimeter of Molly's lot, and by the time we returned to her shop, I was surprised to find that hours had passed. My stomach rumbled and the sun was low in the sky.

"So can I see you again tonight, in dreams?" I asked Molly.

"Of course," she told me. "But what you see in my mind gets left alone. Pretend you didn't see it. We will not discuss my past."

"Okay," I agreed.

As I left, I decided that was probably a good rule all around. If I was going to be inserting myself into people's heads, the least I could do is pretend I didn't know all of their juicy secrets.

Earlier, I'd thought running would be a great idea, and that I'd do it on the way home. But everything hurt and I wished I'd brought my car. I decided walking was good enough, and was proud of myself for not lying down in the grass and calling Evan to pick me up.

When I got home, I found his car in the driveway and the sun setting behind the house.

Ominous music and a woman's scream greeted me when I opened the door.

"Hey, Mom," Evan called from the living room, and turned down the volume of whatever he was watching. "I made spaghetti and already ate. Wasn't sure if you would be home for dinner."

I hung up my coat and slipped off my shoes. "Are there leftovers?"

"A plate in the fridge," he told me as I stepped into the living room.

On the TV, a wave of purple slime slowly crept across a tiny town as people in the street dressed in fifties clothing scattered. The camera did a close up of a woman's face as she screamed, but the TV was muted so I couldn't hear it.

I turned my head away and squeezed my eyes shut.

"You're not afraid of purple goo, are you?" Evan asked, sounding surprised.

"Nope." I shook my head.

"Want to grab your plate and join me?"

I did want to. I really did.

"I wish I could," I told him. "But I need to keep my dreams clear of horror monsters."

"Right," he said. "I'll take the movie to my room."

"No, you stay," I told him. "I'll go to my room. I insist."

I opened one eye, found Evan with his familiar squished face of concern. I was going to give the poor kid premature wrinkles. In response to his frown, I gave him my best reassuring smile, grabbed my plate from the kitchen, and headed upstairs.

The food was good, but hiding out in my room sucked. After I finished eating, I pulled out my scrapbooking supplies. Crafting was always a mood booster.

In the bottom of the sticker box was the pair of glasses I'd been working on for Evan to wear on our movie nights. I'd popped out the lenses and attached short cardstock blockers along the bottoms of the eye holes so I could use the subtitles but Evan didn't have to see them and get distracted. Since I hadn't finished bedazzling them with manly onyx gems yet, I hadn't yet given them to him.

And now we weren't watching movies together anymore.

Later. I'd give them to him later, after I'd mastered the art of not summoning monsters from my dreams. It was decided.

Instead of playing with my scrapbook, I worked on the glasses.

It was good to have Evan home. And before long, I'd drift off to sleep and kick this dream witchery in the face.

On that note, I crafted, I brushed my teeth, and I went to bed looking forward to the new adventures that awaited me, knowing that with the help of my friends, I'd conquer them all.

CHAPTER 14

he coldness of the earth beneath me seeped into my muscles, leaving me feeling like an immovable iceberg. Pebbles pressed up through my dress and into my skin. I could count them by feel—one in my left shoulder, one on my ankle, and one particularly sharp stone stabbing into my right butt cheek.

Tall grass swayed in the breeze, tickling my bare arms and legs as the summer sun softly broiled my skin from above. The broiling was a strange sensation when mixed with the cold from below.

"Hello again, Jenny."

I turned my head toward the voice and peeked through squinted lids. There was a boy beside me. He looked exactly the same age as me, with long bony arms and legs, and no sign of puberty in sight. We both had to be about ten. Yet somehow I also knew the boy was much, much older than he appeared.

Silver-white hair stuck straight up in the center of his head in a short mohawk that I knew I'd run my hand across more than once. Copper sunfires shimmered in the center of his smiling eyes—eyes that drew me in and put me at ease.

We knew each other well, yet I didn't remember him at all.

"Who are you?" I asked.

"This is one of the times you forget." He nodded like that made perfect sense, then sat up and put his elbows on his knees. "That's okay. You always remember when you're ready."

There was a glimmer of sadness in his eyes that betrayed his words, or at least I thought there was. Maybe I imagined it.

I sat up beside him. "What do you mean I always remember? How many times have we met?"

He reached a hand out, as if he wanted to lead me somewhere and show me the answer.

I took it.

As soon as our palms touched, images flashed through my head. Me no older than five or six, pumping my legs on the swings at the park while the boy swung next to me. The two of us were laughing. Then we were teenagers holding hands, flying through the sky. Then we were twenty-somethings lying in the bed of my father's truck and staring up at the stars.

A flood of emotions struck me—closeness, companionship, commiseration, love. It was too much all at once—the memories, the feelings. Glassy tears welled in my eyes. Back in the field, I rolled up onto my elbow, put a hand over his heart, and kissed him.

Suddenly I wasn't a child. He wasn't a child. He was a man—a sexy man setting fireworks off all over my body.

His lips were soft clouds, and he tasted like spiced cider by the campfire, like nostalgia itself and future hopes and dreams. It was little more than a peck, but by gherkin's backside, it felt good to be kissed.

Breathless, I gasped, then I pulled back and stared at the man. We weren't on the field anymore, and we weren't in our forties now, either. We were a little old woman and a little old man together in a set of rocking chairs, holding hands because during the memories and the kiss, neither of us had ever let go.

His eyes were closed, and a look of quiet contentment settled on his face.

"I don't understand," I told him.

"You asked how many times we've met. We've known each other every day of your life."

The look in his eyes told me that what he said was true. It said that he'd been waiting for this moment for a very long time, and now that it was here, it was everything that he'd hoped it would be. I knew everything I was seeing was true, that growing old together had always been inevitable. Understanding the *how* of it all was still just outside of my reach.

"How have we known each other every day before and every day that will be? Are you like me? Are you visiting my dreams because you're a man witch?" I chortled. "Sounds like the sandwich."

He pulled a piece of the arm off the rocking chair and popped it into his mouth. With two short chews, he swallowed the wood. This was exactly how it was meant to be.

His grin spread from ear to ear, and it was as beautiful a smile as it always had been. He was the boy and the teen and the man all at once. He was the wolf and the bear. He was forever my partner, and I didn't even know his name.

* * *

WITH A JOLT, I sat upright in my bed.

Alone.

The ghost of his touch remained on my palm. I squeezed my fingers, trying to hold onto the feeling.

My phone buzzed and jostled at the corner of my nightstand, then dropped off the edge. I dove to the edge of the mattress, shot a hand out, and caught it just before it hit the floor.

Memories from my dream slipped away from my brain, leaving fog in their place along with an overwhelming need to write down what I could before it was all gone.

I hit the green button on my phone and grabbed my dream journal from the nightstand. Paying little attention to the phone I cradled between my shoulder and cheek, I focused on writing down what I could.

> Silver hair, copper eyes
> Rainbow wolf bear is boy
> Is MAN
> All the feels

Words in my ear drew my attention back to the phone. Whoever called and woken me had been talking, and I hadn't been listening.

"Hello," I said.

Remi huffed. "Did you sleep-accept my call or what?"

"Taking some notes, sorry about that."

"It's fine," she said, her voice deflated. "You didn't show last night. Problems with performance?"

The sun was up. The night had flown by like it did if I drank two glasses of wine, and I hadn't met up with my coven in my dreams.

"You think I have erectile dysfunction, but for magic?" I asked, a smile pulling at the corners of my lips.

Remi laughed. "Your words, not mine."

"It's true. I can't get my magic up. I'm not even entirely sure what my magic is supposed to be. You made it look easy when you first got your powers."

"I didn't want my magical erection."

"You wanted limp magic."

"Exactly," she said. "I didn't *want* to be a big flaming ball of fire and brimstone. If I didn't get it together, I would have burned the whole town down."

"Ah, the simpler days."

"It was simpler," she said. "But it was still hard."

I laughed. "Hard as a magical erection."

"That was *not* what I meant. I meant I ended up walking down the street on fire, no idea how to help myself or to stop it."

"And Julian was there for you."

"He was."

Was the Rainbow Wolf Bear my Julian?

Remi said, "But even if Julian hadn't been there, I only had the one thing to learn—fire."

"Dreams are one thing," I said.

"Are they?" she asked. "You see the future sometimes. You can cross into other people's heads. You can manifest nightmares into the real world. I count three things."

"You make me sound more powerful than I am."

"You are more powerful than you think," she said. "And more complicated. How can you expect to master everything all at once? You can't. No one can."

"But if I don't Viagra my powers, and fast, I'll be the one burning the town down. Or vampiring it? I'm not sure what my version of that one is."

"Nightmaring," Remi suggested.

"Yes, that."

"Well, we will just have to make sure that doesn't happen. What are you doing tonight?"

"Meeting you in your dreams so we can kick this dream magic in the face," I said.

"Yes. You had better luck when we were together, right? How about I come over and we start that way again."

"Love it." Already I felt energized and ready to get started.

"See you tonight, say nine?"

"Perfect," I said. "And Remi, thank you."

"That's what best friends are for."

We said our goodbyes, and I peeked between the curtains. The sun hadn't risen yet. The dark combined with the faint beeping of Evan's alarm going off told me it wasn't yet seven.

I took a shower, heat-treated my hair and clipped it back in a chignon, and even applied a pop of lipstick before getting dressed in a nice pair of black pants and a high-necked white shirt and heading downstairs. Even if I wasn't going in to work, it never hurt to look and feel like my best, most confident self. There was something about red lipstick which did just that.

Evan's alarm was off by the time I made it into the hall, but I heard him scuffling around behind his door.

"Morning," I said loudly enough that I knew for sure he'd hear me. "I'm in the mood for waffles. How does that sound?"

He opened his door. A mop of wet hair swept over his eyes. "Sounds great, thanks."

I gave him two thumbs up and turned for the steps.

"Mom."

I turned around.

Evan gave me a crooked grin. "You look nice."

"Thank you." I would tell him he did too, but he was still wearing his pajamas, including the holey shirt featuring the glaring yet half-peeled-off grinning face of Melvin Murderface. I hated that shirt.

136

He didn't wait for me to say anything else before disappearing back into his room. I headed down to the kitchen and got to work on a batch of raspberry chocolate chip waffles.

We didn't have to watch horror flicks together to have nice bonding time. Waffles trumped movies any day.

I whipped out all supplies, threw together the batter, mixed in a handful of raspberries and a sprinkle of chocolate chips, and stirred. A big scoop at a time, I filled the waffle iron and let it do its thing.

While I waited for the last of the waffles to finish, I popped a raspberry in my mouth and bit down. A shot of tart juice sprayed across my tongue. With a wince and a pucker, I decided that a little dusting of powdered sugar was in order for these bad boys, so I coated the heaping plate in a light layer and took a seat at the bar.

Evan bustled about behind me. I looked over my shoulder just in time to catch him reach for the plate, grab a waffle, and turn back for the door.

"No time to sit?" I asked.

"Sorry," he said. "I got caught in this whole group text drama and—"

His phone dinged in his pocket.

He gave me an apologetic shrug.

"Totally fine," I said. "Have a great day."

"Thanks, Mom. You, too."

After he left, waffle bonding turned into a love affair between me and the breakfast confection. Two in, I felt bloated, so I packed the rest away in the fridge for later.

Since most of my current plans revolved around sleep, I didn't have anything special to do while wearing my lipstick and my ready-to-go outfit. Not sure what to do with myself, I shot Jerry a quick text to see if he needed any help with the listings. It was possible business was flourishing and I had no idea. He could be wishing I was with him at a huge showing this very minute.

Hey, how's work?

I waited for a reply. The little dots of typing didn't appear immediately, so I set my phone down. As soon as I rose from my stool, my phone dinged. I checked to see what Jerry had said.

Ho-hum. Painting my toenails for the third time today level abysmal.

I sent back the closest emoji I could find to a pouty lip: :(
He wrote back,

Tell me you're doing better.
    No, wait.
    I want details.
    Wow me tomorrow. Robertini's at one. We'll call it a work lunch.

I'm there.

He sent the blowing kiss emoji, and I slid my phone into my pocket. Lunch with Jerry was going to be a treat. I missed him. But also, I had no idea what details I was going to give him about my life of not-working. It was hardly the glamorous tale he was hoping for.

I went upstairs and looked through the dream notes I'd written in the morning. They were quite a bit less coherent than they'd felt at the time. I mean "is man" and "all the feels" really wouldn't have told me anything had more time passed, but reading them over still kickstarted my memory.

The part that stuck out most to me was playing on the swings at the park with the boy at my side. It had happened before Remi moved to Marshmallow, and it wasn't just a dream. I remembered him. If anyone could help fill in the blanks, it was my mom. She had to have been there with me on the playground. So I called her.

She picked up on the third ring. "Jenny, hi, how are you?"

"Good," I said automatically. Then I reconsidered, and decided to go with the truth. "No, not good. Weird."

"What's going on?"

"Did you know we live in a magical town founded by demons?" I asked, knowing exactly how I sounded.

She didn't answer.

"Magic is real. All the weirdness that belongs in stories, it's in the real world, walking around in people suits pretending."

Still she didn't say anything.

"Are you listening to me?" I asked. "Mom?"

"I'm here," she said.

"So? Did you know?"

"You always did indulge in fantasies. Is this part of one of your games? Have you been reading those books with magic stories again?"

"You mean like *Peter Pan*, when I was seven."

"Yes, like that."

"No."

"I live in reality," she said.

Right. Of course. I could tell her everything, show up in her front yard with Remi on fire and she'd say *oh yes, that's nice, just like your story books* in a condescending tone. Remi could toss a fireball and set her ablaze, and still she wouldn't believe.

"I need to ask you something," I said. "Remember when I was a kid, and you'd take me to the park?"

"You begged me to take you every day," she said. "You liked the swings."

"Yes!"

"What about it?" she asked.

"Was there another kid that I played with? Anyone who made an impression?" It was a long shot, sure. Maybe it had been only once that I'd seen the boy. It felt like more, but memory was tricky that way. And decades later, what were the chances she'd remember him?

"You didn't play with anyone until Remedy moved here, not unless I made you. Even then, it didn't last. Remember Abigail Longsworth? She has always been such a sweet girl. You know she's forty-seven now, and a *doctor*. Betsy, her mother, still brings up that time that you—"

I attempted to change the conversation before I had to hear about the tooth incident again. "Yeah, yeah, I remember."

"You shoved her in the marsh and she chipped her tooth on that rock. Poor thing had to go to the city to get it fixed."

I rolled my eyes and leaned back in my seat. "Yep, well, I'm a monster."

The last fifty times I'd heard this story, I'd defended myself. For one, I hadn't shoved her unprovoked. She called me weird and pulled my hair. She had it coming, but that didn't seem to matter to Mom.

"Jennifer, you should never say such things."

"So, no one?" I asked. "I never played with any other kids? Like on the swings?"

"No one. You were the most antisocial child. It's probably why you made up that imaginary friend."

"Imaginary friend?" That was him. It had to be. "What was his name?"

"Oh, that's right, it was a boy. You called him Baku. You said he had a pink tail and pink wolf ears."

Baku.

"Thanks, Mom."

After my call, I ran some errands and finished bedazzling Evan's glasses. Flipping through my scrapbooking supplies it hit me—my scrapbook was what connected me to my coven when we weren't together. It was my touchstone. Last night I hadn't had it with me, and I hadn't remembered to find Remi.

Tonight would be different. Tonight I'd make sure I was prepared.

I called Remi, told her my plan, and encouraged her to stay home for the night so we could test my theory.

That night, when it was time to crash, I tucked my scrapbook in with me.

* * *

AT THE OFFICE, I spun my chair, kicking off my desk. The swively seat whirled without slowing. I watched Jerry, the door, and the water cooler blend together in swipes of color. This was the part where I was supposed to be so dizzy I was bound to puke. But I wasn't dizzy at all.

I looked down from the swirling room to the heavy object in my lap—my coven scrapbook. Weird. Why would I take this with me to work?

The book demanded my attention, literally.

"Open me. Open me," it said in a voice reminiscent of Angela Lansbury. "Open me. Open me."

"Fine. Sheesh." I opened the book.

Suddenly, I poofed from my office to the forest. The sun was shining, the vegetation was the greenest of greens, and in a clearing sat a red blanket and the strangest tea party since Alice fell down the rabbit hole.

With long blond hair and a Victorian era dress, Molly sat

criss-cross-applesauce. Next to her was purple Fernando wearing a top hat and a monocle. Beside him was the giant with the funny suits who frequented Molly's shop, Murray, only he didn't have whipped cream all over his face, so he looked a lot less Frankenstein than usual. And finishing their circle was what appeared to be a garden gnome statue.

Murray took a sip of tea from a dainty cup, his fingers pinched carefully like he was afraid he'd break it. Fernando lifted a knife into the air. There was a strawberry impaled at the tip. He made a gurgling sound, and everyone laughed and smiled.

Everyone froze, mid-laugh.

The gnome's head spun around on its ceramic shoulders like it was possessed, then it pointed right at me. Its mouth opened and made a siren sound.

The others looked and pointed, too, except for Molly.

It was a little like a horror movie, and this was my cue to run.

But Molly rose from her seat, brushed off her spotless skirt, and walked over to me.

"Time to go?" she asked.

Trying not to be startled by the alarm sounds and all the pointing, I focused on Molly and answered, "Yes."

"Where's Remedy?"

"She's next," I said, and held up my scrapbook to show her.

I flipped open the pages and put my palm over a photo of my bestie and closed my eyes. Air whooshed against my face and then settled once more.

The scents of cinnamon, vanilla, and fresh baked goods filled my lungs.

"This is *not* meant for our eyes," Molly said.

I opened my eyes, because of course when someone says something like that, it was impossible *not* to look.

We were standing in the kitchen of Buckthorn house, like we would for Sunday brunch. Only instead of being greeted by Remi, Julian was there.

Wearing only an itsy bitsy apron.

And nothing else.

He looked at us, smiled, and then flicked his hips to each side to a non-existent beat. He lifted his palms, and a cupcake appeared on each.

Then he started singing that song by Right Said Fred, "I'm Too Sexy."

I practically peed my pants right then and there.

"Remi?" My voice came out a squeak and I tried to look away. It was physically impossible.

Remi appeared in the kitchen between us and Julian as he started singing, and acting out, the part about the catwalk.

"You did it!" She gave me a big hug.

Molly raised a brow and nodded toward Julian.

"Hey, no judgment," Remi said. "It's not like I can control what I dream about. Not like Jen."

"Ha," I said. I was so out of control it was ridiculous.

"Now what?" Molly asked.

"Yeah, Jen," Remi said. "Take us on an adventure."

An adventure? My mind went straight to the first night Remi and I had learned about the existence of magic and gone out to Tergel's armed with garlic leis and a thirst for both excitement and booze. I remembered what Evan had said about adults getting dressed up in costumes and pretending when I'd shown him my vampire booty. And I remembered the dream outfits I'd worn in his jungle dream.

With just those thoughts, the three of us were transported.

The world around us became a vast jungle brimming with vibrant blooms—dreamy daisies? Yes, please. Lush shades of green coated the ground and reached up to the tops of the thirty-foot trees. Pops of pink, yellow, and orange leaves broke up all the green.

My sensible work clothes were replaced by a glittery blue robe. This time it wasn't the potato sack I'd worn in Evan's dream, but a form-flattering version that made me look way hotter than I did in reality. Remi went from wearing sweatpants, t-shirt, and apron to a full suit of red armor. She looked like a mashup of a samurai and a Medieval knight. And Molly wore a leotard of vines and flowers.

"Wow," Remi said. "This is...a lot."

"Awesome, right?" I asked.

Remi and Molly looked at me with flat expressions.

"Come on, it's fun." I looked up, and imagined my crown on the top of my head. It appeared. I held out a hand and my giant golden spork materialized in my grip. "See?"

"The armor's missing something," Remi said.

I wiggled my nose like I'd always imagined witches were supposed to based on my TV-viewing experience. Remi's armor burst into flames.

"Ooh," she said. "That's better."

I looked to Molly for some indication of what she wanted.

"It's fine," she said flatly. "Where are we?"

"Dream jungle," I said. Then I pointed. "That's where I first defeated Dale Corduroy."

We headed in the direction I'd indicated, toward the island where the giant vampire had appeared. Instead of a giant vampire, though, there was only a beach of white sand and crystal-clear water. A cool breeze carried mist from the water and broke the heat from the heavy sun.

"If you could do anything, what would it be?" I asked them.

Remi glanced up at the sun and squinted. "Sled."

"Like down a snowy hill?" I asked.

"Yes. I haven't seen snow since I was little. I always wanted to sled down a giant hill."

"Done." I wiggled my nose.

The hot sun disappeared, as did the sand and the sea.

The three of us blew down an icy mountain slide in giant inner tubes. I had on a snuggly hat, thick gloves, and some kind of puffy one-piece snowsuit. From what I could tell, Remi and Molly were dressed the same. Overcast in a blanket of grayish white, the sky was all clouds. Sharp and cold air bit my nose and cheeks. My tube spun and bumped into Remi's across the snowy landscape. I squeezed my eyes shut to stop the wave of dizziness that hit, and held tight to my scrapbook.

"Yes!" Remi yelled.

I peeked on eye open, and caught a glimpse of a tiny snowflake just before it landed on my nose.

"No. No. Please—" Molly's tube went off the end of a ramp and she went flying through the air. She gripped onto the handles like her life depended on it.

"It's okay," I called out to her. "It's not real."

She landed with a thud and a groan, and all three of us slowed and bumped into each other. At the bottom of the slope, we came to a full stop.

I tried to bounce out of my tube, but apparently my powers did not allow me to reverse the aging process. Instead of popping up, I rocked awkwardly, stuck in the tube, my scrapbook still held tight to my chest. Remi offered me a hand, somehow already standing. She helped me up, then we both helped Molly.

I imagined how amazing it would be to wake to a photo of the three of us just like this.

"That was everything," Remi said.

Molly was still quiet. She looked down at her feet, then off into the distance.

"What about you?" I asked her. "If you could pick anything, what would you?"

A small smile curved on her lips, and she met my gaze.

"You're not going to tell me, are you?" I asked.

She didn't answer, so I put my hand on her forehead, and let her thoughts lead us.

Remi and I appeared in a fancy hall. Instead of outdoor gear, we had on flowing dresses. The fabric was pink, and felt like silk.

Painted portraits lined the walls. There were paintings of horses and dogs, too. Elaborate carpets ran the length of the hardwood floor. Any one thing in here—painting, carpet, decorative outlet cover—was probably worth more than everything I owned combined.

"Where are we?" Remi asked.

I didn't know the answer, but I knew who did, and where she was.

"Ask her," I said, nodding to Molly.

She was sitting in the next room over with her back turned to us. We went in and found her sitting on a throne.

She still had snowboots on her feet, but a dress, too. Hers appeared to be purple velvet. And she looked like she was twenty, with long golden hair and a smug grin of satisfaction.

She waved a hand and the queen of England's royal jewels appeared on her neck, her hands, and her head.

A man in a tuxedo appeared beside her and handed her a tea cup. She took a sip, then pulled a cookie from her purse and took a nibble.

"Now this is what I'm talking about," she said.

CHAPTER 15

ith a stretch and a yawn, I ambled out of bed. My mind raced with dreams and ideas, and my aching body reminded me that I was awake. Maybe that was the key takeaway from my recent adventures—dreams were better than reality.

I jotted relatively coherent notes into my dream journal, then showered, dressed, and made my way downstairs.

It was still dark out, and would be until around seven. That was one of the best parts of this time of year. Sure, short days sucked when you wanted to spend time outside in the evening and it felt like midnight. But short days were awesome when you wanted to spend all of your time sleeping.

Was that a problem? That I wanted to sleep all the time instead of being awake?

My body said yes—move around or you'll get bed sores. My brain said nah, sleep's cool.

Downstairs, I was pleasantly surprised to find that Evan hadn't beaten me to the kitchen for the second morning in a row. I grabbed some vegan sausages from the fridge, along with some eggs and english muffins, and set to work on breakfast.

A few minutes later, Evan jogged down the stairs.

"Morning," he said with a hand on my shoulder as he brushed past me to the fridge.

"Good morning. How'd you sleep?"

"Fine." He poured himself a glass of orange juice and leaned on the counter. "You're...*something* this morning."

"Should I be insulted or do you mean that as a compliment?"

He narrowed his eyes. "It's not bad. You look happy. It suits you."

"Ha."

"It's the boyfriend, isn't it? The LARP one?"

"There's no boyfriend," I told him, again.

"Sure." He grinned, kissed my cheek, and grabbed a warm english muffin from the toaster before heading toward the door.

"Wait."

He stopped and turned.

I carefully stacked an egg, a slice of cheese, and the best sausage veggies could make together on my spatula. Then I crept toward Evan, balancing the stack carefully.

"This is fine," he said, waving his english muffin at me.

"Nope," I told him. "You can at least make it a sandwich. Protein is important."

"Thanks, Mom," he said in a flat tone. He held out his open muffin and accepted the food that I wasn't going to let him leave without. Then he said goodbye and headed off to school.

I lost myself in cleaning and then scrapbooking for a few hours, and before I knew it, it was time to get ready and go to lunch. With a slather of lipstick and mascara—fancy—I met Jerry at Robertini's.

He was waiting for me in our usual booth. When I slid in across from him, we did air kisses, and he passed me a menu.

"Looking fabulous," he told me.

"It's a wonder what a little sleep can do for a girl."

His brows rose and he opened his mouth, likely to snap a witty reply, but my phone buzzed in my pocket. He froze. "Go ahead."

"Sorry," I told him, and squeezed his hand.

Whoever it was, I'd just call back. Still, the mom in me made me check. You never knew when your kid could be sick and need you to pick him up from school. Not that Evan wouldn't just drive himself. It was one of those things, like becoming a light sleeper, that had stuck with me since entering the realm of motherhood.

I pulled out my phone and checked who was calling— Remi. It could be important.

With another apologetic expression directed at Jerry, I answered, "Hell—"

She didn't let me finish my greeting, and cut me off with gravitas, *"Where are you?"*

"Robertini's."

"Look out the window. East side."

Jerry watched me with a look that said he was just waiting for all the juicy details.

I rose from my seat and headed over to the big window. The couple sitting in front of it gave me a strange look.

"Don't mind her," Jerry said. "She's a real estate agent."

The couple looked at him, then back at me, clearly not accepting his explanation. Me, on the other hand, I appreciated the backup.

"Do you see it?" Remi whispered through the speaker.

I looked out the window.

What I saw defied the rules of reality. It was a halo of translucent red that encased the police station.

"Jerry, what do you see?" I asked.

"My very best gal pal acting like a crazy woman."

"And outside?"

"Rain's coming?"

"You two." I pointed at the couple. "What do you see?"

"The bank? The police station?" The woman gave me a look that said I better wrap this up quick. "Uhhhh…"

"We're trying to eat," the man said. He, too, flashed the you're-crazy look. "If you don't mind."

None of them could see the bright beacon of weird that was plopped down in front of them. For the record, I meant the hazardous red glow, not me.

"I see it," I told Remi, and turned from the window.

Jerry grabbed my wrist and led me back toward our table, grumbling under his breath as we went. I caught a word here and there, missing most of them. The standouts included: kicked out, boring people, and sage eggs.

"Give me five," I told Remi.

"Oh you are not getting a high-five for this behavior," Jerry said. "You're scaring people."

"Minutes," I said. "I was talking to Remi. I'll be there in five minutes."

"Good luck with that," Remi said before hanging up.

Jerry crossed his arms and gestured with his brows that I should sit. I didn't.

"You need to tell me what's going on with you," he said. "I'm worried."

I plastered on what I hoped was a reassuring smile. I'd been doing that a lot lately.

"Nope. No lies," he said. "You hate lying, remember?"

"I know." I forced myself to stop chewing my lip and sighed.

I'd regretted not telling Evan the truth. So why not just rip off the Band-aid and tell Jerry? Worst case, he didn't believe me. Or it turned out Remi was right and he would be in danger. But we lived in the magical town of Marshmallow; he was already in danger.

I raised my hands in submission and slid into the booth to make it clear I wasn't bolting. Concern caused a V to form between Jerry's brows on his otherwise lineless face.

I folded my hands together on the table and looked him in the eye. "I'll tell you the truth. You're not going to believe me and you're going to have questions, but I have to go. We'll have to cover the rest later."

"Okay."

"I'm a witch."

He frowned, squinted, and then opened his mouth to ask one of the billion questions I could see churning behind those hawkish eyes of his.

I lifted a finger to stop him.

"My coven needs me." With that I stood and headed for the door.

There was a waitress with dark hair coming in as I was going out, and for a brief second, I could have sworn I recognized her. She slipped away into the kitchen. Letting the passing thought go, I left.

I could feel Jerry's gaze on my back, and I could picture his mouth agape as the sheer badassery of what I'd just told him sunk it. And I felt like a boss as I strolled into the street, and even as I picked up my pace to a run, because there were exactly three witches in this town, and whatever we found, the three of us would face it together.

I hurried around the block to the police station. And then I saw it.

There wasn't a *glow* around the building. It was a twenty-foot-tall, jelly-like blob.

That jaw hanging thing I'd imagined Jerry doing, it was my turn. "What in…"

"Gherkin's merkin," Remi said, appearing by my side.

Molly stepped up on her other side.

"What is it?" I asked Molly.

She squeezed the top of her gnarled cane in her fist. "Nothing I have ever seen or heard of before."

The blob jiggled like it was doing a gelatinous shimmy. Inside its dome-like shape, everything was still—too still.

A nest of angry hornets rattled in my gut.

"What do you think the chances are that the police station is empty?" I asked, in an attempt to channel unfounded hope.

"Zero," Molly said. "I can feel them. Their life forces are strong—for now."

That was something.

"So they don't need to breathe?" I asked. "Because they're magically suspended?"

"We should circle the building and see if we can find anyone trapped who is also visible."

That wasn't the answer I was hoping for. Still, I said, "Okay."

Remi was quiet. She had her fists balled and a determined clench in her jaw. When I was afraid, it was Molly who had answers, and Remi who had enough determination for all three of us.

We'd figure it out. We had to. This time when I told myself how powerful we were, it had a little less oomph behind it, so I kept the sentiment to myself instead of offering lame encouragement.

As we circled around the building, a nagging feeling of déjà vu tickled in the back of my head. Maybe I had seen this blob before in one of Molly's books. But if that was the case, wouldn't she recognize it? Had she read all of the books on the shelves in her shop?

"There." Molly pointed by the door to the police station where a man was standing frozen mid-step.

His back was turned to us, and his arm was reaching out like he was about to grab the handle when the blob had stopped him. We hurried a little farther around the perimeter of the building so we could see his expression.

There was no sign of terror or even discomfort. He had a smile plastered to his face. He was happy.

"Okay, so the people in there didn't see this coming," I said.

"Or at least that guy didn't," Remi said.

"Why would they?" Molly asked. "Most people will live their lives never seeing any of the supernatural world, even when it smacks them in the face."

"Or encases them in gelatin." I held a hand to my stomach where those metaphorical hornets were swarming harder than ever. "How long do we have to fix this?"

"I don't know," Molly said. "The mass has no life force, so I cannot use my magic to drain it. I can make some calls, see if anyone has any idea what this thing is."

Remi scoffed. "Because making calls and sitting around on our backsides worked so well the last time. If we'd acted sooner, we could have spared Evan from getting attacked by that cat demon."

"*Maybe.*" Molly seemed unconvinced. "There's no proof that you wouldn't have made the situation worse. When all else fails, it's the research that we can count on."

Remi sneered at Molly. Molly appeared unbothered.

"Evan's okay," I told Remi.

"And I'm grateful for that," she said. "But it could have gone much, much worse. If we abandon these people like this, who knows what happens to them? I'm not leaving it to chance."

She stormed right toward the blob, fire bursting over both of her hands.

"Wait," Molly said.

But Remi wasn't having it. She thrust her hands against the side of the jiggly dome. The red jelly wiggled and melted, just enough for her hands to slip into the surface.

Yes! Remi was a total boss. I exclaimed, "Take that, blob!"

The liquid jelly seeped down the surface and pooled onto the ground as Remi formed a little dent. That dent grew into a hole. Before long, the melted space was a whole person deep.

I hurried toward her, hoping to follow behind her in the melted jelly path. But Molly grabbed my wrist. I whipped around to ask why.

"It's too late," she said.

"Too late for what?" I pulled free and turned back toward Remi.

With a slurp, the liquid jelly shot up over Remi's legs, her torso, her arms. Before I could warn her, before I could take a single step, Remi was completely encased in the blob.

The surface of the jelly rumbled and inched out, the entire thing seemingly growing larger.

Remi was completely frozen, exactly like the door guy, and her flames were extinguished. I couldn't touch her without jumping into the giant gelatinous mountain myself. Molly was right, I was too late.

My stomach hornets grew to the size of elephants as my body shook with sheer panic.

"Remi!" I screamed.

My eyes blurred. *What was I supposed to do now?*

CHAPTER 16

*M*y eyes burned, tears welling in the corners. I rubbed my sleeve across my face, clearing the emotion that I couldn't afford to indulge.

I grabbed a hold of Molly and shook her shoulders. "We have to do something."

She put her hand on my arm and said softly, "Let go of me."

I did as she said, then sank down into the grass beside the blob, staying as close to Remi as I could without touching the surface of the mysterious red mass and risk getting myself trapped, too.

"I'm going to make some calls," Molly said, and turned to go.

Remi wasn't breathing. She wasn't moving. My best friend was trapped, and I couldn't walk away. I *had* to help her.

I told Molly, "We can't *leave* her here."

"I will do everything in my power to help Remedy and the humans stuck inside the entity."

Molly started walking, and I wanted to protest. I wanted to tackle her to the ground and physically restrain her so she couldn't leave. But tackling wouldn't convince her. I pleaded to Molly, "We're a coven."

She turned to face me. "Remedy is a reckless child. I told her what we needed to do."

"But—"

"Don't be stupid like your friend," she said. "The answer isn't here. It's not linked to emotion. It's out there, and we'll win, but not here. Not like this."

With that, she walked away.

My nose was snotty, my heart a pounding erratic mess.

There had to be something to do here and now. Just like this. Molly was wrong. I wouldn't abandon Remi.

I pulled my phone from my pocket and called the only person I knew outside our little triad who might be able to help—Julian. His phone rang and rang until it went voicemail. Instead of leaving a message, I tried again.

This time he answered right away. "Jen, what's wrong?"

"It's Remi. We need you. Now."

"Where are you?"

"Police station."

"One sec."

There was a scratchy sound and he sounded distant, like he was holding the phone against his chest as he told someone there was a medical emergency and he needed to go. He was at work, being a nurse, saving lives.

"Okay, Jen," he said. "I'm on my way."

After he hung up, I felt a little guilty for making him leave the hospital. But Remi was his world. He didn't even ask any questions about whether or not it was worth his time to come. He dropped everything to help her. Remi was lucky.

Forever and no time passed before Julian arrived. He

found me and offered me a hand up without saying a word. His gaze was set on Remi, and his expression was hard.

"Hey," I said. "I'm glad you're here."

His lips formed a flat line, and his hands were shaking. He squeezed his eyes shut and let out a measured breath, as if it was all he could do to keep his composure.

Wordlessly he transformed into a half-man, half-dragon. His right side turned red and scaly, and a shadow appeared around him, in the shape of wings. Talk about flexing. I could count on one hand the number of times I'd seen him go lizard mode before, each time as mind-blowing as the first.

"How long has she been in there?" he asked.

I pulled my attention down from his ghostly wings and looked him in the eye. "I don't know. It was a little after one when she called me. I was at Robertini's. I met her and Molly here."

I had no idea what time it was now. And thinking too hard was impossible with the mush that was my throbbing brain.

"Where's Molly?" Julian asked. "Is she trapped, too?"

"She left."

Julian gritted his teeth and tightened his shoulders, making the muscles on his neck pop. I felt the same frustration, and also like I'd felt so upset for so long that all that was left was a weird numbness.

"Don't touch the surface," I told him. "That's what got Remi stuck. Then the blob grew bigger to encase her like that."

"Thanks for the warning."

Julian strode forward, fire bursting across his skin. He let the flames loose in a stream against the surface of the barrier. Instead of melting the jelly, the fire glided over the surface and dissipated without leaving a dent.

"Fire worked before," I said, rising to my feet but leaving plenty of space between me and flameball Julian.

"It doesn't now."

Thank you, Captain Obvious. We were on the same team, we both loved Remi. I bit my tongue and kept my snark to myself.

"There's a quality to this barrier," Julian said.

"What kind of quality?"

"It reminds me of the not-vampire, though I can't say why."

A familiar voice came from behind me. "I can."

I spun around to find Evan standing in the grass.

"What are you doing here?" I asked. "Aren't you supposed to be in school?"

"School's over."

"Track?" I was pretty sure this was Thursday and he was supposed to have track.

"Yeah," he said. "I was on the field when I saw the red glow towering over the trees."

He could see it. How could he see it?

"Once magic directly affects a person, they can see it," Julian said, as if reading my brain.

"Right," I said, like this was all totally normal and everything made sense. But the magic that had directly affected Evan? I'd hoped there would be no lasting effect from the cat demon knocking him out. My brain pounded harder. I kneaded between my brows with the palm of my hand.

"You said you knew something about the barrier," Julian said to Evan.

"Yep," Evan said. "It's the wad."

"I was thinking more of a blob than a wad," I told him.

"Not *a* wad, *the* Wad." Evan looked from me to Julian and back again. "From the movie."

Movie monster come alive. Did I do this? *Again?*

"I don't even remember watching that," I said. "How could I have dream-made this thing?"

"You didn't watch it," Evan said. "But you popped in while I was watching it."

"And I saw it."

Now that he said it, it made sense. That's why the blob—the Wad—felt familiar. I'd purposely *not* watched that movie, but it didn't matter. It was my fault that my best friend was trapped, and I had no idea how to get her out.

Julian continued his barrage of fire against the Wad's surface, to no avail. I couldn't blame him for trying again and again. Fire was his strength. And even if it looked hopeless, we *had* to get her out of there.

"What about a rope?" Evan asked.

Smart cookie.

"You're not keeping rope in your backpack, are you?" I asked.

Evan wrinkled his nose. "No. That would be weird, Mom."

"Yes, it would."

"But if we could find something to throw in and grab her—"

"Like a lasso," I said.

"Exactly," Evan said.

I was digging this idea.

The faucet-like sound of Julian's fire stopped. I glanced at him to see what he was up to. He tossed his keys to Evan, who caught them.

"Check the trunk," Julian said.

Evan agreed and hurried back toward the street to check the back of Julian's car. I shot Nurse Hotpants a look when I spotted what was clearly a silky soft bedroom-fun-times rope. He shot me one right back. Mine was full of questions and approval, his was all confidence, just daring me to ask.

When Evan returned, he whispered under his breath, "I'm not going to ask."

Me either.

"Anyone know how to tie a lasso?" I asked.

Evan raised a hand.

"How did I not know that?"

"It was a thing in middle school," he said. "Cowboy week. I hated it."

He tied a loop at the end of the rope.

"Ready?" he asked.

I nodded.

"Go for it," Julian said.

Evan let the hoop loose. I crossed my fingers and my toes and held my breath.

The rope hit the side of the red mass and slid down the outer wall.

"Maybe we need to poke through to put the loop around her," I said.

"Before we go looking for something, we should try something pointy and close by, see if it works," Evan said.

Julian paced back and forth, running his hands through his hair.

Balancing on one leg like a champ, I grabbed my left shoe, a pointed-toe flat, off my foot. Evan held onto my arm when I started to wobble.

Armed with the pointiest thing on my person, I stabbed the wall, careful not to touch the actual barrier. The wall dented and jiggled, like the surface of a Jell-O mold. But it didn't give. I thrust a bit harder, throwing my weight behind it.

"Be careful," Evan said, clearly concerned about my reckless abandon.

"I will." I grunted between gritted teeth. But even with full swinging power behind me, the wall didn't give.

What now? What else could we try?

I looked to Julian and Evan. Julian was losing it. He was pacing faster. "I won't leave without her."

"I know," I told him. "But we need to think. If we just plow ahead—"

His clothes seemed to grow tighter. His chest expanded, as did his arms and his legs. He totally hulked out, his body ripping through his scrubs, human skin replaced by red scales.

"Run," he growled.

I grabbed Evan's hand and I ran. It took Evan a second to start, standing there watching. But as I pulled, he quickly caught on.

We ran half a block away before we stopped to watch Julian's next attempt.

If anything could vanquish a Jell-O colossus, it was an enraged dragon.

Evan grabbed my sleeve as he watched the three-story-tall fantasy creature fly up into the sky.

"The scales were one thing. And I knew, but..." Evan trailed off, his face frozen in awe.

"I know," I said, and patted Evan's hand.

Two stick-thin young women jogged together, in workout clothes and perfect makeup. They looked at us like we were being nutty. They weren't afraid, because they couldn't see any of it. I stuck my tongue out at them as they passed, which did what I wanted and made them leave faster.

"How does it go in the movie?" I asked Evan as we watched Julian rise on his hind legs and tear at the barrier. "How do the people kill the Wad?"

"They don't."

My head spun. Vampires died in sunlight, but how could we defeat an undefeatable blob?

"It just devoured the whole town?" I asked Evan.

"Yeah."

Julian flew up over the police station, did a twirl in the air, and then dove back down at full speed toward Remi.

I cringed at the impending impact.

But he didn't bounce off. The outer gelatinous layer opened for him like a giant mouth. Julian reached a claw for Remi, scooping her toward him, before the mouth closed. Now both Julian and Remi were suspended in space and time. The jelly rumbled and grew, encasing even the tips of Julian's dragon tail and wings. It took over the sidewalks and even parts of the street.

It ate him.

Staring with intensity, I prayed that Julian would move. Just a little wiggle, a blink, anything to signal that his dragon power was far superior to the Wad.

Blurp. The sound of something large pushing against the gelatinous membrane caused me to turn. A ripple waved out over the surface. *Crunch.*

A car smashed straight into the wall of jelly without slowing or swerving. This was really bad.

I hurried over to help.

"We have to call the fire department or something," I told Evan. "Normies can't see the Wad. They're going to hurt themselves."

"On it."

When I reached the car, the driver had the door partly open. The whole front of the car was crushed, and the airbag had deployed.

"Don't move," I told the guy. "Help is coming."

A streak of blood streamed down from his nose. He

squeezed his eyes shut and cupped his face in his hands. "It came out of nowhere. What...it wasn't a person, was it?"

"No," I said. "Everything is going to be okay. You didn't do anything wrong."

He sank down against the side of his car. A vacant look of shock clouded his eyes. "Did I hurt him?"

"No one is hurt but you," I said, softly putting my hand on his shoulder as he tried to get up.

Sirens blared, a sign that the help we needed was on the way. All we had to do now was wait. Then the fire department could block off the area and no one else could get hurt. They'd have to put up tape around a monster they couldn't see, and then I could focus on finding a way to help Remi. And Julian. And the police officers.

My breaths came rapid and jagged. I needed to stay calm, but it seemed impossible.

Shrill and ear-piercing, a scream ripped through the air. I whirled around to see what was the matter, expecting someone must have spotted the giant dragon encased in Jell-O.

But no. It was far worse.

A woman climbed on top of her car as cat-sized balls of fur climbed after her. The two-legged creatures were green, with giant eyes that seemed mechanical when they blinked. One chewed on the tire, quickly popping the rubber, and proceeded to devour the metal. Another climbed up after the woman, and a third clung to her pant leg.

I took a step from the curb in her direction.

Someone moved between me and the woman, causing me to stop. It wasn't a man. It wasn't a woman. It was a skeleton. Eyeless, hairless—only bones. Between the snapping jaw and jigging knees, the skeleton pulled a giant knife from between its ribs.

"Come on, Mom," Evan said, pulling on my arm. "We have to run."

I pulled back. "I can't leave Remi."

"Remi's safe. We're not."

The skeleton dove toward us, blade whipping through the air. All we had to defend ourselves with were a limp rope and a pointy shoe.

So as much as I hated to leave Remi and Julian behind, we ran.

CHAPTER 17

*W*ith every light in the house on, every curtain shut, and both deadbolts in place, Evan and I stared at the TV, waiting for the news people to get through with the forecast and on to the important story.

I should have taken pictures. If I had, we could look back and see everything that we'd forget and any other details we'd missed.

The blond on the TV lifted her microphone to her chin. "Another chilly night. If you haven't already, pull out those thermal pajamas and thick comforters. It's only going to get worse from here."

"Great. Thanks, Holly Weatherby." I scowled at her blindingly white smile and upturned nose. "That's what we want to hear right now."

"It's not Holly Weatherby's fault," Evan said beside me.

It was mine.

"None of them are going to know what's going on if they can't see it," Evan said, clearly not intending the fault comment the way I'd taken it.

I was being defensive, and grumpy, and unhelpful. Some

situations called for less than enthusiastic reactions, and this was one of them, so long as I didn't take it out on Evan.

"I wonder what they see." Evan turned up the volume. "And if cameras can even catch the truth."

"Huh." The camera thing was interesting; I'd assumed they would record everything. "I hadn't thought of that."

"On to tonight's big story," Holly said. "Back to you, Jack."

I rubbed my hands together and leaned forward on my seat in anticipation.

Jack Northam tapped his papers on the desk, and looked into the camera with his trademark no-nonsense stoicism. "Big eyes, wet tongues. They're coming for you."

"Zombies," I guessed.

"Puppies!" Jack said. "There's an adoption drive this Saturday at the..."

I stopped listening and shot up to my feet. "I'm going to call your Grandma and make us some sandwiches. Let me know if they ever get to what's actually happening out there."

"Sure," Evan said.

"Did you call anyone yet? Warn your friends to stay in?"

"I texted."

I paused a moment, wondering what I should tell my mother. Clearly the truth wasn't the key. She'd completely written off everything I'd told her about magic. "What'd you tell them?"

"Gas leak," Evan said. "You tell a bunch of teenagers there are magical horror movie monsters roaming the streets, you think they're going to stay inside? No. They're going out to see for themselves. But you tell them a hallucinogenic gas leak is making people rip off each other's faces, they might actually stay in."

"Smart," I said. But if it had been me and Remi on the receiving end of that story at his age, or our own really, we'd be enthusiastically running out to get in on the action. "Maybe that'll work on Grandma, too."

I left Evan to monitor the news and headed into the kitchen, where I pulled out two plates and all of the sandwich supplies. As I set to work on assembly, I called my parents.

It was almost always my mom who answered, but this time it was my dad.

"Jenny," he said. "How are you?"

I opened my mouth to lie and say fine, the automatic response. But I froze.

"Jenny? Are you there? What's wrong?"

"Hey, Dad," I said.

"You want to talk to your mother?"

"No. I just wanted to check in and make sure you two had heard about the gas leak."

My gut twisted as the lie left my lips.

"Gwennie," my dad yelled away from the phone. "You'll have to wait to go to the store until tomorrow. There's a gas leak."

"It might be later than tomorrow," I said. I had no idea *how* I was going to fix this, let alone *when.*

"Oh. Gwennie, it might be more than a day," my dad said. Then he returned to the phone. "There you go. I told her. But you know how your mother is, she'll only listen for so long."

"I know," I said. That was true not just about my mom, but about Evan's friends. Also, how were we going to get the whole town to stay in? And how long could Remi and Julian remain in the Wad before they ran out of air?

Tears pricked at the corners of my eyes, and my chest tightened. I couldn't panic. Not now.

"Everything else okay?" my dad asked. "Evan still doing well in school?"

"Evan's great," I said. And he really was.

I heard my mother's voice in the background, but didn't catch what she said.

"Your mom wants to know if you've met a man yet."

"I'm not looking for a man," I said.

"I'll tell her." He relayed the message to my mother, who grumbled in response.

I was forty-one years old. By now she should have gotten used to the fact that while sure, it would be nice to have a partner, I wasn't really looking. And I definitely wasn't settling.

The memory of an eldery Baku holding my hand while we rocked in our side-by-side chairs passed through my head. As did the image of his crooked grin and his ridiculous mohawk. I pictured the molten copper of his hooded eyes as his lips sealed mine and stole my words and my breath.

Suddenly I wasn't panicking, or almost crying. I breathed easier. What did that say about me? Taking comfort in the memories of my imaginary friend?

"Mom." Evan waved me over.

"Gotta go," I told my dad. "Love you."

"Love you, too. Be safe, Jenny." My dad hung up.

Careful not to dump our sandwiches on the floor, I hurried back to the sofa. I handed Evan his plate and sat down beside him.

"The gas leak was called in on an anonymous tip," Jack Northam said on the TV. "The caller did mention that he was an employee of the gas company."

I turned slowly to Evan, who was just about to take his first bite of ham and cheese.

"What?" he asked with a shrug. "People have to know to stay indoors. And for the record, I didn't say I worked for the gas company, I just didn't disagree when they assumed that I did."

"You called in to protect the whole town, you sweet-as-pudding freaking genius."

He raised a brow, clearly not thrilled with the compliment. But a smile pulled on his lips as he hid behind his bread.

"We'll go to Meredith North in the field," Jack said.

Evan and I watched as a hazard-suit-wearing Meredith stood right next to the police station, or as close as she could get with the Wad having taken over the entire area. Our first question was already answered. Yes, the video camera could catch supernatural activity. I should have guessed, given I could photograph them.

I grabbed my phone and snapped a shot of the television screen. I'd missed my chance to capture shots firsthand, but this was the next best thing.

"Thank you, Jack," Meredith said. "I'm standing in the heart of Marshmallow, where there have been multiple reports of violence due to the hallucinogenic properties of the gas leak. As you can see, the fire department has taped off the police station and the entirety of this block. People are injuring themselves believing invisible forces are attacking them. The mayor is expected to issue a stay-at-home order for all residents."

In the Wad, I could see Remi and Julian frozen. They looked exactly the same as when we left, which was good, I guessed. The Wad didn't seem to be growing, at least, with no one else touching its surface and getting trapped inside.

The crashed car was right where we'd left it, too. Only now there was a second one smashed against its rear bumper.

Skeletons walked the streets, along with a man in a black and white striped sweater and a catcher's mask.

"Hey," Evan said, pointing. "That's the Barcode Butcher."

"Barcode because of the stripes?" I asked.

He nodded.

"What's with the baseball mask?"

"You don't remember?" Evan asked. "It was one of the first horror movies we watched together."

The guy did look vaguely familiar, which he should, given I'd somehow appeared him out of my head.

"Barry the Barcode Butcher worked at a sports store," Evan said. "It's where he was attacked by that group of 'rowdy kids'—those were your words."

"Oh yeah. They killed him for not being cool, and so he came back and terrorized them one at a time. The story's a lot like *Camp Murder's* Melvin Murderface." The excitement of remembering quickly transformed into a not-so-sweet feeling. "And I let that guy loose on Marshmallow."

There was a flash of movement in the shadows on the screen that I could swear was a twenty-foot-tall spider. But when I looked directly at it, there was nothing there.

"The furben should be less dangerous," Evan said, pointing to the toy-like creatures running across the screen. "They like to cause mayhem. They probably won't murder too many people."

"Uh huh, great. Chinese knockoff version of a nineties toy turned horror movie monsters," I said, remembering that, too. "And the skeletons are from the bone rain in *Upended Undead*." I rose from my seat and headed for the stairs. There was only one thing I could do. I needed to stop all of this before it got any worse.

Evan turned all the way around to watch me. "What are you doing?"

"Getting my spork."

"You can't go out there."

"I have to."

"You're one person, Mom. There are hordes of them. And you're not even trained in fighting."

I stopped on the bottom step, and gripped the railing hard, knowing what he said was true. "I have a pointy weapon. And I'm a witch."

"A dream witch," he said.

"I have to try."

I hurried up the steps, grabbed my spork, and strapped the samurai sword I hadn't used since the Weaty incident to my back. As for fighting experience, I did have a little. I'd survived the vampires. But I'd had Remi, Molly, and Julian with me then. Even when Weaty had me chained in the sewers, I hadn't been alone.

I headed back downstairs, channeling the strength I'd felt when I'd had my friends at my side. They were there for me when I needed them. And I'd be there for them now.

Evan was standing in front of the door with his arms crossed. "I want the sword."

"You're not coming."

"Of course I am," he said. "You saw how bad it is out there. I can't let you face that alone. I can't lose you."

I pulled my brave boy into my arms and squeezed him. *"I can't lose you."*

"Great," he said. "We're on the same page. We go out together, watch each other's backs, maybe save a few stragglers, and when you realize how crazy it is to be out there, we come home."

"I don't—"

He cut me off. "And I get the sword."

Beneath his towering height and behind the manly scruff on his face, were the hopeful eyes of my little boy. Confident, yet a touch unsure of whether or not he was getting his way.

"You can have the sword," I said. "But you're right. It's too dangerous."

The tension in his shoulders eased. "I can't believe I got you to see reason. That was too easy, wasn't it?"

I nodded. "Go pack a bag. The sword is yours after you come home."

He blew out a puff of air that lifted the hair that hung over his face. Without protesting, he did as I said.

We headed straight to my parents' house after that. I thought convincing my parents to leave town was going to be hard, but since they'd seen the news, they were happy to take my credit card and book a set of rooms at the mountain spa about an hour away. They wanted me to come with them, but of course I wouldn't.

The worry on my father's face was nothing compared to the worry on Evan's.

But as they pulled out of the driveway and went on their way, I knew it was the right call. Night had fallen already, and I was no more certain of what to do than I'd been after lunch. What would Remi do?

She'd find Molly and threaten and prod her into doing what she wanted. That wasn't exactly my style. I'd ask nicely. Before deciding what I would do if that didn't work, I needed to try.

There was another car parked in front of the magic shop, an early nineties sedan I didn't recognize. I parked behind it and climbed out, spork in hand for protection.

A figure moved through the shadows around the side of the building. The silhouette was too tall to be Fernando or Molly. And then I caught a glint of light on the figure's blade.

I whipped my spork in front of me. "Show yourself."

"Don't hurt me." A woman with black hair and olive skin raised her hands in the air and slowly stepped out of the shadows. She had on a waitress uniform I recognized from Robertini's. A paring knife remained tightly squeezed in her white-knuckled fist. Behind a pair of red-framed glasses, her hazel eyes were startled globes. *"Jen?"*

It wasn't until she said my name that I recognized her.

"Brianna?" I dropped the end of my trident. "What are you doing here?"

When we'd been chained to the wall of an underground chamber, we'd shared a few words—mostly sarcastic jokes at the vampires' expense. At the time, it was each other's presence that meant more than anything we could have said. Every "lucky for him he has no nose, so he doesn't have to smell himself" was a reminder that we were still alive. We were fellow survivors of Weaty, though she'd been much worse off than me, having spent significantly more time as his captive than I had. And I'd been sure my coven would come for me. She'd been sure we'd never see the light of day again.

She dropped her hands to her sides, mirroring my gesture. "This is where Molly lives, right?"

"You're not planning on stabbing her, are you?"

"What? Of course not. *Are you?*"

"No."

"I'm staying at my dad's place a few miles outside of town," Brianna said. "I saw the news, and Molly didn't answer her phone. So I grabbed a kitchen knife for self-defense and came here to the address on Molly's business card, hoping for answers. But I swear this place wasn't here before."

"Yep. It's a magic thing," I said. "You can't see it until you're connected to magic."

"Like getting kidnapped by vampires."

"Maybe. I don't really know how it works." There was an idea in my head, one I couldn't place. But I had a feeling it was important. "Do you have a chicken farm?"

She gave the look—the one that everyone gave me when they thought I was nuts. It involved brows going up and then down, a twist of the lips, and then a cock of the head. I was used to the look, and I hadn't given a fork about what anyone thought of me in a long time. At least age offered some benefits to balance out the creaking joints and dry hair.

"No. I don't know anything about chickens," she said. "Aside from farmyard books and that they taste best fried. Do you know where Molly is? Or what's going on?"

"Did you try the door?" I asked.

Brianna frowned.

"Okay," I said. "Well, she's doing research, which apparently means dropping off the face of the earth."

"So she doesn't know how to fix this. Or when it'll be safe again? I swear I hate this town."

"Well," I said. "We have some ideas."

"Oh?"

"I have this." I showed her my trident.

"Yeah, I noticed that when you were threatening to stab me with it."

"Right. Well, I also have a better plan, for after. And since it's getting dark, any time now is a time to get to that."

"What's the better plan?" she asked.

"Sleep."

"Well, this has been interesting," Brianna said, and circled me at a wide berth. "I'm going home now. If you see Molly, tell her I'm looking for her."

"I will." Without explaining the whole dream-witch thing, it probably sounded like I was slacking. But Brianna wasn't part of the coven. Molly had called her a potential witch. But if she didn't have powers, and from this strange encounter I was fairly certain being near her didn't boost my powers, she was better off back at her dad's place staying safe, anyway.

After Brianna climbed into the sedan and left, I checked around Molly's place, and tried calling out for Fernando. Neither seemed to be around, so I did a drive through town. The streets were empty, both of Marshmallow's residents, and of any sign of dream monsters. *Where had all the night-*

mares gone? I parked and walked around, and for a long time found plenty of destruction, but zero horror movie monsters. A bent streetlight flickered, strobing the alley below and making the crumpled newspaper rolling across the ground seem like it was jumping unnaturally. The town was eerily dead, like the apocalypse had happened and I was the only one left.

People were safe in their homes. It was a good thing.

The streetlight went out.

I blinked fast, hoping my eyes would quickly adjust, and squeezed the rod of my spork.

A set of glowing eyes stared at me from the under the slightly opened lid of a dumpster. Heavy breathing followed.

Melvin Murderface.

My mind raced, searching for details from his movie. He liked closets, and murder, and his victims were all jerks. The worst thing I could do was insult him. Well, stabbing him with my spork could be equally dumb.

"Hey, Melvin, I think you're super cool," I said, slowly backing away. "I would never make fun of you."

The dumpster lid dropped shut. The only heavy breathing I could hear was my own.

Feeling not so awesome about my not-actual victory, I walked around a bit more, until I found myself back at the Wad, staring at Remi.

"Hey," I said to her. "I need your help. I don't know how I can fix this on my own."

She didn't respond.

"I'm not giving up," I told her. "I'm going to find a way to save you."

Her Jell-O-coated visage remained still. At least she didn't seem any worse off than she'd been earlier. Maybe Molly was right, and we had some time. I hoped that was true.

I had no ideas, my muscles swayed with exhaustion, and

it was getting hard to keep my eyes open. I patrolled the streets a while longer, until the darkness began to lift, and I knew morning would soon be upon us.

There was still one play left before the night was over.

I was glad I hadn't run into anything except for Melvin, and I was also one hundred percent glad to get home and actually do something useful—sleep.

CHAPTER 18

*E*xhausted, I should have crashed as soon as I hit my bedroom. When that failed, I tried a new bedtime routine.

The routine consisted of three steps—scrapbook to relax, take a lavender bath to relax more, and drink sleepy tea to relax so hard I'd knock myself out. It kinda worked. I rifled through my scrapbooking supplies without gluing anything into my book. Bathing soothed my aching everything a bit, and I did my drinking diligence. But instead of feeling relaxed and drifting off to sleep, I ended up writhing around in stress.

Lying in bed with my head swimming in scenarios about how everything had and would go wrong, I eventually stressed myself to sleep, and as I did, I focused on finding the one person, real or imaginary, who might be able to help me —Baku.

* * *

THOUGH THE SUN had taken its rest and the sky was dark,

heat still lingered in the air the way it only did in summer. The world was still except for the singing of crickets and the creak of the metal chains on the bar above.

I squeezed the chains in my hands, finding the metal cool and gritty, and I pumped my legs, dragging my shoes across the rutted dirt as I swung back. If I was going to find Baku, it'd be here.

Anticipation made my palms clammy and my throat dry.

I closed my eyes and imagined Baku on the swing beside me. The image of him in my head was the version I'd met flying through the clouds. Between his button-down shirt, his jeans, and his mohawk, he looked the perfect combination of edgy rockstar and respectable adult—which meant heavy on the rockstar bad boy.

Maybe I was drawn to him so fiercely because I'd spent my entire adult life making responsible choices. Maybe Baku was my midlife crisis. Maybe deep down, I wanted to meet the kind of man whose voice could make my toes curl, whose touch could set my nerves into an electric storm, whose lips could make the world disappear.

Baku could do all of those things, while somehow also inspiring dangerous hope—hope that he could actually be real.

"Hello, Jenny." Baku's deep voice brought a smile to my face and a sense of ease to my tight chest.

I opened my eyes and found him beside me. He wasn't the boy I remembered playing with when I was little, but the man who made my heart flutter. His silver hair caught in the moonlight, while his copper eyes shone as bright as the moon itself.

"Baku." I breathed his name. "You came."

"I'm always here for you."

The truth of his words settled as a warm swirl in my

chest. Still, it didn't offer any answers to my unasked questions.

"Did I make you up when I was a kid?" I asked. "Are you a part of my imagination? The friend I need when I feel so alone?"

He slowed his swing to a stop and cocked his head to the side. "You still don't remember."

"Please," I said. "Just tell me. No games, no riddles. Only answers."

"I am real."

"You're a dream witch, like me?"

"No. I'm...different."

He was nothing like anyone I'd ever met, clearly. But I didn't know what he meant, so I asked, "Different how?"

"I am of the dream world."

"Me, too. This is the only place where life makes sense anymore, as crazy as that sounds. Out there, in the real world —" I sighed, not wanting to indulge in a tangent and change the subject yet. "What do you mean you're *of the dream world?* I still don't think I'm understanding."

He reached out a hand, so I dug my heels into the ground to stop swinging and grab it. When I did, he brushed his thumb over my knuckles. The sensation of it shot warmth up my arm, along with it a sense of everything around me—the air prickling at the back of my neck, the citrus and clove scent of Baku, and how different the world felt when he was around. It was as if he was the light in the darkness, my rainbow wolf bear, a beacon of wild energy.

"You live with one foot in the waking realm and the other foot here," Baku said. "I walk only here."

"But I thought I didn't make you up."

"You didn't," he said. "I have existed as long as children have dreamed. You are coming into your powers now, but the spark was always there. It drew me to you."

"You're what...a dream god?"

"You are more divine than I," he said. "Gods create. I only destroy."

"Creation is overrated," I said. "I could use some well-directed destruction right about now."

Suddenly we weren't sitting on the swings anymore. We were standing in darkness. I held tight to Baku's hand, not afraid of the dark, but not wanting to let go.

I never wanted to let go.

How did he manage to be both calming and exhilarating at the same time? He was a balm I needed to bottle and carry with me always.

Images appeared around us in a column, giant rectangles like curved television screens. We stood in the center as different scenes silently played out in each. In one, a pink wolf sucked an entire beach scene, along with a giant, into his mouth. I recognized it as when I'd gone into Evan's dream.

In another, a rainbow bear winked at me in a field where raindrops were frozen midair.

In a third, we lay together on the floor of a forest. I looked terrible with leaves in my hair and dark circles around my eyes. But Baku looked drool-worthy amazeballs. No, amazeballs was an understatement for the tantalizing image in front of me.

He was completely naked.

Broad shoulders tapered down to narrow hips. The journey my eyes embarked upon led from over tan planes of muscle and through the valleys between. I took my sweet time, searing the scenery into my brain. This would be a trip I'd look back upon over and over again.

As it turned out, Baku was a show-er, as opposed to the deceptive grower where it was impossible to tell what you were going to get at game time. I stared at the image of his impressive manhood, and upon discovering an abundance of saliva lingering on my tongue, I swallowed and forced myself to look away.

I looked up at the real Baku and squeezed his palm, while trying really really hard not to think about what lay beneath his button-down shirt and distressed jeans. My voice was tight and husky as I asked, "What are you trying to show me?"

"I didn't do this." Amusement sparkled in his eyes as little lines formed at the corners of his lids. "You did."

It was just like me to make up a scene where I could stare at him naked. Still, I didn't remember dreaming up any of this. A little worm of concern wiggled through my brain.

"No way. No freaking way. How am I supposed to fix all the problems I've caused out in the real world if I can't even control what I do here? You know I somehow made a bunch of monsters appear out there? They're roaming the streets, doing who knows what, and I did it. And I don't know how. Tell me how to fix it." I grabbed Baku's arms—his very muscular arms. And I tried not to ooh and ahh about how wonderfully firm and amazing they felt under my fingertips. I cleared my throat and looked him in the eye. "Please, Baku, help me learn to destroy."

"It's not possible to teach a fish to fly."

"Great." I scoffed. "I'm a fish now. I think I preferred when you called me god-like, even though it had no basis in reality. Maybe I did make all of this up. Maybe this is one of those dreams where nothing makes sense and I just can't tell until after I'm awake. I mean, you *can't* be real."

"Why is that?"

"First off, you've shown up different times in different forms—total red flag. Plus, have you seen yourself? You're too gorgeous to be real. I should have seen it sooner. If I was going to make up the perfect man, he'd be somewhere between modern day Henry Cavill and *Dirty Dancing* era Patrick Swayze. Throw in a dash of those scoundrel brothers from *Prison Break.* Boom—it's you."

"I don't know who those people are."

I waved away his objection. "You're there when I need you most—something no real man ever is. And thinking about you makes me happy—again, football-field-sized red flag. The only thing that doesn't make sense about this is why I would dream up such a smoking hottie and *not* do exactly what I want to him—you. It's like I choose to torture myself even here, in my own dreams. When all I want to do is—"

His Adam's apple bobbed in his throat as he whispered in that dark and daring voice that stirred a side of me I never indulged, "What do you want?"

In answer, I grabbed onto Baku's shoulders and pulled myself flush against his hard chest. He tilted his chin down so our lips were only inches apart and spread his hands over my back, holding me close. His pupils dilated, showing me the hungry predator inside of him.

Shallow breaths and unwanted clothes were all that was left between us. I could explain to him my vanilla history in the sack, or more accurately a spot of mediocre action here and there over a long orgasmless timeline. I could tell him I wanted to end the Sahara of a dry spell, or how all I really wanted was to feel as desired as I did when he held me just like this. But most of all, I didn't want to talk.

All hesitation and concern melted as my mouth crashed over his. He tasted like mint and bliss. And he felt like home.

He deepened our kiss, teasing me with the tip of his tongue, then nipped my lower lip. The animalistic moan that followed most definitely came out of me. I mauled his freaking face.

It didn't matter if he wasn't real. He was everything I

craved, everything I needed, and if I couldn't make myself let loose in my dreams, what was the point of dreaming at all?

* * *

I FLINCHED and opened my eyes, confused as to why I was awake and alone instead of asleep and tangled up in Baku. Then the disappointment hit. My dream had ended prematurely, and I had no idea why.

A knocking sound carried through the no-longer-dark house. It sounded like a jackhammer. Was there construction going on outside...first thing in the morning? Was there a horror movie villain that used a jackhammer to kill his victims?

I stretched my sore everything and tried to remember the different horror films I'd watched. Honestly, I hadn't remembered half of the movie monsters until I'd seen them in the street. My subconscious was tricky like that, apparently, holding onto things my conscious self had forgotten.

With the snuggly heat of my blankets gone, my room felt like a freezer. I threw my robe over my tank and sleepy pants, and slipped on my favorite bunny slippers.

As the banging continued, I grabbed my spork and headed for the stairs.

The sound grew louder.

I crept down the steps, spork at the ready. The front door quaked under the assault of something inhumanly powerful. Whatever it was, it would soon bust the door from its hinges.

With my feet shoulder-width apart, I stood six feet back, the pointy end of my golden weapon aimed at whatever was out there.

The banging stopped. And a voice boomed, "Open."

It sounded like Frankenstein's monster, like the too-deep command was difficult to produce.

I hurried to the living room window to see if I could get a glimpse of what I was up against before it broke in. Careful not to obviously disturb the curtains, I peeked through.

Morning light illuminated a massive, hunch-backed figure in a lemon-colored velvet suit. Only one person in Marshmallow, and probably the universe, looked like that —Murray.

Murray was Molly's friend, or at least her acquaintance. She'd kicked Remi and me out of her shop when he'd arrived once. As for what I knew about Murray, he had a penchant for slathering whipped cream on his face and hands while wearing the ugliest suits in existence. And this was the first time I'd heard him speak. I had assumed he didn't, whether because he couldn't, or because he chose not to.

I hurried back to the door and opened it, no longer annoyed that I'd been woken, even though that had been an awesome dream. This visit was sure to be a delight, if only in that I had no idea what to expect.

Murray filled the doorway in his signature whipped cream mask and a cardboard box cradled to his chest.

"Hi," I said.

He said nothing.

"You're Murray, right? I've seen you at Molly's magic shop before."

He said nothing.

"What brings you to my doorstep at—" I glanced back at the clock on the living room mantel. "Nine-thirty in the morning?"

A shot of worry hit me that I hadn't woken when it was time for Evan to get ready for school, before I remembered that he was safely with my parents and out of Marshmallow.

Murray shoved his arms straight forward, nearly smacking me square in the nose with his box.

I took a step to the left and tilted my head to see around

the cardboard to his whipped-cream-covered face. "Is that for me?"

His eyes bulged. "Take."

"Okay." I accepted the box, but I bumped his hand as I did. Something wet and cold got onto my finger. I smiled and pretended not to be disgusted while I waited for him to say something, anything.

Instead, he turned to go.

"Thanks for the—" I looked inside the box. It was brimming with individually-wrapped fortune cookies. "Fortunes."

He lifted an arm in a clunky, dismissive wave, but didn't turn back.

I would have thanked him for the cookies, but I remembered what Molly had said about them. *Murray excretes them.*

Yeah, I would not be eating these cookies. Still, Remi had told me it was one of Murray's fortunes that had guided her in finding me when I was held captive in the sewers. So somewhere in this box could be my lucky break for the living nightmare predicament.

Clearly Murray thought I needed answers now. Lots of cookies' worth of answers. Couldn't argue with that.

CHAPTER 19

$\mathcal{T}$he first thing I did after locking up was wash my hands. The wet stuff that came off of Murray definitely looked like whipped cream, and it smelled weirdly tropical, but if the dude excreted cookies, who knew what that stuff on his skin actually was, or where it came from.

The second thing I did was grab my phone. My first instinct was to call Remi. Remi wasn't available. So next, I wanted to call Molly. She'd been notoriously difficult to reach as of late, and she'd ditched me when I'd needed her most and hadn't checked in since, so I wasn't sure how this would go. But I dialed her anyway.

It didn't even have a chance to ring before she answered.

"You're awake," she said.

My jaw dropped. She actually answered. It took me a moment to let out a lame, "Yes."

"Good. We have work to do."

Had she known I'd been up all night patrolling the town? She could probably guess. Either way, she said we had work to do, so yay for finally being on the same page. With a burst of excitement, I said, "We're finally clearing the weirdly empty streets and saving Remi! It's such a relief, I can't even—"

"No."

"What do you mean, *no?*"

"Did you or did you not receive a delivery?"

I glanced over to the cardboard box sitting on my kitchen counter. "I did. How did you know?"

"It wasn't easy to get Murray to help us on such short notice. We need to examine those fortunes. There's no time to waste."

At least we could agree on something.

"I'm on my way to your place," Molly said. And she hung up.

Finally, I was going to find a way to save Remi.

I wanted to be bitter that Murray had woken me from an amazing meeting with Baku. I wished that dream had answered all of my questions and offered the perfect, simple solution. But the truth was, I'd gotten a little sidetracked. Plus, if Baku wasn't real, he didn't have any answers for me. If I'd made him up, he could only know what I knew. So that was a bust of sorts, though a hot one.

Since I clearly wasn't going back to bed anytime soon, I got myself dressed and started a pot of tea, and set myself up with a cup of chai. It was the perfect blend of warm flavors and caffeine boost to get my tired butt moving.

Right after the tea was ready, there was a knock at the door. This time, it was a human-sized knock, not an elephant-sized one.

When I opened the door, Molly pushed in past me.

"Where is it?" she asked, scanning the living room with sharp eyes.

I pointed to the kitchen, where I'd set the box on the counter. Molly hustled over and peered into the box, shuffling around the contents with one hand.

Molly looked me up and down, then pursed her lips. "This is more than he produced over Weaty."

"Okay…" I couldn't help but feel a bit judged. It was fair, I guessed, given the whole monsters-roaming-the-streets fiasco was entirely my fault. Still, I wasn't used to this brusque side of Molly. I was a little afraid to ask, but I had to. "What does that mean?"

"I'd say it means the answer to our latest problem is less certain, but the way Murray spoke on the phone—"

"Wait." I held up a finger and leaned on the counter beside her. "You're telling me he can actually hold conversations?"

She furrowed her brow. "Of course he can. He's just particular about who he speaks to. He's shy."

"Right." I guessed that made sense. "So why did he show up here? Why not give the cookies to you instead?"

"That's the interesting part," Molly said. "There are multiple questions that require answers this time."

"What questions?"

"You tell me. All of the questions belong to you."

Well, I did have plenty of questions. And who didn't love answers?

I snatched the box from the counter, delivered it to the kitchen table, and dumped the contents all over the surface.

We took seats and surveyed the mess. There had to be at least one hundred cookies here. I wasn't sure that I had *one hundred* questions.

I laced my fingers, stretched my arms, and rolled my neck. "Let's get cracking."

We each took a pillowy package and broke into the plastic and cookie, revealing tiny slips of white paper.

"A finger of time is a finger of whiskey," Molly read, then looked up at me like she wanted to know if it meant something to me.

"We should drink some liquor?" I shrugged, then read out

loud the fortune I was holding. "You will find what you seek the last place you look."

Molly was still staring at me, that inquisitive expression on her face.

In answer, I told her, "I don't understand that one either. Of course when you're missing something it'll be found the last place you look. You stop having to hunt for it. Duh."

"Not all of the fortunes will be relevant," she said.

"Well, that sucks."

She folded her hands on the table top, her usual grand-motherly expression bringing a smile to her eyes. "Our best predictor of what the future holds isn't found in a cookie. It's in you."

She of course was the one who'd insisted the cookie-thing was our highest priority.

"I've been *trying* to work on my dreaming powers." I deflated in a puff of air that raspberried through my lips and sank back in my seat. "The dream-walking thing is cool. Maybe that's what I need to try tonight. Maybe I could reach Remi that way."

I bolted back up.

"*That's* what I should have been doing last night. Instead, I was searching for answers from my imaginary friend Baku. I'm supposed to have my life figured out. I mean, I'm middle-aged, for gherkin's sake. I shouldn't be playing pretend. I should be able to clean up the messes I've caused. I should—"

I stopped when I caught sight of Molly's face. She looked awfully pale.

"Are you okay?" I asked.

"Did you say *Baku?*"

"Yeah...so?"

"You have been visited by the Baku?"

"Molly. Seriously." I banged a hand on the table, jiggling all the cookies around. "What do you know about Baku?"

"The Baku is one of the oldest mythical creatures," she said. "The books suggest it may predate even the kukudhli."

"You're telling me I *didn't* make him up?" Memories from my quite invigorating dream kiss flooded back, and with them a flush of heat crept up my neck.

"No, you did not make him up. Though you certainly are capable of creating anything your mind can dream."

"Baku said I was a creator," I whispered more to myself than to Molly.

"Where did you see it?"

"Him," I said. "Baku is definitely a man. And a hot one at that. I mean, you should have seen..."

Molly's gaze sharpened in that predatory way it did every so often. I had no idea what she was thinking, other than that she had *thoughts* on my situation.

"In the dream or waking realm?" Molly asked. Her tone was soft, too soft, like my answer meant everything.

"Dream."

She exhaled slowly, and resumed her soft, grandmotherly expression. "Good," she said. "Very good."

But my takeaway was different than hers—Baku was real. And it was possible to bring him here.

"Be careful," she said. "The Baku is a dream eater. He is the antithesis of you."

"Balance for the win." I nodded and opened another cookie. "Yin and yang."

"You understand he is dangerous, right?"

"Yin and yang." I showed her the fortune that said those exact words, choosing to ignore the further push to discuss Baku as anything but amazing. We were forever—he'd shown me that in my head. He'd been with me since I was a kid, and he'd be with me when we were old. Or when I was old. If he was as old as time, I guessed that made him old already. Either way, I had his back, just like I knew he had mine. And

I didn't need to hear anything else about what I should or shouldn't do with him.

I set the yin and yang fortune close to me on the table, and pushed the fortune about finding things to the middle to start a junk pile. Then I grabbed another cookie.

We both got to work opening cookie after cookie. I could feel Molly's gaze on me when she thought I wasn't looking. She could think what she wanted. It changed nothing. By the time we were done, the junk pile had evolved to discard mountain, and the number of possible winners was measly.

You'll wish you had shoes.

The dream is mightier than the spork.

If you can't take the heat, get out of the basement.

Fortune favors the cold.

The two temperature-based fortunes left me to wonder if they had something to do with Remi and her fiery powers.

Molly scooped a handful of papers from the center of the table. She deposited them back in the box and said, "We should keep these for now. It's possible we've miscategorized something."

I grabbed a fresh trash bag and swept up the cookies and wrappers inside. I repeated my favorite of the rejects, "Never underestimate the pungent pickle." Then I waited with my arms crossed and a smile on my face for Molly to argue.

"Maybe not *that* one," she said, with a smile back.

"But I've been thinking about the one that said 'believe it to be real and it will be,'" I told her. "And it's the same as what —" I almost mentioned Baku, but instead quickly corrected, "—you said about me being a creator. What if the fix we need is for me to make *more* dream creatures real?"

"Double down on what caused this issue?" Molly asked.

"Kind of. But instead of monsters, maybe I watch a bunch of happy movies. And then those happy creations defeat the bad ones. Right? *Right?"* With exaggerated enthusiasm I tapped her arm with my elbow.

She swayed her head from side to side, considering. "More than likely, you'd be throwing gas on the fire."

"Psh. I'm a creator. I'm supposed to create. The fortunes told me so, and so did you. I believe this to be true, so it will be." I waved away her concerns with my fortune-quoting prowess. "I'm going to order a salad because it's already lunchtime and I'm starving. And then I'm going to binge watch the happiest, fluffiest, cringe-because-it's-the-cheesiest flicks I can find. Of course you can leave if you want, leave me to pick what to watch and decide the fate of the world alone. *Or* you could join me, impart some of your benevolent wisdom, and make sure I don't screw this up."

I flashed a competent smile at her as she narrowed her eyes at me.

"What do you say?" I asked.

"You win this round, Jennifer," she said. "But we're ordering Robertini's. I can't stop thinking about those sage eggs."

"Deal."

CHAPTER 20

*J*t was funny how slugging around could hurt just as bad as—if not worse than—overexerting. But the most painful part of the binge-fest was the movies themselves.

I slowly stretched as I paced around the living room, careful not to block Molly's view of the TV. The truth was, if I had prevented her eyeballs from having to ingest even a few seconds of this garbage, it would have been a kindness.

Molly held a pillow over her face. Her muffled words still came through clear. "This is torture."

"I know," I said. "Thank you for suffering through it with me."

She dropped the pillow. "I don't know how much more I can stand of...what even is this? We've been staring at these flailing men in colorful Styrofoam costumes for hours, and I still haven't deciphered what they're meant to be."

I grabbed the remote from the side table and paused the film. The screen froze on a close-up of one of the characters mid-song. It was the pink, log-shaped one with lumps all over it. His unblinking Styrofoam eye stared at the camera, right through my soul.

I shivered. "I imagine that one is an evil penis."

Molly raised a brow at me, her subdued version of when anyone else would be gaping in shock and horror. "You believe this children's program features genitalia."

It didn't seem like a question, but instead, more of a judgment on me personally. I didn't mind.

Bluntly, I answered, "Yes."

"Why?"

"Isn't it clear? He's pink. He's got the one eye," I went up closer to the alienesque penis character and pointed to his large, dome-like lumps. "And he has some kind of sexually transmitted disease. These lumps make it clear that he needs to see a doctor."

"I—" Molly bit her lips. "I don't know what to say to that."

She rose from her seat and walked to the fridge. "I require quite a bit more alcohol in my system if I'm going to keep suffering this garbage with you."

"More alcohol?" All I'd seen her drink was tea and water.

She retrieved two beers from the fridge and brought them back to the living room with her. "I carry two flasks on me at all times. I drained them both during the first film. What was it—the one with stuffed animals who lived in the clouds and kept hugging each other." Her expression soured.

"You don't like Feeling Friends?" I couldn't help but take that personally. "They're the best."

"If you say so." She popped open her can and took a seat again. "You can have the other one if you want, or leave it for me. I'll drink both."

"Seriously? You don't even like Wishing Walrus? He has that cute lisp and he helps people make their dreams come true. We're looking for nice magical happy things, and it doesn't get nicer, happier, or more magical than Wishing Walrus."

"I don't find the use of a speech impediment for entertainment charming in the least," she said. "And their voices overall—they're grating."

"I can agree Gratitude Goose is a little harsh to listen to. But, Wishing Walrus, he was my favorite when I was a kid." I even had a plush of him in a box in the attic. "What did you watch when you were young?"

"Life," she said. "I lived it."

I rolled my eyes, grabbed the other beer, and sat down beside her. "Don't think I missed that two flasks comment, either. You're sneaky. I didn't even see you pull one out."

She smiled behind her drink before taking another sip.

"And for the record, I lived life, too. Sitting down for thirty minutes a week to watch nice stories about nice characters didn't prevent me from going to playgrounds or spending hours exploring the woods."

"I'm sure it didn't," she said with sincerity. Then she tapped my knee. "Should we continue with the film?"

"I really don't wanna. Let's see what else there is." I exited to the home screen and scrolled through lines of children's films, looking for something decent. "The documentaries are nice, but not magical. The talking pet ones are okay, too, but also not helpful. What about this one with the unicorns?"

I imagined riding on the back of a unicorn through the streets, crown on my head, spork in my hand. I'd vanquish every nightmare creature with sparkling pizzazz. The resulting scrapbook page would be epic.

Molly said, "And if your plan half-works, and the children's creatures go bad—"

My imaginary scenario transformed to me crying in the street while the unicorn trampled back and forth over my mangled body, and then jabbed me full of holes with his glittery horn. Much less charming.

"Yeah, I don't want anyone getting trampled and stabbed. I guess we stick to the one-eyed-wonder weasel."

"Tell me that's not a Feeling Friend," Molly said with a flat expression.

I shook my head and pointed to the pink guy on the show selection screen. "Penis guy."

"I don't really want to see that in the streets either," Molly said.

I laughed. "I don't know. It would be interesting."

She shrugged and smiled.

With that, we restarted *The Wigglers Nine: Pokey's Birthday.* It was nice getting some time in with Molly. We still didn't know each other as much as I'd have liked. She wasn't much of a sharer. Still, I couldn't help but wish Remi was here with us. Or Evan. Or Remi *and* Evan.

We ate some snacks because the movie seemed to last forever, and then when it was over, I was sure that if I never watched another children's movie again, it would be too soon.

"I'm done," I told Molly.

"Good."

She didn't move from her spot on the sofa, even as I got up and stretched. Again.

"Should we set up in the living room like last time?" she asked.

I had no idea what she was talking about.

"Hold hands so you can more easily find me while we sleep?" Her brows shot up and she leaned her head forward, a confused look on her face.

And it clicked. "Oh. You were thinking of spending the night."

"Clearly that was not what you were thinking."

"No," I said. "I hadn't thought about it."

"What is there to think about? Your whole plan revolves around manifesting the children's characters into the world. And your power is stronger with my help."

Everything she was saying was true. But that wasn't all I had to think about. I had gleaned a key piece of information much earlier in the day. And as much as I knew Molly was right, my intuition told me there was something more pressing—finding Baku.

"Jennifer?" Molly was staring at me, waiting.

"No," I said. "There's something else I have to do first. Then I'll find you and we'll do all the things. But I need to sleep in my bed so I don't wake up feeling like I was run over by a truck. And I'm going to do it alone."

She folded her lips into a line, making her mouth practically disappear.

"You don't have to agree with me," I told her. "It's what I'm doing."

"Why?"

I didn't want to get into it with her about Baku again. So I used my mom voice and my favorite mom line. "Because I said so."

The line didn't solve anything, and was never well received. But it successfully ended the conversation, making it clear I would hear no further arguments. And just like it did with Evan, the line worked on Molly.

She put on her shoes and her coat.

I got mine on, too.

"I can walk," she said.

"No. I will drive you."

"You've been drinking."

"I had two sips of a beer," I told her. "And it'll be a lot safer for me to drive you than for you to walk home alone in the darkness with nightmares on the loose. Even if your powers worked on them, I'd insist. And if you say no, I'm going to follow you the whole way there and back anyway, so you might as well say yes."

She opened the door and gestured for me to come with her. And again, mom moves for the win. Being a parent had strengthened me in ways I'd never expected. It was hard, but nothing worthwhile in life was easy. I just needed to remember that when I failed over and over again with this whole witch thing. Get back up, and try again until I figured my power out.

After a quiet and uneventful drive to Molly's place to drop her off, I gathered a box full of supplies and returned to the center of town. The streets were deceptively quiet again, but I knew the living nightmares were still out there. With one eye perpetually checking over my shoulder, I lugged my spork and box of random household goods as close as I could to my best friend.

The Wad was exactly the same as I'd left it. Remi and Julian remained suspended as they had been, too. The man by the police station door still stood with his hand held out for the handle. No one looked particularly starved of oxygen or any worse than they had when they'd been trapped.

"Hey, Remi." I set down my box by the edge of the gelatinous red mass. "It turns out my rainbow wolf bear is real. His name is Baku. I'm going to visit him again tonight, and maybe he'll be able to help me figure out how to help you. Molly doesn't like him."

Frozen in Julian's dragon claw, Remi couldn't respond. If she could, I knew she'd say something nasty about Molly and tell me I should get some of that fine old-as-time dream man.

"I'm going to try to find you in the dream world, too. So if you're there, we can talk. Be on the lookout for me, okay?" My throat tightened, but I didn't want to be emotional. Crying wasn't going to help Remi. "And I brought everything I could think of to try and reach you here and now."

The spork was first. I stabbed the pointy end as hard as I could at the surface of the Wad. Thwarting my attack, the Wad made the tips slip and my arms recoil.

"Pointy is out," I told Remi. "Let's try chemicals."

I pulled spray bottles and scrubs from my box and assaulted the Wad with rain and globs of every cleaning agent I'd had in my closet.

"Jell-O, meet Drano!"

My war cry and chemical weapons didn't even make a dent.

Disheartened but refusing to admit defeat, I packed up, said goodbye, and returned home to try a different strategy.

Before I could attempt dream work, I texted Evan. He was fine, just worried about me. I took a bubble bath and went through my bedtime routine a little earlier than I would have on a typical night. And a little quicker than on a typical night, I drifted off to sleep.

* * *

STARS TWINKLED, sprinkles of color and life in the black void. With my scrapbook clenched to my chest, I flew through space with rockets on my feet. I closed my eyes and pictured my best friend. I focused on her fiery red hair, her guarded emerald eyes, her genuine scowls and smiles. I focused on her band t-shirts and sweatpants, her vegetable muffins, and the way she made me feel like I never had to face any trial alone because she was always in my corner.

In the darkness, I expected to see a glowing fireball that was Remi, much like the thorny mass that I knew represented Molly.

But Remi wasn't there.

* * *

THE THRESHOLD BETWEEN HOT, dry sand and cool, wet sand was a matter of a single step toward the ocean. The earth was hardpacked, giving only a little under the weight of my bare feet. Sunlight warmed and blinded me, reflecting off the whites and blues of the surface of land and sea. Out of every sensation the beach had to offer, it was the sound that soothed me most.

It didn't surprise me that Remi wasn't in the dream world. I hadn't expected her to be, I'd only hoped. Not finding her made my next move clear.

Caws and clucks came from the seagulls. The waves purred and whooshed as they lapped up onto the shore. The air whispered sweet nothings as it wisped a cool salt mist from the sea.

I soaked up my surroundings and breathed them in. There was a sense of calm here which seeped from every particle of the scene into the bone. Strange, given the panic and purpose I felt as I clenched my scrapbook to my chest. I *would* get my answer tonight, and I'd save my best friend. When I exhaled, I spoke his name.

Baku.

The fin of a great shark popped out of the water, halfway to the horizon. A crab the size of a small horse scuttled out of the sea. The sand coiled and writhed, like a creature was coming. Each disappeared before the next arrived.

I knew in a way I couldn't explain that all of them were him.

"Baku," I said to the beach. "I'm here searching for you."

I had questions for him. I needed to know how to find my dream solution to my dream-created problems. I needed to know why Molly thought I should be afraid of him. I needed

202

him to help me figure out what to do next, and how to free Remi.

Awareness roamed across my skin, the very core of my being in tune with his presence. I turned slowly, knowing I would find him standing there.

The breeze carried hints of orange and spice, skin and memory. My brain filled with whispered sensations of *the kiss*. It hadn't been a friendly locking of two sets of lips. It had been an epic joining of two mouths, the likes of which the world had never seen. The scrapbook slipped from my hands.

No. I tried to catch it, but it disappeared as soon as it left my fingertips.

Hard lines and a soft smile met my gaze. With a single glimpse of Baku, my mind went blank and my mouth went dry.

Shadows sculpted his collarbones, peeking out through the open neck of his button-down shirt. I imagined what his skin would taste like there, how it would feel against my tongue.

"When you call for me, I will always come," he said in that rough voice of his.

Cotton and denim may as well have been chocolate, with as desperately as I wanted to tear them off him using my mouth.

I was supposed to say something now.

The sensation of his touch was all over my skin, the heat of him mirrored in the beating sun. I could feel his hands sliding over my back, even though I could clearly see he had them casually in the front pockets of his jeans.

When I needed him, he'd always been there. I believed him when he said he always would. And I needed him now.

But what I needed him for exactly was fuzzy. One thing I wanted him for was certainly clear—I wanted another kiss-to-end-all-kisses like our last. I wanted to pick up right where we'd left off before I'd last woken.

"I'm here for pleasant dreams," I said. I was pretty sure there was something else I was supposed to say. Something about solutions. Something that sounded less sexy.

"How can I help?" he asked, taking a step closer. His gaze flicked to my mouth and darkened.

It felt almost as good as a kiss.

Electricity filled the air, snapping between us like a livewire. If I didn't touch him, I might combust.

A whimper seeped out between my lips as I tried to focus my brain on what I was supposed to say. Was it something to do with unicorns? I could certainly have some fun with his horn.

I laughed, grabbed his shirt, and sealed my mouth to his.

He slid his hands up my arms and into my hair. With a gentle tug, he angled my chin to his liking and delved his tongue into my mouth deepening our kiss so much that I wasn't sure where I ended and he began.

I tore at his shirt, freeing buttons from their threads to go rolling and get lost in the sand. Smash and grab—I was a thief stealing everything I could from him before reality could interfere. He swallowed my pleas for him to never stop, as he lay me down on the sand and tore open my clothes. I twined my arms around him, and held tight as he nipped a line down my jaw and neck.

With hungry hands and needy moans, I spurred him on. There was only Baku and me, skin on skin, and the crash of the waves on the sand around us.

Yes. This certainly felt like a pleasant dream.

CHAPTER 21

*W*ith a stretch, I woke in a giggling fit. I was in my bed, not on a beach, and there was a lot of light bursting in through my blinds, suggesting I'd been asleep for a freaking eternity. And I'd needed it.

Sure, the z's contributed to making me feel ten years younger. But more than the rest, it was the sexy dream shenanigans with Baku. I hadn't enjoyed anything more than a fling with a man since Evan's father, and that was half a lifetime ago. I'd never found the big O with anyone but myself before, and oh-my, Baku had *a lot* on my battery-operated boyfriend, even if he was only in my dreams.

Did dream sex count as real sex? I guessed it depended. People in waking-world relationships would probably say no. Then again, I was a dream witch, and I made my own dream rules. So, I decided that I most definitely was counting what happened as getting laid.

There was no walk of shame after, or awkward conversation, because Baku was safely tucked away in the dream realm. When I woke, it was just over. And something told me there wasn't going to be an awkward conversation with him about defining what we shared when I returned tonight, either.

I grabbed my phone to text my best friend, because I *had finally gotten laid!* But when I held my phone in my hand, reality struck with its nasty reminder stick.

Remi was frozen in a gelatin hell.

Poop. The scrapbook—I'd dropped my scrapbook in the dream. I was supposed to get answers, and instead I'd gotten the shaft.

I set the phone back down without even unlocking the screen and headed downstairs, a mix of emotion boiling up inside of me. I yelled to my empty house, *"I got laid, and I'm so freaking mad about it!"*

When no one is home, there generally is no answer expected to these things. Still, it was slightly disappointing that my proclamation was met with silence. I wanted someone to scold me for being selfish, for being a terrible friend and forgetting that I needed to help my best friend.

There was a knock at the door.

Maybe someone did hear me, and this was my next-door neighbor Mr. Geffin coming by to congratulate me on the timely end to my somewhat unintentional celibacy. Maybe he'd yell at me, which I really deserved right about now.

I opened the door and was pleased to find it was not Mr. Geffin standing there waiting to greet or berate me. It was Molly. In a thick white coat with a collar of faux fur that perfectly matched her hair, she looked like an ice queen.

"Hey, Molly," I said, with my still-thinking-about-orgasms frown. Under any other circumstances, it would have been a smile. "I got laid."

"Congratulations," she said without blinking. "Is that why you haven't answered your phone? Never mind. I don't want to know. Get dressed, we have to go."

It only then occurred to me that I'd promised to meet her

in the dream world last night. Had we also made plans for the morning?

"Uh, sure. Want some tea first?" I stepped back and opened the door wide so she could enter. "We can hash out our plan for rescuing Remi. For the record, Drano is a no-go. Even the spork didn't work. Now that you're here, though, we have more options, right, some kind of magic solution I haven't thought of yet and—"

"There's no time." She followed me in and pushed me toward the steps. "Daytime clothes. Go."

She was surprisingly strong for someone so petite, and for someone so advanced in years. When I grew old, I wanted to be just like her. Maybe a little less serious, though, as she never did seem to loosen up completely.

Instead of rushing to do what she said, I turned around on the first step and put my foot down. "I'm happy to put on clothes, and to go wherever so long as it's related to saving Remi, but I think it's fair to expect to be told what's going on."

Molly stared at me a moment, then she answered in a curt, clipped tone. "There is mayhem in the streets. I called multiple times to tell you."

Okay, maybe I could agree that the best thing to do was go see and try to deal with this mayhem instead of standing around talking about it. So I hurried upstairs, threw on some jeans, a long-sleeved blouse, and some flats, then I came straight down after. I grabbed a straight-from-the fridge wheat bagel and held it between my teeth as I tied my hair in a low-ponytail and returned to the door where Molly was waiting for me.

She handed me a coat and stepped outside. I slid on the coat and locked the door. "So this mayhem—"

Behind Molly stood a towering pink cylinder with arms and legs.

"One-eyed wonder weasel," I whispered.

"What?" Molly turned around, following my gaze. She sucked in a sharp breath and said softly, "It's him. The foam penis man."

He stood like a statue. His giant eye didn't blink as he stared right back at me. I slowly reached behind me for the door handle.

"If this goes wrong," I said, trying not to move my lips, or anything else, more than I had to. "My spork is in my room. Upstairs, second door on the right."

Molly flexed her fingers and tilted her shoulders toward the penis man instead of away. "Ready."

The way she said it, and the way she spread her feet like she was steadying herself, made it seem like her plan was not the same as mine.

I reached for her shoulder. "Molly?"

"I'm not—" She started, but stopped when Mr. Wonder Weasel turned on his heel and started skipping down the street, arms swinging. Molly breathed out a slow breath. "The penis man does not appear to be hostile."

He weaved from the center of the street toward the sidewalk and started whistling.

High-pitched barking filled the street. Straight ahead of the penis man was a tiny dog, dancing back and forth in his yard, hair raised.

For a panicked moment, I worried the penis man would hurt the terrier. But instead, he reached down, patted the dog on the head, and returned to his skipping.

"I thought no one could see the dream creatures," I said to Molly.

"Animals are more perceptive than humans."

That made sense. We were supposed to be the smart animals, but it was dogs who could sniff out cancer and bombs. I said, "Good smellers."

Then I looked back to Molly who had already slipped down the sidewalk and had circled around the driveway to the passenger door of my car.

"Come," she said. "We have no time to waste."

I unlocked the car with my fob, then hurried back into the house for my phone and spork before joining her. There was no good way to hold a six-foot long weapon while driving, so I settled Sir Pointy McStabberson on the back seat.

"Downtown," Molly said as I climbed into the driver seat and started the car.

"Okay." I backed us out of the driveway and headed toward Main Street, snacking on my bagel as we went. "So what exactly did you see this morning?"

She didn't answer, and instead stared out the passenger side window.

"It had to be bad, right? To walk to my place and for this grand sense of urgency?"

"We'll see how bad it is soon," she said.

Molly's disappointment and displeasure had fallen on Remi before. Remi had complained that Molly was cruel, and I still didn't think that was the case. But I was seeing a different side of her than I had before. She was colder.

"Are you mad at me?" I asked.

"No."

"You seem upset," I told her. "Why not just tell me what's going on?"

She finally turned to look at me and patted my hand. "I'm unaccustomed to our coven's level of willful disregard of my opinion."

"Try living with a teenager," I told her. And as soon as the words left my lips, I immediately regretted them. "I am *so sorry*. That was a stupid thing to say."

She shook her head. "It's fine."

"Really," I said. "I should have thought about it first. Sometimes words come out of my mouth before I have time to think about them. I didn't mean—"

"Jennifer," she said. "I'm fine."

Maybe she was and maybe she wasn't. But I still felt terrible. I should have thought about the fact that she had once had a daughter. I didn't want to hurt her.

"There." Molly pointed out the window to a parking spot in front of the candy shop.

I pulled in and clicked off the car. I turned to Molly to further apologize, but she climbed out too fast. I grabbed my spork and followed after her as she headed in the direction of the police station.

"Is what you saw related to Remi?" I asked. "Did you figure out what we need to do to help her?"

"No."

We turned the corner and found the blob exactly where it had been before, exactly the same size as it had been before. Somehow, though, it felt more imposing. It was like it had taken a shot of angry cola after the Drano incident.

On the street, a group of fuzzy toy-like monsters tumbled and tore at each other.

It was a stuffie rumble to the death, with a group of furbens tearing at...no, it couldn't be...Wishing Walrus.

I gasped and tried to run to help him, but Molly grabbed my arm.

Another of the Feeling Friends, Gratitude Goose, joined the mix, jumping down from the roof of the town hall and landing elbow first—or whatever the wingy goose approximation was—on the group of furbens. I'd never been happier to hear the grating honks of the plush fowl. The furbens, stunned and knocked down, did nothing to stop Wishing Walrus and Gratitude Goose from returning to their feet.

The two friends stood back to back and kicked the furbens as they scrambled to get back up.

"It worked," I said. "I cancelled out the bad dreams with nice dreams."

Molly grunted, clearly not agreeing.

"What?" I asked. "It's a good thing."

She pointed to the little building attached the town hall. "The side window is broken. The walrus did it."

I cringed, guilt rattling through my brain.

"The news showed it dancing around inside, while people appeared startled that the table fell over on its own. They're talking about whether it was a ghost or if the residents are mentally unstable."

"But it was neither."

"The news implied they were crazy," Molly said.

"That sucks, but I mean, after this is all over, I can have all the problems fixed. I'll pay for their window and—"

"When will it be over?" Molly asked. "What happens when your creations stop fighting each other and return to fighting the town?"

"Well—"

"They won't disappear on their own, will they?"

Maybe? I didn't know. There was so much I didn't know. This was a play-it-by-ear kind of plan. It was a desperate no-one-else-seems-to-have-answers-either kind of plan. It was an at-least-I'm-doing-something kind of plan. And it was all that I had.

At my speechlessness, Molly continued. "This is why it's important to do research before acting. There are answers in the books, in my contacts, and in the cookies."

"Well, we did open the cookies," I said. "And honestly everything of value the cookies told us I already knew from Baku and from my own intuition."

At Baku's name, Molly tensed. I didn't care what she thought about him, or about me for trusting him. Okay, so I cared a little. It would have been nice for Molly to be on team Jen, cheering for me and backing my decisions. Remi would be.

And then it hit me. I needed another dream solution for my dream problem. I should have thought of it sooner. It was so obvious.

I headed straight for my best friend, and for the Wad who held her captive.

"I made you, Jell-O monster," I proclaimed with the shake of my fist. "And I can unmake you."

Momisms for the win. I'd never said that particular phrase to Evan, but my mom had definitely used it on me once or twice.

I dropped to my knees and gave that Jell-O gherkin a reason to quake and jiggle. That's right, I was going to eat his jiggly ass.

"Don't!" Molly said from behind me.

But I wasn't going to argue or listen to her tell me not to. She could research if she wanted. But the research wasn't doing Remi any favors. The best thing to do generally wasn't sit around waiting for someone else to solve your problems for you.

I looked at the gelatinous red monster in front of me. "You are Jell-O. You taste like strawberries." Then I closed my eyes, opened my mouth, and I bit him.

Slimy gelatin filled my mouth, with an artificial sweet fruitiness—cherry. I wasn't sure what to make of the Jell-O being the wrong flavor, but even so, it worked.

Molly pulled me away, and slapped my back. "Spit it out."

I swallowed.

"I can't believe you just did that, silly girl." She put her hands on the sides of my face, and her palms grew unnaturally cold. "You're as reckless as Remedy."

Remi was as brave as brave could be. To compare me to her was a compliment, and I was happy to accept. I said, "Thank you."

Molly squeezed her eyes shut and held my face, and then let go and sat down in the grass. "It's not making you sick?"

"No," I said. "I'm fine."

"It's not poison? And it's not consuming you from the inside out?"

"No," I said. "Clearly I'm consuming it. You should join. We'll reach Remi faster that way."

She shook her head. "This is going to take forever."

"Then we should get some help." I looked around, and spotted the diner. Brianna worked there. Maybe I could get her.

"I'll go to Tergel's," Molly said.

The bartender had a tail, and apparently connections. I hoped he also had a big appetite.

"Great. I'm going to try for Brianna."

A sadness glistened in Molly's eyes. "Good luck. You'll need it."

"You, too." I was curious why the idea of asking Brianna made her sad. Probably because the two of them had been friends before the whole vampire abduction thing, and Brianna didn't seem too jazzed about hanging out with us after what happened.

We split up and I hurried over to the diner. Inside, I found Brianna talking to a couple at a table. I waited until she finished before ambushing her.

"Hey," I said.

"Leave me alone."

"You've seen it, right?"

She glanced to the window to where the blob blocked out the freaking sun. "Nope."

"You can," I said. "I know you can."

She inched her way around me.

"We need your help."

"Look," she said. "I'm working. And even if I wasn't, I'm not like you."

"You can see it. You have a mouth. You can help."

"Please," she said. "I have enough to deal with. *I can't.*"

Her last two words were a plea desperate enough that I could feel them squeeze my heart. So I let her go, disappointed, but understanding. After what we'd been through, I couldn't blame her for wanting to distance herself from the magical world. But it wouldn't happen, not with her staying in Marshmallow. I wished for her sake that she'd figure out how to move forward, one way or another, so she didn't have to live in fear anymore.

When I returned to the Wad, Molly was already back. Tergel was there, too. I recognized the bartender from his stumpy stature and abundance of hair. It was thickest not on the top of his head, but on the bottom half of his face and leading down his neck.

Five clones of the guy were there, too, only they were half his size. And they had just as much hair as Tergel himself.

"Kids?" I asked, and looked to Molly for confirmation.

I'd never seen such epic beards on children before.

She nodded. "Watch."

Tergel and his mini-mes chomped through the Jell-O like they were wood chippers and the Wad was a forest.

"See," Molly said. "It's better not to try to do everything alone."

"I'm happy to have the help," I said. "And if I hadn't jumped in there and taken that first bite, we'd still just be waiting."

She considered my words a moment then said, "Fair enough."

I figured that was as close as I was going to get to her telling me I was right about something, and I gladly took it.

Quickly, the Tergels reached Julian and Remi. One of the mini Tergels bit the edge of the dragon's wing. Julian twitched. Mini Tergel backed up quickly.

Air hit Julian's wing, just a tiny spot, but it was enough. He returned to human form, still holding tight to Remi. Neither Julian nor Remi seemed to be moving, or talking, or waking aside from Julian's transformation.

In the dragon-shaped hole, the two collapsed, still unconscious. We moved in, all of us working together to pull Remi and Julian out onto the Jell-O-free grass.

I dropped down beside Remi and listened close to her face. At least she was breathing. And Julian was, too.

"Hey, bestie." I pet Remi's gooey red hair. "You were so brave going in there and fighting the Wad, putting others first because it's who you are. You're the bravest person I've ever met. You're strong, too. Use that strength, because it's time to wake up now."

Hope and fear mingled as a strange cocktail in my insides. There was something peaceful about unconscious Remi, like even though she wasn't dreaming, whatever she had been experiencing while trapped in the Wad wasn't so bad.

Molly touched my shoulder and bent down beside me. I made way for her and her healing awesomeness. If anyone could fix Remi, it was Molly.

"You can use some of my life if you need it," I told her.

She didn't say anything, but reached for Remi's face and closed her eyes. She lingered there, doing her life-force probing thing. Then she pulled away and sighed. "This will take time."

"How much time?" I asked.

"As long as it takes."

It wasn't an answer I liked, but it was still progress.

"Okay," I agreed. "Now what? We just hang out in the grass for a while? I could go get the glow worms if that would help."

"We go back to your house," Molly said.

"Oh."

Molly nodded to Big Tergel. She directed, and the Tergels did the heavy lifting, loading Remi and Julian into my car.

I glanced around, wondering what people would think if they saw us. No one seemed to be watching, which was good. Piling a couple of unmoving bodies into your car was generally a bad look.

Molly shared a few words with the Tergels. I waved and thanked them.

"They're going to stay and finish the job," Molly said, joining me by my car. "Let's go."

Were the Tergels staying because Molly had offered them something, out of the goodness of their demon hearts, or because they really loved Jell-O? No matter the reason, I was glad for the win, and I looked forward to getting Remi home and awake.

I parked in the driveway and glanced around before climbing out. Molly didn't seem to share my concern about onlookers, as she was already opening Remi's door. An unconscious Remi leaned against the window, tilting like she'd fall.

"Geez." I hopped out of my seat and hurried over as soon as I realized what was happening.

Molly let the door go, and Remi with it. Remi fell right onto the pavement, but Molly caught her head before it hit.

What are you doing?

"What does it look like?" Molly said. "She's fine."

"She could have cracked her head open." I reached down and inspected Remi's arms and legs. No way she wouldn't have a few scrapes and bruises.

"Let's get this done." Molly wrapped her arms around Remi from behind.

Remi's arms stuck up like she was on a rollercoaster. Molly pulled, and I caught Remi's feet before they, too, smacked into the ground.

Molly said, "You're going to have to unlock the door."

Easier said than done while trying to awkwardly lug one-hundred-and-however-many pounds of Remi.

We waddled our way to the front door, where I shifted my weight, tucking Remi's legs in along my hip.

"Hurry," Molly said, her grip slipping.

"I'm trying!" I jostled my keys searching for the right one. Red for realty. Blue for bed. There. I thumbed to the blue one and shoved it into the lock. Remi's legs began to slip, so I squeezed her tighter.

We hurried inside and deposited her onto the chair.

"Now, Julian," Molly said.

I let out a puff of exasperated exhaustion and followed her back outside.

Molly reached through the already open door, and backed up, pulling one of Julian's feet along with her.

"We need to watch his head," I reminded her.

"I know."

I grabbed his calf and helped her pull. Julian was *heavy*. We'd barely made it inside with Remi. There was no way we were going to be able to carry Julian all the way to the living room. If we were lucky, we'd carry him a foot or two before dropping him. And that was probably overestimating how it would go down.

Julian's butt slid from the edge of the seat, halfway out the door.

"We're going to have to get his hands," I said, letting go of his leg. "Drag him that way."

Molly stopped pulling and set down his foot. "Agreed."

The two of us stood there a moment, taking a breath, before I leaned over Julian and grabbed one of his arms. I bent and pulled it out, offering it to Molly. She took it, and I grabbed the other.

Then we not-so-gently lowered him to the ground before dragging him across the lawn for the door. His head fell back, dangling down a few inches from the ground and aimed at us like he was staring at me, only his eyes were closed.

I looked away, only to catch a glimpse of Mr. Geffin gaping at us from the center of his yard.

"Hi, Mr. Geffin." I gave him a friendly nod and a smile.

"Is everything...okay?"

"No worries," I said. "It's, uh, he drank too much."

Molly leaned closer to me. "Ignore him. Worst thing he does is call the cops. They're encased in gelatin, or looking like our dragon friend here."

"Thank gherkin for that."

We worked in jolts and heaves. With no small sum of effort, we eventually reached the open door and delivered him with a big lift, a push, and some shoving, onto the sofa.

"There," I said, and wiped my hands against each other. "We did it."

My phone rang. I pulled it out of my pocket and checked who it was—my mom.

"Hey," I said. "What's up?"

Molly shut the door and took a seat on the edge of the sofa by Julian's feet.

"It's Evan," my mom said.

Panic flooded through my veins. "What about Evan?"

"Something's wrong with him, Jenny, he—"

She screamed.

And the call cut out.

CHAPTER 22

*A*t times I could be calm and calculating, weighing possible choices before coming to a reasonable solution. This was not one of those times. As soon as there was a whiff of anything dangerous or upsetting involving my son, mama bear instinct took over.

I left Remi and Julian in Molly's capable hands and tore through the streets. Driving through downtown was so automatic, my frantic brain didn't register the path at all. But the drive from the edge of Marshmallow to the mountain spa was much less familiar, so with my white-knuckled fists clenched to the wheel, I let my phone's navigation guide me.

The cheery British robot lady led me across a series of little roads through the forest and up the mountain. What should have been an hour-long drive took closer to thirty minutes. Wind howled around the car as I drove and pulled the tree limbs. If I hadn't been in a frantic rush, I may have appreciated the mountain views and impressive expanse of sprawling log cabin-esque luxury. As it was, I had tunnel vision for reaching my son. I threw my car into park and hurried toward the spa. My arms were shaking as I dialed my mom's cell.

While the phone rang, I ran to the revolving front door of the towering building.

Pick up, Mom. Please pick up.

As I pushed the glass door around in a small circle and entered the spa, cold air and howling wind were replaced by warmth and soothing music.

A woman in a flowy white dress appeared out of nowhere and held out a glass of water with fruit slices floating in it. "Welcome to Everpeak Spa. Ginger lime water?"

"No. It's an emergency. Can you tell me what room—"

"Jennifer?" My dad finally answered the phone.

A small line formed between the spa greeter's brows, the only sign that she ever felt anything but the tranquility she was selling.

"Yes, I'm here, Dad," I said into the phone, and turned away from the woman so she couldn't distract me. "What room are you in? What's going on? Is Mom okay?"

"Room one-oh-three," he said. "Are you here?"

"Yeah," I said, and ran down the hall. "Be right there."

There were only two ways to go, one hall marked *Spa*, one marked *Rooms*. Easy choice. A door opened, and my dad's shiny head popped out into the hall. His cheeks were red, and his eyes were teary. Seeing him like that was a punch to the gut. All the manic energy that had carried me here was gone in an instant.

Tears welled in my eyes, and my breaths came short. Dad pulled me into a hug and squeezed.

"Where's Evan?" I said, my voice shaky. "Talk to me."

He squeezed me harder then let go. "He's gone."

"What do you mean *he's gone?*" Throbbing pressure crept up the back of my neck.

"Come on," Dad said, leading me inside the room.

With an ice pack held to her forehead, my mom was sitting on the edge of the mattress. Her shoulders curled in, making her look smaller and frailer than I was used to seeing her.

I rushed to her and dropped down beside her. She lifted her chin and met my gaze, her eyes imploring.

"It all happened so fast," she said.

"What did?" My voice rose three octaves. I gently moved her wrist, pulling the icepack away enough to see the egg forming on her face. Her pupils were even, so that was a good sign. "Where's Evan?"

"He was sitting at the desk over there." Dad pointed to where Evan's laptop and backpack were left open. "He stood so fast he knocked down the chair and started for the door. Your mother asked where he was going and stepped into his path."

"His eyes were red," Mom whispered.

"He knocked your mother over," Dad said. "I went after him. Asked him what was wrong. I yelled."

"Why were his eyes red, Jenny?" Mom asked. "I don't understand."

I understood. And I'd been a fool. I'd thought everything was fine after the kukudhli had touched him. I'd wanted to believe it. And instead of keeping him close where I could be there for him, I'd sent him away.

"It's magic, Mom," I said. "I know you don't want to hear that, and that you don't believe me, but—"

"I believe you," she said.

Dad touched my arm. "Me, too."

All it took was my kid getting possessed.

"Where is he now? I have to find him before—" Before he hurt someone else. Before he hurt himself. I couldn't say the words.

"I followed him out into the hall, but he disappeared," Dad

said. "I wanted to follow him, but I couldn't leave your mother like this."

"I understand," I said. "You did the right thing. I'm so sorry."

"You have nothing to be sorry for," Mom said. "And neither does Evan. He wasn't himself."

Of course he wasn't. Evan was the sweetest. He would never ever do anything like this. It wasn't him. It was that winged kitten from hell.

"Have a doctor look at her," I told my dad.

"I'm fine," Mom said. "Or I will be. You find Evan. And, Jenny, be careful."

Worry for my mom was trumped by the need to find my kid. My dad would take care of my mom, and she'd be okay. She had to be. I hurried back the way I had come, yelling for Evan as I went.

"Evan!"

The reception woman stayed back this time when she saw me. "Are you looking for someone?"

Duh. The fact I was yelling his name should have made it obvious. But she was trying to help, so I needed to keep the snarky commentary to myself.

"My son. He's tall." I gestured with my palm up a few inches above my head. "Shaggy hair. Have you seen him?"

"Oh yes," she said with a bright smile. "He's here with his grandparents, right? I saw him yesterday at evening tea. He ate all of the chocolate macarons."

"Today." I rubbed the blooming stab of pain between my eyes. "Have you seen him *today?* Like within the past hour?"

"No," she said with hesitance. "But I'm sure he's okay, and perfectly capable of looking out for himself."

I wanted to punch her in the nose. Her comment was not even a little bit helpful.

"I need a piece of paper," I told her instead of doing the whole punching thing.

She grabbed a pen and a pad with the name of the spa printed on the top of it. I scrawled my number on it, and told her to call if she saw my son. She reluctantly agreed, probably just to get me out of there.

Back outside, I filled my lungs with cold air. Tears stung in the corners of my eyes. I balled my fists and I yelled. "Evan!"

The only answer was the wind. Sadly, it didn't tell me anything except that I needed a scarf.

If the kukudhli was in control of Evan's body, he could be anywhere by now. Since no one had seen him since he stepped into the hall, there was no reason to believe he couldn't have popped away, teleporting through thin air, just like the demon could. He could be in Marshmallow. He could be lost in the woods. He could wake confused and lost, and have no idea where he was or how he'd gotten there.

Fingers fumbling like clumsy sausages, I pulled my phone from my pocket.

Molly was at my place. If Evan returned home, she'd be there. I shot her a quick text.

Evan's missing. He's not himself, could be dangerous. Call if he shows up there.

And if he didn't go home, where would he go? There was that girl in his dreams. Clearly he thought about her *a lot.* She deserved a warning. But I didn't have her number, or even know her last name. But I did have Brandon's number, so I called him.

"Hello?" he answered.

"Hi. It's Ms. Jameson, Evan's mom."

"I know. It says on the screen when you call," he said. Then after a pause, he added, "Is everything okay?"

"No. Evan's—" Uh, what was I supposed to tell this kid? Explaining the truth of the world to Evan, or my parents, or even Jerry was one thing. Telling someone else's kid about monsters didn't have the same must-not-tell-a-lie ring to it. Also, Evan wouldn't exactly be thrilled about his mother spewing her crazy everywhere. This time, sharing the truth was an all-around bad idea.

"Did something happen? Is he hurt? Ms. Jameson?"

"Yeah, no. Evan's fine," I said. "Kind of. He's sick. He's having fever hallucinations."

"That's awful. What can I do?"

"Actually," I said. "He walked out of the house in a fever haze while I was at work. And it's not safe to get close to him. It's a super contagious virus. So, call me if you see him, but stay away."

"Okay..." he said. "But I thought he was going to a spa with his grandparents."

"Change of plans. Nasty bug. You wouldn't believe the vomiting." As soon as I said that, I cringed. Evan was not going to like that I'd told Brandon that. But hey, at least I hadn't said diarrhea. "And please tell all of your friends to do the same. Especially that girl—" I snapped my mouth shut to stop myself from finishing my sentence. I probably shouldn't say he liked her. I cleared my throat. "Don't forget that girl...Erin?"

"Yeah, okay, Ms. Jameson. I'll let everyone know. I hope you find him soon and everything's okay."

"Me, too. Thanks."

We hung up. I headed out into the woods, circling the building in a spiral pattern so I didn't miss anything. I walked until my legs burned and wobbled. I called for my son until my voice cracked and my throat burned worse than my leg muscles.

I tried to think if there was something else I could do—something smarter than wandering the woods. I didn't feel particularly smart at the moment. I didn't feel anything but numb and lost and trapped in paralyzing fear that my son was gone and I had no idea how to find him.

What good was being a witch if I couldn't use my powers to protect my own kid?

No good at all.

Maybe someone had called, and I'd missed it. I slid my phone out of my pocket and checked. Nothing.

I walked some more. I called out for Evan, and I cried.

Time lost all meaning through my raging pulse and fruitless hunt.

At some point, the mountain and the forest began to darken. I was no closer to finding my son than I'd been when I'd arrived at the spa. My head spun and my chest clenched. And suddenly I wasn't standing anymore.

My head hit the ground in a sharp bite of pain and cold. My eyelids were heavy, and muscles I didn't know I had ached.

No. You can't sleep, not yet.

Everything went numb and black.

CHAPTER 23

*W*ith my heart pounding and my skin coated in a sheen of sticky sweat, I raced barefoot through a dark forest. I knew my feet should have hurt, but they didn't. There was no pain, only numbness. My only internal sensations were fear and dread.

Darkness boiled across the sky and snaked through the trees. I knew what the darkness was. I knew what it felt like to be caught in his grasp. I wouldn't let Weaty capture me again.

I told myself there was a bubble around me, a giant ball of protection that the smoke couldn't pierce. And then there was.

Weaty was forever trapped in a kitty cat cookie jar. This experience wasn't real. This was a dream, and in the dream world, I was queen.

Though I knew the smart move was to keep running, I forced myself to stop. My muscles jittered, but I steeled myself with the clench of my fists. I turned around slowly to face my foe.

"We've already seen how this ends," I said. "My coven wins."

The darkness—dream Weaty—whispered back, "Your coven isn't here."

I didn't need to be saved this time. "I'm enough."

All the emotions swirling inside of me were fuel I could wield. It was energy. Power. Summoning everything to the surface, I thrust my hands forward. In a shockwave, the bubble around me shot out in every direction, shoving the darkness from the forest and the sky.

And I was alone.

I sat down in the dirt, knowing defeating Weaty should have left me feeling on top of the world. But it didn't.

There was a tightness in my chest. I rubbed my breastbone with the heel of my palm. It didn't help.

Something was still wrong.

Everything was still wrong.

I closed my eyes and reached out for the lifeline that I knew was out there somewhere, waiting for me.

Baku.

I could feel him even before I opened my eyes. And when I did, I found him sitting on the ground beside me. His feet were bare, just like mine.

This was the part where I usually lost my focus. When I saw him, I tended to want to tear off all of his clothes. This time, I appreciated the size of him, the warmth of his closeness, and the way sitting side-by-side made me feel a little better.

"Hey," I said.

"Hey."

"You're a dream god, right?"

"Not exactly."

"But more or less," I said. "So do you know everything that happens here in the dream world?"

"Not everything." He grabbed a small stick, popped it in his mouth, and ate it.

He always seemed to be eating something. It was weird. "So, even if you don't know everything, you know most things," I said. "Like who is dreaming of wild sex with a stranger, or more interestingly, with someone forbidden in their life."

He brushed his thumb over the top of my hand. "What is it you truly wish to ask me?"

He was right; that wasn't what I really wanted to know. I held my palm over my heart, where the ache seemed to be growing larger and stronger. What was I supposed to ask him?

"Something's very wrong," I said.

He nodded. He had that sad look in his eyes again, like he was waiting for me to say or do something, but I didn't know what.

"I think...I think it has to do with someone I love."

"You remember," he said.

And then I did. Evan.

I was supposed to be finding Evan.

"I think I passed out when I was looking for my son. Is he here? The last time something happened to him, he came here."

"He is," Baku said, and closed his eyes. His expression tightened.

"It's the cat again, isn't it? I can't believe I fell for those cute baby eyes and fluffy fur."

Baku frowned. "I cannot see Evan. He's shrouded in black smoke."

Like I had been, with Weaty. No, this was different. What was happening to Evan was nothing like what had happened to me. I'd been kidnapped. He was possessed.

"It has to be the cat demon," I told Baku. "Evan's eyes

turned red and he hit my mom. He would never do something like that."

"The darkness is much like it was when you visited his dreams."

"Wait. You came into his head, too. I remember you were all cryptic and creepy, and then you ate Dale Corduroy."

Baku had a peculiar expression on his face.

"No offense," I said, referring to my creepy comment.

"I followed you there," he said. "I could not have broken through on my own."

Huh, that was interesting. I'd just assumed Baku could go anywhere in the dream world.

"You were trying to warn me, and help me," I said. "I just didn't see it then."

"Always."

I grabbed his hand and squeezed. "Help me now."

His expression was earnest, his copper eyes filled with compassion. The sadness I'd thought I'd glimpsed before was gone. "What can I do?"

I didn't really have an answer. I just knew that if Evan was dreaming, I had to go there. I knew how to find him, and I didn't want to do it alone.

With a little tug on Baku's hand, I leaned my head on his shoulder. We'd shared so much, more than I could remember, but the echo of those experiences remained. There was nothing I couldn't tell him, and no one I'd rather have with me for this. So I told him, "Please come with me."

He nodded and threaded his fingers in mine. "Anywhere, any time."

There was reassurance in his touch, a promise of solidarity, of being my partner, my friend, and my confidant no matter what life threw my way. I could borrow his strength, and I would.

The way this worked, I needed to close my eyes. I needed

to picture Evan not only in appearance, but focus on everything that made him who he was.

Staring at the back of my eyelids, I pictured my little boy running to me, dirt in his hair and snot all over his toddler face. I imagined the infant who cried every time I put him down, and the weight and warmth of him as I rocked him in my arms through a string of sleepless nights.

I envisioned the young man who took time to fold laundry when I didn't ask, who fixed the sink before I could make time to call the plumber, and who let me join him in watching his favorite movies. When he decided to be on the track team in middle school, he'd faceplant every time he tried the hurdles. Instead of crying and quitting, he'd try again, over and over until he conquered the challenge.

"Jen," Baku whispered.

I peeked through one eye and found Baku and I had been transported to Evan's room. Evan was sitting in his chair, slumped down, facing his computer screen.

I reached for his shoulder.

"Wait," Baku said. He took a step forward, positioning himself between me and my son, but not blocking my line of sight. Baku looked up slowly.

I followed his gaze. Strings rose from Evan's shoulders, his hands, and his head. Floating in the air above, a kitten with fairy wings pulled the strings.

Evan whipped around, twisting his chair to face us. But the person in the chair wasn't exactly Evan. He had glowing red eyes and a tiny pink nose. A blanket of black fur covered his face, and pointed black ears stuck out of the top of his head.

He was *half cat.*

Cat Evan hissed, in sync with the cat in the air above him.

The air whipped out of my lungs like I was hit in the chest with a concrete bat. I flew backward. It was like that hiss was a tornado-level wind. I didn't understand it, but dreams often had a way of making zero sense. Sucked back away from Evan, I reached out for him.

I should have hit the wall at the back of his room, but there was no wall. There were only flashes of images racing past. Clawing at nothing, I tried to find something to hold onto. My hair lashed against my face.

And then everything was still. I landed exactly where I had started, barefoot in the woods. Alone.

With a dizzy head, I looked around, searching for Evan and Baku.

A second later, Baku appeared beside me.

I released the heavy air from my lungs. It was good that he was here. "You didn't eat Evan, right?"

Baku leaned back on his hands, stretching his torso and flexing his arms. "Of course not. Evan isn't a nightmare."

"But what's happening to him is," I said. "What kicked us out? Did the cat do that? Or was it Evan?"

"Evan's no longer in the dream world," Baku said. "He's awake."

So we were kicked out because we couldn't hang out in Evan's dreams if Evan wasn't dreaming.

"I need to be awake too, then," I said. "At least I have some idea where to look now. He was on his computer in the dream. Maybe he's going home."

I hoped he was going home. Then I could find him and help him.

"I wish you could be there with me," I told Baku, catching my reflection in his eyes.

"Me, too."

"Goodbye, Baku." I kissed his cheek, and told myself it was time—time to wake, time to put on my big girl pants and finally solve the dream problems I'd caused, time to find my son and save him for good.

My eyes shot open. Through the blurry branches of the forest canopy, the afternoon sun blinded me. I rubbed my eyes. Clouds came into focus, puffy cotton pillows meandering across the blue sky. High-pitched yips echoed through the trees, some kind of wild predator. A rustle told me something small and close scurried through the leaves.

In an attempt to bolt upright, I rolled partway to a sitting position. My body ached, my throat was dry.

I was on the ground in the forest, not the dream forest, but the real one on the mountain side by the spa. The discomfort of sore joints pretty much always meant I was awake. I rolled my neck slowly, careful not to wrench the too-stiff muscles. And then I saw him.

Beside me was a very naked man, a man who belonged in dreams, a man who wasn't supposed to be in the real world.

Baku.

CHAPTER 24

"*B*y gherkin's merkin." My mouth dropped open as I stared at Baku lying on the ground.

He wiggled his fingers against the fallen leaves. Then he tilted his head and looked up at me, brows furrowed. "Where are we?"

"Welcome to the waking world," I said.

He rolled up to a sitting position, showing no sign of the stiffness and inflexibility I had when I'd attempted the same move. "This can *not* be."

"I know, right?" I grabbed his shoulders and squeezed. "It's freaking fantastic."

"I didn't know it would be now that I'd find myself here." He lifted his hands out in front of him, flipped them over, and said, "There are so many new sensations. The waking world bites at my skin. Is it an invisible plague of tiny insects?"

I looked at the goosebumps on his bare arms. "Oh, no, nothing is biting you. It's just the cold."

"Cold. I like it. And the ground beneath my feet?"

"Also cold," I said. "And hard. And wet."

"Wet," he said, as if trying out that word for the first time, too. "I do not like that as much."

My face pulled as I grinned from ear to ear. "I can't believe you're actually here."

"It's unfathomable," he said.

Unfathomable, extraordinary, too good to be true—having Baku here was a lot of things, all of them thrilling.

"Come on," I said, rising to my feet. I would like to have said I popped up, but I didn't exactly pop anymore, unless you counted the crack in my hip and the awkward stretch I had to do after where my elbows cried out, too.

"We have to find Evan," Baku said, standing up beside me. He popped, and so did his biceps.

I was going to really enjoy that. If dream Baku was hot, then real Baku was scorching. I could not believe he was real.

Apparently when he was on the ground, he'd decided to take some leaves with him, because I watched in horror as he lifted them to his mouth.

I tried to warn him. "Don't—"

Too late.

He spit and blew his lips and made a sour face. The leaves floated back down to the ground where they belonged.

"Yeah, I have noticed the way you're always eating things. It's like you have this weird oral fixation. You can't do that here."

He smacked his lips together and looked at me with big sad puppy eyes.

"General rule for the waking world—don't eat anything you find on the ground."

"Noted," he said, and wiped his tongue on his arm.

"This way." I grabbed his hand and led him up the mountainside toward the spa, and my car.

Baku stopped and hissed. "I don't like this hard ground at all."

He lifted his foot, where a small, thorned vine was stuck into his skin. He pulled it out and threw it. Blood pebbled on his skin.

"The ground is a jerk," I agreed. "I might have an extra pair of Evan's shoes in the car that you could borrow. Hopefully something else for you to wear, too."

Baku looked down at my feet, to where I had on shoes, unlike in the dream. "Shoes would be nice."

I nodded. "Watch out for vines, rocks, sticks, oh—and *snakes*. You do *not* want to step on one of those. Way worse than thorns. Trust me."

"I do," he said, and followed me up the slope a little slower than before.

Eventually we made it up to the parking lot. Baku stepped even more gingerly across the stones than he had in dirt. I popped open the trunk and looked through the hodgepodge of just-in-case things I'd stashed inside.

Too bad we didn't need promotional postcards, because there was a whole box of those. There was a first aid kit, so yay for that. There was also one of Evan's old coats. No shoes.

I grabbed the coat and offered it to Baku. "Evan wore this a year or two ago. You're a lot bigger than he is though."

"Thank you." Baku took it and slid his arm in, then he awkwardly tried to stretch the coat around his back to get his other arm in.

With a crinkle and a rip, the fabric tore. Baku froze, and his eyes went wide.

"It's okay," I said. "It's an old coat."

I circled around to his back and found the coat almost completely torn in two. Only the neck held the two pieces together.

"I would offer to replace it, but I have no means to create in my world. And here—?" He said the words as a question. Neither of us knew what he could do in the waking world.

"I don't make coats either," I told him. "I buy them."

His forehead wrinkled in a way I had never seen him do before. We were so far out of his element, he was lost. It'd be all right. I could be his anchor.

"I'll teach you all about consumerism later," I said. I put a hand on the lid of the open trunk, then reconsidered the box of postcards. Yes, that could do nicely.

I grabbed a fistful of them and a roll of duct tape because that stuff was the magic fix to everything that actual magic couldn't fix. The end of the tape was folded in such a way, that it wasn't difficult to start a strip. An audible zip accompanied the unrolling.

"Can you tear me strips about like this?" I asked Baku.

"Happy to."

I handed him the roll and situated the first of the postcards over the tear in his coat. He passed pieces of tape over his shoulder and I plastered the images of me and Jerry in a triangle over his back. Before looking down to his bare bum.

It really was a nice butt—tight, pinchable. Sadly, he had to be freezing while completely exposed like this. Plus, if Mr. Geffin hadn't called the police on me before, when I showed up in my driveway with a pantsless linebacker, he was totally going to call.

"Give me a bigger one," I said. "Really long."

Why did everything sound so dirty? Right. Because Baku was here. And he was still mostly naked.

He looked over his shoulder, checking if he should stay still.

"You can turn," I told him.

And when he did, I tried really hard not to stare at his frontside nakedness.

He held out a long piece of tape. I accepted and attached a

row of postcards to each other, then another and another. I'd never been a seamstress, but I was a boss crafter.

I fastened the makeshift kilt to Baku's waist and admired my handiwork for all of about two seconds before remembering we most certainly did not have time for admiring or ogling.

"Let's get in the car," I told him. "I need to bandage your feet."

We climbed in, and he lifted his hurt foot up for me to see. It was worse than it had looked outside, mostly because he'd scraped up his toes and heel more on the walk up the mountain. I put some ointment and a bandage over the cut.

"Any more spots that need mending?" I asked.

"I'll be okay," he said. "Thank you."

He was so freaking polite. It was hot. Touching his feet was hot. Holding his hand as we'd walked was hotter. I was going to combust like a horny teenager because my fake boyfriend was now my real boyfriend and I could actually touch him in the waking world for the first time.

I giggled.

Baku grinned, just a hint, enough that I found myself staring at his mouth. I really wanted to kiss him to see how much better that was than touching feet. A lot, I would wager, as I wasn't a feet person.

"We should start driving so I don't maul you again," I said.

"That sounds painful."

"Maybe a little. But in a good way," I said. "I just can't believe you're really here."

"It was inevitable," he said.

The dueling thrilling and soothing nature of having Baku with me was tempered by the panic in the back of my head. Evan was still missing. He was possessed. And instead of staying laser focused, I was enjoying myself. It made me feel like a terrible mother, but even that couldn't steal the grin from my lips.

I buckled up, and Baku did the same, watching and taking his cues from me. I started driving, forcing myself to keep my hands on the wheel, and my eyes on the road.

"If you're here, does that mean I've stolen you away from your sacred duty of helping people in the dream world?" I asked, glancing over at him for a second before returning my attention to the road ahead.

"I don't know."

"Would that screw up the cosmic order? Leave children unprotected from their nightmares?"

"Everyone has nightmares, whether I am there to devour them or not," he said. "It's a universal truth."

"Nightmare law," I said. I guessed it was okay not to feel too guilty about taking Baku all for myself. People woke from nightmares. Plus, he was supposed to grow old with me, right? I'd seen it in my dreams.

If that was true, that meant he was for keeps. Right now, for always, he was mine. After everything else that had happened recently, I held onto that glimmer of hope and positivity.

The drive felt like it took no time at all, in a totally different way than it had when I'd been heading in the other direction.

Empty gravel roads were replaced by busy pavement. "Busy" in Marshmallow meant a few other cars were going to and fro, because it was a Saturday night and everyone wanted to make the most of the remaining scraps of daylight.

"This is home," I said, as I pulled into the driveway and turned the car off. "Let's go."

Baku followed me as I hurried up to unlock the door. Inside, Remi and Julian were right where I'd left them, unconscious on the living room furniture. Molly was probably still around somewhere, but I didn't take the time to look for her.

"Evan?" I called as I raced up the stairs.

At the top, everything was quiet. I went right for Evan's room, steeled myself with a deep inhale, a mental reassurance that I could do this, and threw open the door.

His room was empty. He wasn't here.

The intestinal hornets returned in full force, buzzing and stabbing and twisting in my guts.

"Poop." I blew out the hope I'd been carrying in an exhausted breath. Evan was supposed to be here. Lost, I asked the empty room, "Now what?"

Scuffling sounds carried up the stairs.

"Stay back," Molly shouted.

Well, that wasn't good. I hurried back downstairs and found Molly standing in the living room between unconscious Remi and Julian, a scowl on her face. Fernando was by her feet, a kitchen knife in his hand. He waved the serrated bread blade in front of himself with unprecedented ferocity.

Only then did I realize the target of their wrath was Baku. He seemed unfazed, standing a few feet away, leaning on the wall by the coats.

I should have warned her when I'd gotten in that I wasn't alone, but I'd been focused on checking Evan's room and hadn't thought of it.

Molly sneered at Baku, her voice low in warning. "The wardings seem to have failed, but I won't."

"Hey, hey, Molly." I positioned myself between Baku and my coven and raised my hands in defense. "We're all friends here."

"Jennifer," Molly said, her expression softening.

Fernando lowered the knife for a moment when he spotted me before lifting it once more.

"A nightmare has breached the wardings," Molly said. "Can't you see it?"

Wardings? When did that happen?

"You mean Baku?" I pointed and looked over my shoulder at him.

He smiled at me. It was a make-my-insides gooey in a good way smile.

"You *didn't*," Molly said in a flat tone.

I shrugged and returned my attention to her. "It appears that I did. I brought him into the waking world, and I'm not sorry."

She sighed and gestured to Fernando to lower the knife. He squinted his giant eye at Baku, then popped the knife between his lips and smiled with a menacing mouth of sharp teeth.

"I heard you call for Evan when you burst in," Molly said. "Does that mean you found him? I didn't see him arrive."

"No," I said. "In the dream realm I found him here, which is why I was hoping he'd be in his room. But he's not there."

"Did your parents say what was wrong with him?" Molly asked.

"Yeah, as best as they could," I said. "And my dream confirmed—it's the kitty."

"Lingering influence from the incident before or a new act of control...it doesn't matter," Molly said to herself. She tapped her chin and sat down on the sofa by Julian's feet. Then she looked back up at me. "It's impossible to guess what the kukudhli intends to do without consulting the cookies."

"You think the answer is in one of the fortunes Murray brought by?" I asked. We'd already gone through all the cookies in the box once. Good thing we hadn't thrown the fortunes away.

Baku stepped up beside her, looked at her, and pulled a

piece of tape out of nowhere. He slowly lifted it toward his mouth, then looked at me. I shook my head no.

"Possibly," Molly said, purposefully not looking at Baku. "You start there, and I'll call him, see if he has any insight to offer."

I agreed, pulled down the box from on top of the fridge, and set it on the table.

Before Molly had a chance to walk away, I asked, "How's Remi?"

"Improving," she said. "They both are."

At least something was going right. The sooner the two of them woke up, the better.

A rumble seemed to shake the whole kitchen. I turned to Baku, who was standing by the counter.

"I think the noise came from inside of me," he said.

"You're hungry," I told him. And then, really looking at him, I realized I still hadn't adequately clothed him. Seeing my smiling face plastered all over his man bits was kinda awesome, but also not the best I could do now that we were here.

"Come on, let's find you something more fitting to wear, then I'll get you some food, and you can help me with the fortunes."

Molly said, "Have fun with that. I'll step outside and make that call to Murray."

I led Baku upstairs to Evan's room. It felt like an invasion of Evan's privacy, with him not here. But I couldn't very well make Baku roam around in a paper kilt and bandages on his feet. There was nothing to do about the tattered jacket until we had time to go shopping. While Evan had giant feet, and would hopefully be a decent match for Baku in foot-size, Evan was tiny compared to Baku's massive frame. Any other coat or jacket I offered Baku would end up just as over-stretched and torn up as the one he was currently wearing.

Careful not to dig through anything I didn't have to, I grabbed a pair of socks and shoes for Baku. Then I remembered the extra clothes I'd started keeping for Remi and Julian in the hall. Julian had to be a better match.

I grabbed a t-shirt and jeans, and handed them over along with Evan's shoes.

Baku gladly put them on, sitting in Evan's chair to do so.

"Okay?" I asked.

"Tight," he said, looking down at the shoes. "But better."

"Great. I swear once we find Evan, and the whole night-mares-roaming-the-streets thing is resolved, I'm taking you shopping."

"It's strange not knowing things. There is much in your world that I am unaccustomed to."

"I look forward to showing you," I said. And I did, but I also needed Evan safe before I could truly appreciate my new reality of Baku being in my life full-time. I spotted the sword I'd told Evan he could keep leaning against his desk. I grabbed that, too, and handed it to Baku. "Let's go back down. You can read me the fortunes while I make you a sandwich. You can read, right?"

"Yes."

"Great." I grabbed his hand and led him back to the steps. We headed down and found Molly in the kitchen holding up a slip of white paper.

With a smug expression, she said, "If you can't take the heat, get out of the basement."

I recognized the saying from one of the cookies we'd opened together before. Reciting one of the others, I said, "Fortune favors the cold."

Molly nodded. "One of my loans came through from the library. Murray was there to accept it for me."

"And you found a connection by doing this your way, research and peopling over jumping into action, so you're going to tell me why you were right the whole time," I guessed.

"I'm not so petty as to rub salt in a wound." Her grandmotherly expression of sweet innocence implied what she said was genuine.

"Okay," I said. "I don't care how we get there, just tell me how it all meshes together and how we can save my son."

"We're looking for dark and hot. Research shows that's where the kukudhli make their nests. It's where we'll find Evan."

Yes. I had Baku. I had a lead. Something inside of me clicked, and I knew everything was going to work out.

CHAPTER 25

I couldn't wait for Remi and Julian to wake. I hoped they'd be up and moving sooner rather than later, but I couldn't spare another minute. Evan was out there, possessed, and he needed my help.

How exactly I would de-possess him, I had no idea. But I'd never sweated the details before, and I wasn't about to start now.

With my spork at the ready, a backpack filled with supplies, and a sword-wielding Baku at my side, I headed out into the quickly-darkening streets.

"Molly said dark and hot, so I'm thinking we check the basements downtown first," I said.

Baku asked, "People will let us into their homes?"

"No, probably not. I'm more hoping we get lucky and that we only have to break into a few of the public buildings. Better if no one is there."

"You have experience in breaking and entering," he said. It wasn't a question, because he knew all kinds of things about me through our years dreaming together. Because this was Baku, there wasn't judgment in his statement.

"Yep. It's a handy skill in real estate."

If Evan was here, he'd give me a disapproving glare. If Remi was here, she'd make a crack about me flashing my realtor badge at the cops as they arrested me. Baku, who actually was here, nodded his understanding.

Even though the nightmare monsters had been chilling somewhere on the down low, I watched every sign of movement with suspicion. Out there somewhere, they were still around unless my dream magic expired at some point and they turned to dust, poof, gone forever. That was probably too much to hope for. More than that, I didn't care for the implications given I'd also brought Baku from the dream world.

People walked around, mostly heading to Tergel's for a drink or Robertini's for a meal. They drove by, too, heading home from whatever non-magical people did with their daylight hours, to tuck in safely behind locked doors and under fluffy covers.

I eyed the buildings with a different kind of suspicion. Each was a potential target as I looked for which would be empty. Two blocks from my house, it hit me— I didn't need to break anything. I just had to make a call. I squeed and pulled my phone from my pocket. Baku ate his sandwich and watched with interest as I dialed Jerry.

"Jen," Jerry answered. "It's about time you called."

"Oh?"

"You left me hanging at lunch days ago. I tried calling you a few times since, and you never called me back."

"Did you leave a message?" I asked, raising a brow he couldn't see.

"You *know* I didn't."

"Well," I said, "seems I'm off the hook then."

"You can be, *if* you tell me everything. Work is boring

without you. Tell me a fantastic tale of your magical adventures."

"Well, funny you should ask," I said. "I'm calling to invite you on one."

"Perfection," he said. "Tell me where to meet you. I'll grab my coat."

I gave Baku an enthusiastic thumbs up. Then I said to Jerry, "Town Hall. Bring Tess's keys."

She had access to every government building in the city. It shouldn't have taken me so long to think of this.

"See you in five. Kisses." Jerry hung up.

Baku was looking at me, a sparkle in his metallic eyes.

"That was my business partner, Jerry," I said.

"I got that."

"The kisses thing, it's like the French," I told him. "Wait, *not* like French kisses. Next to the cheek, air kisses. I would never slip Jerry the tongue."

I shivered at the thought.

Baku's smile widened. "I know."

"Right," I said. "Because you know everything about me. You've seen my dreams for forty years. You know me better than anyone."

"I don't know everything," Baku said.

"Oh yeah?"

"I don't know the events that have happened to you in the waking world that you have not dreamed about."

"Interesting. You didn't know what hunger feels like, but you do know all about my friends and family."

"Exactly."

We walked a few more blocks. I enjoyed the different explorative expressions Baku made while he ate on the way.

Up ahead, Jerry was waiting for us at the Town Hall. He was leaning on the stone building, holding up a ring of keys. He said, in his teasing tone, "Took you long enough."

I gave him the oh-puh-lease look. "You've been here, what, two minutes?"

"Clearly you should have driven instead of walked," he said. "And when you said to meet you, why didn't you mention your *friend?*"

"Jerry, this is Baku. Baku—Jerry." I did the whole intro thing, and the two shook hands.

"And that *handshake.*" Jerry gave me an oh face and bumped his shoulder into mine. He smiled at Baku. "Tell me you two aren't just friends. Please. This woman is overdue for some...happiness."

"Baku just got here," I said.

Baku slipped his hand around my hip, and I melted against his side.

I said, "We're figuring it out."

"Exotic, international boyfriend," Jerry said. "Good for you."

"Not exactly." I snatched the key ring from him and unlocked the door to the building. "But he's not only good— he's *great* for me."

I stepped inside and held the door for Baku and Jerry. Baku entered. Jerry didn't.

"You don't think I'm trespassing with you, do you?" Jerry asked.

"I assumed. You seemed eager for adventure on the phone."

"Keep the keys. I want to hear all about this, but after the danger's over. I'm more into vicarious adventure, where I don't end up spending the night in a jail cell." He whipped out his phone and snapped a pic of Baku and me. "Don't worry, I'd never use any of the evidence I have against you. This is for later."

"I'm totally reassured," I said. "And what do you mean later?"

"You'll want the photo," Jerry said. "Trust me. With the way he's looking at you—mmm."

I grinned. "Okay, I'll let you know how it goes."

"And don't lose my wife's keys."

"I promise not to lose the keys."

With that, Jerry left. Baku and I made our way into the dark building. I pulled my trusty flashlight from my backpack to light our way. Government buildings were all halls apparently, and no stairs. To get dark and hot, we needed to find the old furnaces in the basements.

"Sorry about Jerry," I told Baku.

"Don't be."

"He's a lot," I said. "Which is why I love him so much. Again, in a platonic way."

"I'm not threatened," Baku said.

"Is that so?"

"I'm disconnected from the dream world while I'm here," he said. "But while I was there, I lived without time. I've lived the past and the future with you in dreams. While I am there, I know what it is to have been married to you just as I know what it is to meet you for the first time."

"That's crazy," I said. "Crazy awesome. But to be clear, when you say we're married in the future, you mean in the real world, right? You're one-hundred-percent not going to disappear back to the dream world?"

"I'm not going anywhere," he said. "You saw. Remember the dream? We grow old together. If I were to live only in the dream world, I wouldn't age. I am one-hundred-ten-percent certain we will share a life here."

That seed of doubt, squashed, I felt way better.

Baku said, "One thing I didn't know from the dream realm was that Jerry would have keys to the city."

I waggled my brows and held up the ring. "Good stuff,

right? Well, his wife is the head of the cleaning crew for all the city buildings."

Baku raised a brow.

"I know," I said. "Surprising someone would marry him, right?"

"It's not that," Baku said. "I was just imagining the conversation when she realizes he's taken her keys."

I laughed. "Yeah, I'm glad I won't be there for that."

"There." Baku pointed down one of the halls to the stairwell we'd been looking for. We hurried over and headed downstairs, side-by-side.

If it weren't for Baku being here with me, I would have been a complete mess. My insides were still clenched up and my head still hurt. Both grew worse with every minute that passed that we hadn't found Evan. But Baku was great company, and his presence kept me from focusing on the panic. It was freak-out on the back burner, drool over bonding with my hottie on the front.

At the bottom of the stairs, the labyrinth of halls ended. We'd found the basement. I flicked the switch on the wall, clicking on lines of fluorescent lights. It was a big, packed space. Shelves upon shelves stood in rows throughout the room, filled with file boxes. So far, there was no sign of the giant furnace that had to be down here somewhere.

"This can't be the whole basement," I said. "It's too small. And there's no furnace."

We walked the perimeter of the room.

"There's a doorway," Baku said, pointing through a path between lines of shelves.

I turned and headed that way. The temperature change hit me halfway across the room. Each step became a few degrees warmer than the last. And there were noises—scratching, snorting, scuffling noises.

I readied my spork as we reached the open doorway.

There was a furnace, for sure. The giant, ancient machinery dominated the smaller room, and it roared like hellfire. Sweat beaded on my forehead and made my grip on my golden rod a bit clammy.

And something was squirming around behind it. Sadly, that something was way too big to be Evan.

"If it's a rat back there, I'm stabbing it," I said to Baku over the clanking of the furnace.

"It's not a rat."

I was about to ask how he knew what it was when a streak of green fur zoomed out into the open, aiming right for me. *Furben.* The nightmare's mechanical eyes blinked out of sync as it opened its beak-like mouth and sailed through across the floor. Clucking chicken noises, so deep in tone it sounded like maniacal laughter, came from the nightmare toy.

The furben dove at my shoe, taking the toe end into its mouth and squeezing. I shook my foot, and the nightmare fell off. It raced back toward me.

I whipped around my spork, putting the pointy end first.

The furben stopped right in front of the stabby tip and looked up at me, giant eyes wide. Another fluffy creature inched out from behind the furnace.

Wishing Walrus. One of his tusks was missing, and his purple fur was torn and matted. Stuffing popped out from his seams. But it was undoubtedly him.

My favorite childhood character dove at the furben, catching the creature by surprise. The furben's already-wide eyes went wider as he was tackled to the ground.

Clucking turned into a long crackled cucaaawwwww before cutting out completely.

I held my spork steady, looking for an opportunity to catch the furben without hurting Wishing Walrus.

"We sood awl be frens," Wishing Walrus said, just before the furben caught a chunk of his stuffing and pulled.

"No!" I couldn't watch this happen. It was torture.

Baku touched my shoulder. "Step back."

His voice was soft, his gaze kind.

I did as he said. "What are you—"

He opened his mouth and inhaled. His chest expanded as the heat in the room was sucked into his magically vacuum-like lungs. The tumbling walrus and furben scrambled for something to hold onto as they were lifted up into the air. A plastic shopping bag whipped up and around before getting sucked toward Baku's mouth. Two more furbens appeared from around the furnace. They slid and grappled with the slick floor before they were sucked up, too.

All of them flew into Baku's face, shrinking as they grew closer, and disappeared into his mouth.

There was a rumble. Baku put a hand over his stomach.

He looked at me and said, "I much prefer the flavor of your sandwich."

CHAPTER 26

*M*outh agape, I stared at Baku. "You can devour dreams here."

"It seems so."

"Not just the nightmares," I said.

"That's a good thing, right?" Baku's brows dropped, and he frowned with concern.

I wasn't sure what my expression was telling him, but clearly it wasn't good. If I had to guess, I'd say he could tell that I wasn't one-hundred-percent jazzed about seeing my favorite childhood character get—for lack of a better word —eaten.

"Yes," I said. "It's probably good."

"I thought you wanted the dream creations removed from existence."

"Maybe not Wishing Walrus," I said. "I liked him, or the cartoon version of him at least."

"I apologize. I misread the situation. It seems I don't know what you are thinking as well here as I do in the dream world."

"No, it's for the best," I said, as much to myself as to him.

"Who knows what kind of problems happy dreams would cause."

I guessed I did have some idea. Fighting between the good dreams and the bad dreams had caused damage and confusion, broken windows and the like.

"Plus," I added, "this one wasn't the cartoon from my childhood. He was a dream, a dream whose fluffy insides were sticking out. What about the plastic bag? I didn't know you could inhale non-dream objects."

"Neither did I."

"Interesting." I bumped his arm with my elbow and grinned up at his ridiculously handsome face. "We're figuring all of this out together."

"Yes we are."

A scratching noise came from behind the furnace. Something else was here. Another furben? Baku and I exchanged a knowing look, then he circled the furnace slowly. I followed, spork aimed at the floor, ready to stick whatever nightmare or rat or whatever other basement monster we uncovered.

There was a square hole in the wall too small to walk through, but large enough to crawl. We knelt down to look inside together.

"Well, that's creepy," I said. "I can just imagine climbing in there and getting mauled by a bunch of rats who are lying in wait."

Baku stuck his head in, and I cringed, expecting him to pull back at any moment, his head covered in spiders.

"It's hot inside," he said.

"It's hot out here. That's the not-so-secret power of the furnace."

"But the heat doesn't dissipate through here. It's a tunnel. This could be where we find Evan."

I grumbled. "You had to use the magic word—*Evan*. Fine, yes, I'll take a rat mauling, or spider coat, but I won't like it."

The corner of Baku's lips lifted in the grin that made my brain go all melty. Shadows highlighted the pleasant width of his jaw, the chiseled lines of his nose.

"I'll go first," he said.

I handed him my flashlight. "I love you so hard right now."

"I love you always. I have since the moment you were born. I didn't understand it at the time, or for a long time after. I wasn't ready to admit it before, but it's the truth." He kissed my forehead, then crawled into the dark tunnel.

Always. I loved him always, too. Huh, funny how that happened. It had snuck up on me. I'd already planned on keeping him, but thinking in terms of love was new. It was true, though.

I crawled after him, holding tight to my spork and trying not to think about what might be lurking in the hidden recesses of the creepy tunnel. The scratching noises up ahead did not make me feel any better. I told myself it was just Baku, and not a writhing mass of murder rats, and that maybe helped a little.

Shreds of light pierced the little gaps between Baku's giant frame and the walls of the tunnel, suggesting the darkness was coming to an end. He shot up to his feet and bolted from my line of sight.

There were grunts and scuffling sounds.

"Baku?" I froze. "It's not murder rats, right?"

He didn't answer.

What was I thinking—even if it was murder rats, I had to help him. This was Baku.

I scurried forward with a battle cry and jumped to my feet, ready to stab every rat in the face.

There weren't any rats.

Weirdly, I noted, the room had no furnace. It did have a set of stairs and was attached to another doorway.

Baku struggled to free himself from a mess of skeletons. One yanked on his arm, another had its legs around his neck and its hands pulling on the corners of his mouth. A third tugged on his leg, leaving him to struggle for balance on one foot. Two more shoved each other as they fought over a chain that was wrapped around Baku's skeleton-free arm.

"Not on my watch, bone breath." I stabbed at the skeleton perched on Baku's head. Of course, ribs had holes between them when there wasn't any flesh filling the gaps, so the stabbing plan wasn't the best.

Its jaw dropped open, dangling half-off, and turned its eyeless gaze on me. A curly mustache and pointed beard decorated its face.

I cackled at the revelation. "This one has facial hair!"

Beardo grabbed my weapon with a surprising grip, given the dude didn't have any muscles. I didn't let go, though. I twisted, knocking the pointy part of my weapon into its bare ribs and hoping torque topped stabbing.

One of its fingers flew off and clattered to the floor in two bits. They wiggled like little brittle worms.

Beardo turned its eyeless gaze on me and shoved the rod of my spork. I stumbled back. It dove. Baku fought to try and stop it, but with so many other skeletons all over him, he had enough to deal with.

"Jen, find something to grab onto, and—" Baku's words cut short when another skeleton grabbed his face.

Beardo slammed me back into the stone wall, knocking the air from my lungs. The skeleton landed on the ground a few feet in front of me. I squeezed my spork and swung like it was a baseball bat.

The golden rod made contact with shoulder blade, clattering Beardo's entire arm to the floor. But it wasn't enough. It looked to where its arm flailed on the ground. Then it looked back at me.

I lacked the mad skills needed to twirl my spork in a way that looked remotely threatening. So when the skeleton lunged at me, I grabbed my spork in both hands and slammed it straight out.

Beardo slammed strait into the golden rod and threw its broken jaw around in front of me, spraying rancid green fluid across my cheek. I snapped my eyes and mouth shut hard. Peeking back out through squinted lids, I successfully held him back with the rod of my spork.

In the sounds of the scuffle was a rush of footsteps, and a woosh of cold air.

From the corner of my eye, I caught movement by the stairs.

"Jen!" Remi said.

Beardo stumbed back, its only hand wrapped around my staff. I wiped my eye on my shoulder, leaving the gross goo on my shirt. Better than having it in my eyes.

Remi had the skeleton by the hips, and she shook it. Its legs flailed and rattled. Molly beat on its hand with a baseball bat.

Beardo let go, and Remi tossed it across the room.

I grabbed both women and pulled them in for a reunion hug. "I am so freaking glad to see you." Then I let go and turned to Baku, because I wasn't the only one who needed help.

Julian was already by his side, helping. He tore the skeleton's arms from Baku's face, freeing his mouth.

"Hold on," Baku said.

I grabbed Remi and Molly's hands.

Baku opened his mouth, sucking in the skeletons that held onto his arms and legs. Beardo squirmed and scrambled for purchase as it slid across the room.

"What do you call a skeleton that's happy to see you?" I asked Remi.

"Boner," she said with a grin.

"Children." Molly shook her head.

Beardo grabbed on Julian's shirt. Julian's feet slid across the floor, as the skeleton pulled him toward the magical vortex that was Baku's mouth. He reached for something to hold onto just as the skeleton had, his free hand scraping on the rough stones of the wall.

Remi bolted toward him, pulling Molly and me with her. The suction toward Baku was gentle, but constant. For Julian, it seemed much stronger. It must have been because the Beardo, a nightmare creation, was holding onto him.

"Peel its fingers off," I called to Julian.

He let go of the wall and twisted his body toward Beardo. Large red wings burst from Julian's back. He lifted up off the floor and pulled Beardo along with him, away from Baku. Then he grabbed the skeleton's forearm and snapped.

Instead of dislodging himself from Beardo's grip, he ripped its arm apart. The hand still clung to him, but the skeleton was sucked into Baku's mouth.

Baku closed his jaw, and with it the portal.

"What the hell was that?" Remi asked Baku, a ball of fire in her palm. "And why shouldn't I toast you where you stand?"

"Whoa, whoa." I put myself between my best friend and my boyfriend, arms out in defense. "This is Baku. He's a good guy."

Molly grumbled something under her breath.

I shot her a scowl, then looked back to Remi. "Baku's been with me my whole life, in my dreams. He's here because I brought him here. He's here because I need him."

Remi dropped the ball of fire and her expression softened. A smile slowly spread across her face. She pointed at Baku. "I remember you. You're cloud guy." Then she pointed at me. "You're doing the Talladega tango with rainbow wolf."

I nodded. "Yep."

She raised her hand for me to high-five. Our palms met with a satisfying smack. *This* was the congratulations I'd been waiting for.

"This isn't the time," Molly said.

"She knew, didn't she?" Remi asked me, and then shot Molly a glare. "And she didn't tell me on the way here. This is big news."

"Yeah," I said, "but Molly's right. We'll have all the time in the world to catch up. Right now we—"

"Have to find Evan," Remi said with a nod.

"We're going this way," I said, pointing to the far end of the room where there was a doorless entry leading who knew where. "It seems that at least a few of the basements here are connected."

Baku and Julian led the way, neither seeming to mind that one of them had almost just eaten the other. Molly walked behind them, leaving Remi and me to take the rear.

"How did you find us?" I asked.

"Molly said you'd be in the attached basements under the public buildings. For whatever reason, she knew the library would be open, so that's where we came in."

"I wish I'd known we could have gone up and around before crawling through that dusty shaft. You don't see any spiders on me, do you?"

She gave me the once over without commenting on the fact that I'd said *shaft.* "Spider free."

The doorway led to a tunnel, and I was struck with an eerie sensation. This was similar to when I'd been dragged underground, chained to the wall, and held as a vampire snack. The stonework was the same. So was the smell, damp and cold and undead.

"Is it just me or is there a weirdly high number of underground spaces beneath this town?" I asked, my chest growing tight.

"Marshmallow was founded by demons," Molly said. "Some of them can't handle daylight. Naturally a demon town would host a town's worth of tunnels beneath the surface."

Remi rolled her eyes. *"Naturally."*

"There's something ahead," Julian said, slowing the group.

The tunnel opened to a larger room. This one, too, had a furnace roaring in its center. We stood together in a line and looked over the scene.

It was pure mayhem.

Feathers floated down from above as a half-plucked Gratitude Goose flew across the ceiling, a pair of furbens clasped onto his legs like murderous boots. In black and white stripes and a catcher's mask, the Barcode Butcher rode on top of a giant rat. In the center of a mass of skeletons, foam penis man swayed back and forth, dodging grasping boney fingers.

Remi summoned flames in both hands. "Let's do this!"

Wings burst from Julian's back, and his entire person burst into flames. Both ran ahead, catching both dreams and nightmares alike in flames.

Molly hung back, smashing anything that came her way with her cane. As the end came down onto the head of a charging furben, one of the green creature's mechanical eyes popped off. The lose eye clattered to the ground and in a rapid burst of blinks began to smoke. The furben stopped in its tracks, wobbled on its feet, and then fell flat on its face.

Baku opened his mouth, sucking in charred nightmares. The breeze pulled gently on my jacket and pants.

I dove in with my spork, knocking one of the skeletons from the dancing dick. But before I could move on to the next, there was a tickle in my brain, a sensation that told me to turn, that there was something I needed to see.

In the corner of the room floated a small ball of black fur, its blue wings fluttering at its sides.

The kukudhli.

$\mathcal{T}$ime stood still as my heart tried to beat its way out of my chest. Flashes and crashes still happened around me, but all the noise and motion seemed to fade away as I was locked in a staring contest with the demon.

And then it blinked.

And it turned.

The floating kitty flew out of the room.

I ran after it, not waiting to see if anyone else would follow.

All I could hear was my pulse. All I could feel was the frantic energy surging through my veins. I couldn't let it get away.

My feet pounded against the stone floor, numb. I caught a glimpse of the fairy wings just before they disappeared around another turn. No matter how fast I ran, I was no closer to catching the demon.

Out of breath, and legs aching, I turned another corner, bashing my shoulder as I went.

I hissed and cringed, but the pain was soon forgotten

when I saw that the kitty fairy had stopped. I gasped when I saw who it was with—Evan.

Cords lay strewn across the floor of the huge basement room, connecting heaters haphazardly to extension cords. In the center of the space, by the biggest furnace I had seen, sleeping bags had been braided together into a bird-like nest.

Evan, his back still to me, tucked one of the ends of the sleeping bags in, like he was arranging the space.

I stood there staring, unable to find my voice. I shook my head.

"Evan, I'm so glad I found you." I took a step closer.

Evan snapped around. The kitty demon was perched on his shoulder. Both of them had glowing blue eyes, but as they looked at me, that blue turned to red. The kitty disappeared with a pop, leaving me alone with my son.

"I know you're in there," I told him. "And I know you didn't mean to hurt anyone. It's going to be okay."

I set down my spork and raised my hands to show I meant no harm. I took a step closer to my son, and then another.

He watched me approach, the glow of his red eyes burning rings into my retinas. I was afraid to blink and risk him disappearing like the demon had. If I could only touch him, maybe I could reach beyond the demon's control to the real Evan underneath.

"Stop." Evan's voice boomed through the room, seeming to come from everywhere at once.

I stopped.

"It's me," I told him. "Mom. I would never do anything to hurt you. I love you."

If I couldn't reach him, I couldn't help him.

"Try to remember," I said.

I shifted my weight to take a step forward. My feet

wouldn't move, like they were cemented to the floor. I pulled harder, shifting my weight forward.

Evan stepped out over the lip of the nest, turned, and started to walk away.

No. I couldn't let him go. He was so close, I had to stop him. I couldn't allow anything else to happen to him. I had to get to him *now*.

As Evan turned his back, I fell forward. I stumbled to find my footing as I ran wildly toward him.

He whipped around just before I could grab him, and swung his arm. He hit me in the shoulder. Pain radiated down to my elbow as I knocked into the wall.

Without a word, he kept walking.

I couldn't take him in a fight, because I couldn't make myself purposefully hurt him, even if my life depended on it. I would die for him. But I didn't want to die, either. I wanted both of us to walk away from this ourselves. I wanted to introduce him to Baku and watch the two of them get to know each other. I wanted all the conventional family moments, even if my little family was anything but conventional. All of that meant I needed to make Evan stay. And I needed to survive the encounter.

That left one move.

I thrust off the wall and dove at him. He started to turn, but I reached for his head and touched him before he could fully twist around. It was instinct, because I couldn't explain how I made my power work, even after all the practice.

Dream magic wasn't about control. It was about intention and submission to the flow of the wild world where anything could and would happen.

So I held onto my intention with everything I had, and I grabbed onto Evan, hoping it would be enough.

Everything went black.

* * *

MY HEAD STUNG and my muscles ached. I needed to open my eyes. Something was off. Why was my bed so cold and hard?

Stretching my hands out, something rough and crumbly met my fingertips. I really needed to stop eating cookies in the bed.

There was a feeling in the back of my head, and not just the hard coldness that was there. It was a notion, something I was supposed to remember, something urgent.

I pushed away the thought and relished the cloudy haze at the front of my mind. Lazy as a sloth, I opened my eyes. Instead of my ceiling fan, I found the midnight sky full of stars.

Weird. Maybe it wasn't just cookies I needed to quit, but alcohol, too.

I rolled slowly up and ambled to my feet. Everything hurt. The sense of urgency returned.

There was something important I was supposed to be doing instead of drunk sleeping under the stars.

I brushed off the draped fabric of my robe. Wait. I looked down at myself again.

This was familiar, and not because I kept a rainbow-swirl wizard outfit stashed in my closet. I didn't. Though maybe after this, it was worth considering. I was rocking the shape-less sack outfit like the boss that I was.

I looked around at the black and gray landscape. I stood at the foot of a mountain cliff. At the peak there appeared to be a giant fire. Generally, I knew it was good to flee fire. But that was the way I was supposed to go. I didn't know why, but I knew it was true.

Scaling cliffs was not exactly a specialty of mine. Not having a fear of heights was helpful, though. I put one hand in front of the other as I started climbing.

A few feet up, and everything hurt. My arms burned with stress and fatigue. My feet were sore and my legs were, too. Good thing there were only a few hundred more feet to go? With a cringey grin, I whispered to myself, *"Yay."*

I reached for my next handhold, but the rocks broke under my grip. They tumbled as they fell, clacking against the rockface just like I would have if that rock had been holding my weight. I swallowed down the lump in my throat and kept going.

Something important was at the top of the cliff. No, not some*thing,* some*one.*

How did I know that? Where was I?

A few feet farther up, and I caught a glimpse of the moons.

Moons—plural.

Two celestial bodies floated above, one pink and one blue.

The pink one had a familiar face. She was Evan's friend Erin.

Moon Erin winked at me. "Hey, Mom."

As realization struck, all the pain and weakness drained from my trembling limbs. There was no reason to follow the rules of the real world.

This was a dream.

As the Queen of Dreams, I made the rules.

CHAPTER 28

"Hi, Moon Erin," I said, waving a greeting back at the pink moon.

She winked and smiled.

Strangely, none of this seemed weird to me. *Because dreams.*

I let go of the rockface, knowing I wouldn't fall. I floated back and then up, flying into the sky.

"What are we looking at?" I asked the moon.

"Fair skies," she said. "Raging flames."

"I'm here for Evan," I told her, realizing the truth of my mission as I spoke the words.

Memories flooded back into my head, of the kukudhli, of the nest and the basement, of Evan possessed and how I'd grabbed him, throwing both of us into this dream. Well, I hoped it was both of us. Either we were both here or I was lying on the ground with a head injury all by my lonesome.

"He is here," the moon said.

"He's in the fire, isn't he?"

She nodded in a weird face-shifting-up-and-down-the-surface-of-the-giant-space-ball way.

Rising into the sky, I whooshed toward the raging flames fist-first, summoning superhero energy as I went. As I thrust through the fire, I didn't burn.

The moon's last words followed me. "Be careful."

Careful was for suckers. Bold action was the way to shape the world—dream or real.

The fire yielded to me, breaking apart to let me through to what appeared to be a double stack of giant glass balls. There was a hole in the center of one of the giant balls above me when I landed, slowly seeping sand down onto the ground below. It was an hourglass, and time was ticking.

A lump sat in the center of the building sand.

I ran for it, for him, knowing that Evan had to be inside.

With both hands, I scooped wildly at the sand, digging to find him in its depths.

My fingers met flesh.

I grabbed onto him and pulled with the superstrength I told myself I possessed, and I freed him from the sand with ease.

His eyes were closed, but he was breathing. I carried him to the edge of the hourglass and set him down.

"It's time to go," I told him. "We'll wake up together."

I squeezed his hand, but he didn't open his eyes.

A shadow grew, covering the ground and everything with it. I turned and discovered a towering black cat. Its ears brushed the top of the glass bubble, and sand cascaded down over its head. It sat like a normal cat would, with its glowing red-eyed gaze set on me and its tail curled around the side of the hourglass, flicking in agitation.

I rose to my feet and positioned myself between Evan and the demon. "So we meet again."

"The boy is mine." The cat's voice vibrated everything, from the glass, to my arms and legs, to my vision. It was deep and cutting, and absolutely terrifying.

I cleared my throat and stood taller. "You can't have him."

The corners of the cat's mouth rose in the creepiest grin the world had ever seen. "I wasn't asking for your permission."

Quick as, well, a cat, the giant feline pounced. Gargantuan black paws smacked me down without warning. Claws as long as my arm pinned me in place, and the cat pressed down, squishing, smashing me against the ground.

But I wasn't afraid. The crushing pressure should have snapped my spine. But it didn't. My spine was steel. My skin was diamond. I was invincible, because I was the Queen of Dreams, and this was my realm.

Heat poured over everything, because that's what the demon needed. Heat, fire. I knew what I had to do.

I breathed in like Baku would, sucking in not the dreams or the cat, but the heat. I took every ounce of warmth from my body, then from the air.

The paws shivered. The claws recoiled.

I rose from the ground and stood taller than ever before, growing twice my size. And I inhaled the fire.

The dream was frigid.

The sand stopped falling.

The cat shrank to normal kitten size, its fur tipped in frost. I didn't stop. The tiny cat fairy sat on the ground shivering. The black faded from its fur, replaced by a bluish white sheen of frosty crystals.

With one last inhale, I took the remaining heat from the kitten. Frost hardened to ice. I'd created a frozen statue of what had been a mind-controlling demon. Winner winner chicken dinner—me! I shrunk back down to normal-sized me and did a little victory shimmy.

"Mom?"

I whipped around and found Evan standing behind me. He threw his arms over my shoulders and squeezed.

I hugged him, too, relieved that it was finally over. I'd done it. I had my Evan back.

"I'm so sorry I hit you." His eyes grew into glowing orbs of concern. "And Grandma—is she okay?"

I smiled at him and let him go. "She'll be fine."

We all would be.

"I'd like to go home now," he said.

"Samesies."

I took his hand.

"Wait." He pulled away, ran over to the frozen kitten, and smashed it to pieces with his heel. Ice shards scattered, leaving nothing resembling a cat, only bits of frozen fur in sand.

"Okay," Evan said, and grabbed my hand. "I'm ready."

I closed my eyes and willed us to wake.

Waking up was harsh. My side hurt. My head hurt. My hip hurt. And there was a heavy weight smashing me. I opened my eyes and found Evan half on top of me in the tunnel where I'd grabbed him. The furnace still roared, and my head still throbbed.

"Are we—" Evan rolled off of me and groaned. "This has to be real. Everything hurts and it smells awful."

"Mm-hmm," I agreed.

I rolled my neck and stretched my arms.

A flutter of movement above me caught my attention.

I looked up.

Floating there, completely not frozen or smashed was the winged kitten, eyes glowing red.

"Oh, poop."

CHAPTER 29

*W*ith a graceful crabwalk, I inched slowly away from the demon. Evan, ever the faster of the two of us, had already made a mad dash across the room and snagged my spork while I was busy doing the whole inching thing.

The demon loomed, its furious red gaze set on me.

"Hey," Evan called. "Over here, fur ball."

Inwardly I wanted to scream at him not to call it. The last thing I wanted was for it to touch him again. Still, I was grateful for the distraction when the cat snapped its attention up.

I scrambled up to my feet and waved my arms around at the cat. "Nope. Not him. Back over here."

The demon looked at me.

"That's right," I said. "Ignore him."

I had nothing on me to defend myself, and my magic was useless here in the waking world, so I clenched my fists and bounced between the balls of my feet. A well-placed punch could kill a demon. Maybe. Probably not. But it could buy us time if I startled it.

From the corner of my eye, I caught Evan trying to move in.

"Stay put," I warned him, keeping my focus on the cat.

Evan grumbled but did as I said.

I could live with him being mad at me. I couldn't live with losing him.

"Here, kitty kitty." As the words left my lips, I was entirely sure my lack of plan was bonkers. *Punch the demon in the face* was not a plan.

Life had taught me three things: trust in friends, magic will always keep you on your toes, and when life gives you pickles, you don't make pickle-ade. You fashion yourself a slimy vinegar-soaked pantsuit and rock that gherkin garbage like it was Prada.

My plan was the pickle plan.

"Mom?"

The soft, higher-than-usual pitch of Evan's voice made me pause. I turned to see what was wrong, and found a towering black pole emerging from the shadows in front of Evan that hadn't been there before. Except it wasn't a pole. It was hairy, and it had a giant insect-like foot attached to the bottom.

As I watched, horror-stricken, the foot wiggled.

Without waiting to see what the leg belonged to, I darted into action and ran for Evan.

The giant leg was joined by seven more giant legs, all attached to a black ball covered in eyes. It was the nightmare to rule all nightmares—a giant spider.

To my credit, I didn't pee my pants. But I most definitely did scream.

I ushered Evan toward the door. The demon appeared in the doorway, floating right in the center. I squeezed Evan's wrist, probably too tight, and slowed so we wouldn't smash straight into the demon.

With a thwack, something came flying at me from the corner of my eye.

I ducked and whirled around just in time to see a long, thin pink tube fly over my shoulder where my head had been.

The long, whip-like appendage came from the center of the spider's face. Instead of hitting me, it stuck to the demon.

The tube snapped back just as quickly, snatching the cat and pulling it into the giant spider mouth.

"Was that—" Evan trailed off. "That was a spider tongue. You have got to stop having nightmares."

"I'm trying," I said. "It was probably from before." It wasn't like I'd continued creating nightmares since the first mass of them. At least I didn't think I had been.

The spider ground its jaw, crunching the demon. Then it gulped.

I shivered. "Let's not wait to see if it's still hungry."

With a yank, I led Evan toward the doorway. Two steps away and a familiar wind pulled back against us. It was a gentle suction, and welcome. We grabbed onto the doorframe and turned around.

Baku stepped in behind the spider, his mouth open. The nightmare creature scrambled to get away, but its spindly legs quaked. One after the next, its feet lifted from the ground. It scrambled for footing until it was clear it had no chance of escape. Huge to miniscule, the spider disappeared into Baku's mouth.

A wave of relief washed over me.

Evan was still tense as I let go of the doorway and relaxed. "It's okay," I told him. "It's over."

He let go of the doorway, but he pursed his lips and his eyes teared up. He looked to his feet and hugged himself.

Remi, Molly, and Julian poured in around Baku. I touched Evan's shoulder.

"I'm okay," he said with a smile. "I will be. Really."

The second part, I believed. I gave his shoulder a squeeze, then turned and hugged Baku. Any lingering concerns melted when I was in his arms.

I squeezed before letting him go and digging through my backpack. I pulled out a piece of gum and handed it to him. "Chew, don't swallow. For the spider breath."

His lips quirked around the gum.

For the record, his breath was unaffected by eating spiders and skeletons and every kind of nightmare I'd created.

"I swear I didn't make that spider up on purpose," I said.

"It's not new," Remi said, understanding my concern. "We followed it here. It was down here as long as any of the others."

I turned from Baku back to Evan.

Baku was the first man in my life to make it to this stage. I wanted to introduce him to my son. It was a little scary, but also exciting. "Evan, I want you to meet—"

"Are those my shoes?" Evan chuckled.

"I didn't come to this world with protection for my feet." Baku bent down and started untying the laces.

I shot Evan one of my best mom expressions. It was the look of disapproval that also said *hey, stop what you're doing and apologize right this second.*

Evan looked from me to Baku, and back again.

"Keep them," he said. "Really."

"Thank you," Baku said.

"You said *you're not from this world?*" Evan asked.

"That's right. I am of the dream realm."

It was Evan's turn to give me a look. It was an eyebrows-up, caught-me-doing-something-I-shouldn't look. It was a I'm-going-to-hold-this-over-you-whenever-I-want-some-thing-for-the-foreseeable-future look.

"Baku's my forever friend," I told Evan.

"Friend." Evan's grin spread from ear to ear.

He had eyes, of course he'd know I was into Baku.

"Have you two been *LARPing* the whole time you sent me away with my grandparents, *for my own good?"* Evan teased, air-quoting "for my own good" and saying LARPing like it was the dirtiest word in the dirty-word dictionary.

Remi chortled.

I shot her a look.

"What?" She shrugged her shoulders, looking completely unashamed.

"We've been busy fighting monsters, saving the world," I told Evan. "You know, mom stuff."

Evan laughed and offered Baku his hand. "Nice to meet you."

"You, too."

They shook.

"Well." Evan smirked at me. "This is going to be interesting."

CHAPTER 30

There was no way I could sleep after all of the crazy excitement we'd endured. Or so I thought.

Drooling, I crashed in the passenger seat of my car on the drive home. Fortunately, Evan drove.

I peeked here and there, as Baku carried me up the stairs to my bed. After tucking sleepy me in, he started for the door. Even three-quarters asleep, I wasn't having it.

He whispered something about offending my kid's delicate sensibilities or something silly like that, before accepting my undeniable force of will and climbing into bed beside me.

When I woke, I was tangled in bedding and in Baku, and completely aware of my surroundings. I was home, and I could feel it on a bone-deep level. The homecoming feelings weren't just because this was my bed, but because everything was how it was meant to be. Most of all, because my family was here.

I ran my palm across Baku's chest and squeezed the leg I had thrown over his hips tighter. He felt so freaking good, it was beyond comprehension.

"I still can't believe you're really here," I told him.

He rolled to his side and pulled me into his arms. "Always."

I looked into his smiling eyes and kissed him, sure I would never ever leave my bed again. Showers? Nah, I liked him dirty. Food? Eh, who needed to eat when they could lick Baku instead? I did just that, exploring his mouth with my tongue.

"Heading out. Breakfast is in the oven," Evan called from downstairs.

I froze. Then I slowly peeled myself from Baku. I cupped my hands and called back down to Evan, "Wait a minute."

I scrambled out of the bed, trying my best to ignore the way the cold air bit and the way my body begged me to stay in bed. "Sorry," I told Baku. "I just need a minute."

"You don't need to explain yourself to me," he said.

And I loved him for it. I just loved him.

"Thanks," I said, and grabbed my robe as I hurried out the room.

From the top of the stairs, I locked eyes with Evan, who was standing by the door in his coat, with his gym bag slung over his shoulder.

"Good morning," he said, as I hurried down to meet him.

"Good morning," I said as I hurried down. "You could stay home today, you know. With everything you've been through, it wouldn't hurt to take a day and skip track. I could write you a note and—"

"Mom." He put his hand on my shoulder. "I'm fine. After having to go to Remi's place, and then the spa, I could really use some normal."

"That makes sense." It did. And I understood, but I still selfishly wanted to keep an eye on him and keep him home. "What about Baku? You haven't gotten a chance to really talk to him yet. I want you to get to know each other."

"We talked," Evan said. "Last night."

"What?"

"You fell asleep. He came back down, and we watched *Camp Murder*."

"Without me?" I could feel my mouth dangling open, so I shut it, but I left my hands in their natural offended position on my hips.

"You were sleeping."

"Well, yeah. It was a long day."

"We'll watch something else tonight," Evan said. "If you think you can handle it."

"Handle it? I'll show you what I can handle with my spork."

Evan laughed. "What is that even supposed to mean, Mom?"

"It means watch yourself, mister," I said in the sternest tone as I could muster with a smile pulling at the corners of my lips. "It's good to have you home."

"It's good to be home. Now let me go or I'm going to be late for track."

I hugged him. He was so big, so grown up. "Fine. Go. Be responsible."

"I will. Love you."

"Love you, too."

Evan stepped outside and almost closed the door all the way before I realized there was something else I needed to say. I grabbed the knob. "Wait!"

Evan sighed, clearly done with my shenanigans. "Yes?"

"Why not invite Erin over for the movie tonight? We could get pizza."

He shook his head and headed down the sidewalk. In a flat tone and with a dismissive wave, he said, "Bye, Mom."

Instead of worrying that our dynamic was changing, and that he didn't need me anymore, I smiled. We were both going to be fine.

I closed the door and locked up, then headed back upstairs to find my sexy man where I'd left him. But he wasn't there.

The bed was empty and straightened up, the blankets squared and pillows fluffed to hotel-level perfection. The sound of water raining down against glass led me to the bathroom. The glass was steamy, but I could easily make out Baku's impressive silhouette.

"I hear you and Evan had a chat last night," I said, leaning on the door frame. "Bonding and all."

Baku turned, his shape facing me. "We watched a movie."

I was happy watching *this* scene play out, the way his thick arms moved and his torso stretched in the awesome v that led from broad shoulders to narrow at the hip.

"How was it?" I asked, no longer caring at all about the movie.

"The movie was interesting, much like a dream. As for the conversation, we didn't talk much, but I already know Evan from your dreams and his," Baku said. "He's a good kid."

"He is," I said, shedding my clothes. "I think you two will get along just fine. Let's talk about something else."

Naked, I opened the shower door. Baku's muscular body glistened with water. I hadn't thought it possible, but he looked even hotter wet. Droplets streamed down over his face, his jaw, his pecs, his abs.

"Better yet," I said, "I don't want to talk at all."

* * *

AFTER OUR SHOWER, and a few rounds of hanky panky, I placed a phone call to my parents to check in on my mom. She was totally fine, and I let them know that Evan was safe and himself again. Then, I left Baku by the TV and headed in to work.

Jerry had left about fifty bazillion texts, wanting to know all about the action of the evening, so I decided to give him the rundown in person instead of over the phone. Plus, I had to return his keys. I was a little surprised he was at the office instead of at home, given it was a Sunday and we'd had zero business as of late.

On the drive, I swung by the police station and was surprised to find no sign or evidence of the nightmares I'd created. Even all of the gelatin was gone, which I guessed meant the Tergels *really* liked Jell-O.

I sat in my spinny chair across from Jerry. He leaned his elbows on the desk, and cupped his hands over his cheeks.

"Tell me it's not true," he pleaded in response to the details he'd begged for. "Or I'll never sleep again."

"Well, it's gone now," I said. "Baku ate the spider, and therefore also the demon in its stomach."

Jerry shivered. "I don't know how you can kiss a mouth that has eaten spiders."

"I don't know," I said. "It's pretty amazing when he does it. Like it's this vacuum vortex superpower. He destroys bad dreams. I think that's heroic and sexy."

I skipped the part where I'd given Baku gum.

"If you say so." Jerry whirled his chair around and grabbed some folders from his desk. "I have news, too."

"Oh?"

He splayed out the folders in front of me. "The whole newsworthy incident downtown that you caused is turning fabulous for business. Pretty much everyone downtown is selling."

I added, "Because who wants to live where people go crazy, crash their cars into nothing, "ghosts" wreck houses, and people lose days of time when they try to visit the police station?"

"Turns out, weird AF out-of-towners do. I don't know if

it's a new hipster obsession or something more...in your crazed magic realm, but apparently we made statewide news, and it was enough to attract a whole mass of new buyers."

"That's fantastic."

"I need you," Jerry said. "There's no way I can handle this alone. It was one thing when nothing was moving, but now is a different story. Also, you're not allowed to say no, seeing as how this huge boost in our business is all because of you."

I considered a moment, though really what was there to consider? I'd taken off to work on becoming a powerful witch. And now I was.

"I'm in."

"Mimosas!" Jerry called out. "If that wasn't clear, we're celebrating."

How could I say no to my favorite celebratory drink?

"Just one," I said. "I promised my coven we'd do brunch."

"Fine, fine," Jerry said, pouring me a glass that he seemed to have ready to go under his desk the whole time. He raised a toast, "To your freaky nightmare magic, and to the future."

We clinked and drank, chatting for a few minutes about the exciting turn of events. Then I hurried off to Remi's place, wondering if I should bring Baku along. I decided to give him a call as I drove.

Baku was happy to stay in, and planned to explore town a bit. After my brunch, I'd take him shopping. He still had nothing to wear that belonged to him, and I looked forward to righting that wrong. He encouraged me to have fun with the girls. So that's exactly what I decided to do.

Julian's car wasn't in the driveway when I pulled in. I parked in his spot and knocked on the door. A moment later, Remi opened it and greeted me with a huge hug and the scent of amazing baked goods.

"Where's Baku?" she asked.

"Good to see you, too," I teased.

She pushed my shoulder. "You know what I mean. I'm thrilled *you* are here."

I nodded. "He's watching some TV and then he's going to walk around town."

Remi pulled me aside and whispered, "Heads up, Molly's here."

She said it like I should watch what I said, but I wasn't planning on bad mouthing Molly anyway.

"Great," I said, knowing I needed to say something.

We went into the kitchen, where there was a fabulous spread of sage eggs, fruit, fresh-baked cookies, and more mimosas.

Before we could really dig in, something smacked into the glass back doors with a bang.

We all turned.

Bent over and holding her stomach was a woman with black hair. As soon as we spotted her, she fell to the ground.

Remi ran for the door, with me on her heels. Molly took her time climbing off her stool and following us. Remi opened the door. The woman was curled up in a ball like she was in agony. When her face moved to the side, I realized I knew her—it was Brianna.

Molly pushed us out of the way.

"Brianna? What's wrong?" Molly asked.

"It hurts. Everything hurts." Brianna's face was contorted in agony.

"What do we do?" I asked.

Molly reached a hand down to touch Brianna's forehead as she did when she was going to do her magic healing probe thing.

But before Molly could touch her, Brianna popped up on hands and knees. There was a flash of light, and Brianna wasn't Brianna anymore.

She was a chicken. Feathers, beak, everything. She gave a plaintive *cluck*.

If it hadn't been for the pile of clothes under her orange feet, and the fact that I'd seen it happen with my own two eyes, I wouldn't have believed it was possible.

Molly fell back, and Remi covered her mouth as she whispered, "What in gherkin's name—"

I remembered my dream where I'd found a hen in a field. I'd known her, and I'd known her name was Brianna. I'd even asked her about it when I ran into her at Molly's place.

I'd foreseen this happening, even if I hadn't realized it until now.

I pointed at the familiar fowl and exclaimed, "I knew you were a chicken!"

Bird Brianna scratched at her pile of clothes, then spread her wings out like she was throwing her fists at the sky in anger. She belted out an agitated *buck-buck-buck.*

I had no idea what was going to happen next, but I couldn't wait to find out.

ABOUT THE AUTHOR

Sassy. Snarky. Supernaturally Sparkly.

Keyboard ninja, late-blooming bibliophile, proud geek, animal lover, eternal optimist, visual artist.

USA Today Bestselling Author Keira Blackwood writes exciting paranormal romance with all the snort laughs and all the feels.

www.keirablackwood.com